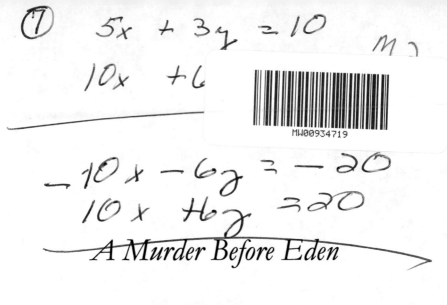

① $5x + 3y = 10$ M

$10x + 6$

$-10x - 6y = -20$

$10x + 6y = 20$

A Murder Before Eden

A Nonfiction Novel

$0 = 0$

infinite solution

Alison Pratt

Lulu Press

ISBN 978-0-557-72658-5

Published by Lulu Press

www.lulu.com

Cover design by Steve Hetzel.

The events in this story were originally published as:

Pratt, Alison, "A Murder Before Eden," *The Journal of Rockingham County History and Genealogy*, Volume XXXIII, 2008 issue, published in June, 2010.

To Tom and Nettie, Jake and Josie, and Dad and Mom: thank you for your sacrifices for your children.

Acknowledgements

Nearly sixty years after the fact, this family story begged someone to write it down. My dad, Herbert T. Pratt, didn't hesitate to help me do it. As a native of Rockingham County, he provided insight into local history, technology, and folkways and paved the way for interviews with fellow his North Carolinians. Dad and I spent hours in North Carolina libraries, pored over crackling microfilm, tromped through overgrown cemeteries, walked around abandoned houses, and dug through dusty court archives. Dad taught me how tobacco was grown and what winder operators did in mills. A true historian, he edited the text with his precise comments and suggestions. We had a great time. Thank you, Dad.

My mother, Mary S. Pratt, gave me suggestions on Southern dialect, but more importantly, insisted that I stick to my guns (the best advice, ever).

If Dad was my historian, Eric Ries was my copy editor. Eric's objective eye and contributions made this a better book. Eric's enthusiasm for the project kept me moving forward when I was grinding to a stop. His sense of humor kept me sane. Referring to me as "Nancy Drew" actually *did* help.

Warren Pratt, an attorney and my brother, reviewed the manuscript for the accuracy of the legal terms and proceedings, and he researched the North Carolina "outlaw" statute. Thanks, Bro.

Dennis Maneri got me talking about these family events and made me think that other people might want to read the story. My brother-in-law, Jack Hetzel, suggested the title. Bryan Brown sent me poetry. Thanks to all of them for their enthusiasm.

Bob Carter of the Rockingham County (N.C.) Historical Society and Rockingham Community College provided assistance with fact-finding and was a careful editor. The Honorable J. Mark Pegram, Clerk of the Superior Court for Rockingham County, was extremely helpful in navigating court and trial records. Ms. Pamela Robertson, Clerk to the Board of the Rockingham County Commissioners, assisted with archives.

The web site www.leaksville.com gives a nice overview of the town I remember from my childhood visits and provided good background material.

Carl Thompson was a distant cousin to one of the people in this book. Carl kindly listened to this story and became equally interested in the project. He, too, did some sleuthing and gave me information about the Thompson family that I could not have found anywhere else.

My great-aunt Custis Clifton and my cousins Colleen Shropshire, Ray Turner, Hazel Estes, Winfred (Wink) Hoover, and Emma Joyce all remember this story; some of them were there, and they all knew my great-grandfather, Tom Pratt. They gladly shared with me what they knew. They also gave me a connection to my own family history that I had not known.

I interviewed other people who were kind enough to give me their time and input into this story, but who preferred to remain anonymous. I thank all of them for their contributions. I also thank many enthusiastic friends whose kind words and interested questions got me writing and kept me writing.

My husband Stephen Hetzel and his mother Jane, who always loved a good mystery, were the first to point out to me that I should write this book. Steve gave me good ideas about how to present the story and opened my eyes to the larger historical context. My young son Reid Hetzel connects the past to the future, and he will carry these stories forward. My thanks and love to them for their patience and support.

4

Author's Note

This story is true. Every named person lived and no characters were invented. All the major events occurred as I have described them. My sources were newspaper articles, court documents and people who remembered it. In Part 1, for the sake of carrying the story, I have invented dialog and internal thoughts of the characters. I have speculated on some events where I did not have the information. Part 2 contains strictly factual information with no embellishment. The chapter notes provide additional background information and clarify fact from fiction in Part 1. If you like a mystery, I suggest you save the notes for last. A bibliography is provided for other historians who would like to follow my trail.

$$3x + 4(2x+1) = 15 \qquad (4)$$
$$3x + 8x + 4 = 15$$
$$11x = 11$$
$$x = 1 \qquad (1,3)$$

$$\frac{z}{0} = 3$$

$$4x + 3y = -11$$
$$-4x + 5y = 35$$

$$8y = 24$$
$$y = 3$$

$$4x + 9 = -11$$
$$4x = -20$$
$$x = -5$$

$$(-5, 3)$$

22) $7x - 2(3x - 2) = 7$

$7x - 6x + 4 = 7$

$x = (3, 7)$

$(3, 7)$

Part 1

The Murder

$3x + 5y = 37$

$2x - 5y = 8$

$5x = 45$

$x = 9$

$27 + 5y = 37$

$5y = 10$

$y = 2$

$(9, 2)$

$$2x + 3y = 11$$
$$3x - 6y = 6$$

$$4x + 6y = 22$$
$$3x - 6y = 6$$

$$7x = 28$$
$$x = 4$$

$$8 + 3y = 11$$
$$3y = 3$$
$$y = 1$$

$$(4, 1)$$

Chapter 1

Junior Edd Thompson

Wednesday, September 3, 1947

Junior Edd Thompson raced through the Virginia woods with the sinking feeling that they were catching up with him, but still he pushed on. Nine days earlier, in the middle of the night, he had taken off, heading north, seven miles across the state line from North Carolina to Virginia. He had thought maybe the sheriff wouldn't come looking for him in Virginia. His friend James Penn had taken him in, but when he heard the dogs barking he knew it was the bloodhounds. His blood ran cold and his feet caught fire. He ran out the back door just minutes before the sheriff and the dogs were coming in the front.

Of course they would blame him. Negro people didn't stand much of a chance against white people anyway, and they'd say he'd done it. It wouldn't matter if he'd done it or not done it, they'd say he did. He'd be lucky if he wasn't shot or the dogs set to him. He was trying to think of a plan, but the trees and the earth under his feet were all a blur. Just keep moving, keep going, fast now, faster, go, run, go!

His whole family had been awakened by hollering from the house behind them and all the commotion that came after that. Sam Turner had banged on their door asking for a flashlight, and Junior had given it to him. "What's goin' on?" his daddy had demanded to know. "Tom Pratt's been attacked by somebody, 'bout near killed him. Bunch of us are goin' to find him." Sam had hurried out. A stunned silence filled their room as if Sam had just sucked all the noise out of their house when he left. A dark look passed between Junior and his dad; a look, no words. Junior couldn't stop thinking of that look on his daddy's face as he ran deeper into the woods. That look had been haunting him for nine days now. Daddy and Mama had said nothing as Junior had made his decision. Weldon and Big Pete were talking nonsense: "What you doin', Junior? Where you goin'? Don't go out there now." Tying his shoes, throwing on his jacket and grabbing some cold biscuits from the kitchen, Junior gave his mama a quick hug, looked at all their worried faces one last time, and bolted out the door.

Junior had known the Pratts his whole life, had played with Tom Pratt's grandchildren in the orchard, and sometimes helped with the apple picking. Old Mrs. Pratt had died when he was five, and then Mr. Pratt married a young wife. Now Mr. Pratt was dead and it was going to get put on him. Running now, like he had run before. Maybe he had gotten too full of himself and thought he could always run his way out of trouble. Maybe he still could.

He lived with Mama, Daddy, Weldon, and Big Pete on Price Road just in front of the Pratt property. Now 17, it seemed to Junior he had always been in some kind of trouble. Daddy and Mama had given him plenty of lickings but it didn't do any good. Daddy would talk about how hard he worked over at Fieldcrest, and how hard work was what kept them in this house and food on their table. Mama would praise his little brother Pete and his big brother, Weldon, as if they'd never done a thing wrong in their lives. But Junior hadn't listened. His daddy starched cloth at the mill to make bed sheets, day in and day out, and what did it really get him? Always having to answer to somebody else. By the time Junior was 13, he was looking into the future and not seeing a thing he liked. He couldn't sit still in school, left it for good that year. What would be the point anyway? To pick worms off of somebody else's tobacco? To mop the floors at somebody else's store? To clean spittoons in a barber shop? For what? No, he had wanted some kind of real life, and there was no way he was going to work so hard, *so hard*, and then be told he should be grateful for the chance. That's what he had been thinking when he was 13. By the time he was 14 his rebellion had turned into a solid determination to take what he could get however he could get it. Only ignorant people lived by rules that did nothing to help *them*.

That was when the real trouble started. January 11, 1945. He remembered that date as it was his unlucky day. He got caught robbing a house in the middle of the night, stealing a pistol and a box of cartridges. Sheriff Barnes had caught him right off, one, two, three. Life changed after that. Next thing he knew he was being sentenced to four to seven years in prison. He was put in the Montgomery Correctional Center, the minimum security prison in Troy, North Carolina. He had thought he was a real tough guy going in, but he soon learned he wasn't as tough as he thought. There were other boys there, even grown men, but he was among the youngest, and as skinny as a rail. Most of the other prisoners were as mean as the guards, making him do things, pushing him around, beating him up if he resisted. Life in prison teaches you things you could never learn on the outside. One thing is, you've only got yourself to count on. Nobody's gonna help you. Nobody can be trusted. And if you try to follow the rules–and who can follow all those rules anyway?–it won't get you anything. Nothing's better for following their rules. Make your own rules; that was his motto.

From the moment he had arrived in Troy all he could think about was getting out. Freedom and home. It hurt all the more when other prisoners got released while he had to stay behind. He didn't make any vows to be good, he just vowed to stay low, out of sight, not to let anyone take notice of him. He couldn't stand the thought of wasting his life there. He'd already served nearly two years; the thought of staying for five more was just too much. He thought about it every day: stay low, keep watch, find your chance. And one day, by God, he saw his opening. They'd been taken out of the prison to work on the road, busting up pavement. A chain gang, but with no chains. It was a crisp October day, 1946. The guards worked them hard that morning, fed them some dinner, and set back to work. It was getting close to quitting time, and Junior just couldn't bear the thought of going back inside those walls. The lure of freedom was coming from just beyond those trees over there. If he could just make it into those woods, they wouldn't miss him until head count, and it would soon be getting dark. As the guards started to get tired themselves, Junior saw a way to slip off unnoticed. By the time the head count started on the bus, Junior was miles away in the dark woods.

He didn't know anywhere to go but home. When he got home a few days later, he made up a lie about being let out of prison early, and his parents had accepted it. A week went by, then two. Nobody came to take him back to prison, and before you know it, he had been home ten months without a problem. Maybe the law didn't care. He started to breathe easier and went back to seeing his friends, and quit worrying about hiding. He bragged about his prison exploits. He was still a kid, after all. What he had done, robbing a house, wasn't all that bad. Lots of people did it. If they hadn't come looking for him, they must not have cared very much that he ran away. Just one more nigger they wouldn't have to feed in jail.

But now, this. When all that noise started up the road at the Pratt house, he had to run. He'd run because he was scared to see the sheriff, had run to avoid going back to prison with a jailbreak to answer for. But then it got worse. It had been in the news that Mr. Pratt had died. Now everybody was looking for the killer, and he had been named. That new Mrs. Pratt, she had blamed him. Open and shut, whether for jailbreak or murder, they'd have him one way or the other. And he didn't want to go back to prison in any case. He thought that if he could just hide out until all this commotion died down, he could come back home later. Or maybe he could find work in Virginia and just disappear for a while. They'd find somebody else to blame and forget about him.

Running now, in the hot September sun, he still tried to figure a way out. In the thickets and hollow woods, maybe he had a chance. He heard the dogs barking behind him, closing in. He had left James' house without grabbing his coat and sweater off the porch, just took off running, hoping to have a head start, hoping they couldn't track him. But he was pretty sure that the sweater and coat had given the dogs the scent, and they were right behind him. Damn! Why didn't he grab those clothes? Why did he get so comfortable up at James' house? He should have kept moving north, maybe up to New York City, someplace far away. He could have made it on his wits; he always did. And if wits didn't work, sheer guts. He was a little guy, but he had never backed down from a fight. He was fast, he could throw some good punches. But now, now, how was he going to get out of this one?

He had been running for an hour now. The trap he was in became ever more obvious. Sweat pouring off of him, his shirt sticking to his back, his legs feeling like wood, his mind racing in terror, he knew he was running out of steam, out of time. The barking got louder. Plowing through a cornfield in an effort to hide, he dove into a thicket and waited, trying not to breathe. He was hot, tired, hungry, and defeated. He thought he might throw up. There was no more he could do.

The bloodhounds were barking furiously. A loud shot filled the air that rang in his ears as the noise pounded in his chest. His blood ran cold. He prayed that the shot would be the last. These men had him cornered and he would have to give himself up.

"We got him! Junior Thompson! Come on out here!"

He had lost this race, and if he didn't come out, the dogs would come in. Terrified, his legs feeling like rubber, Junior stood. The dogs, barking and straining at their leashes, were menacing. In front of him stood two men, their guns drawn and aimed right at him. He walked slowly toward them, trying to think of a new plan, trying to look totally innocent.

"Junior Thompson, you are wanted for the murder of Tom Pratt." He looked at the triumphant white faces of the two men and felt their sense of power over him. He knew they could do him harm in an instant and nobody would question them for it. No use trying to fight. He'd lie.

Looking them square in the eye, he said, "My name's James Price, Jr. I don't know no Junior Thompson. I'm not who you're lookin' for."

"What were you runnin' for then?"

"I was just comin' home from work in Martinsville. I heard the dogs. I just got scared."

"Well, that's funny. Obie, ain't that funny? This boy says he's not Junior Thompson. Know why that's funny, boy?" One thing he had learned in prison was to be quiet when the taunting started. He kept his mouth shut. The man continued, "Because we have a picture right here of Junior Thompson, and he sure looks just like you." The man held it up. Junior looked at the circular–wanted for murder and burglary, it said. Escaped con. They had the photo from his time in jail. He sighed. He was caught. It was all stacked against him: these men, and the others who must have been close behind, their side arms, their dogs. He couldn't talk his way out of this one.

"I didn't do nothin'. I didn't do nothin'."

They were placing handcuffs on him and shoving him forward, a gun aimed at his back. "Like you didn't do that robbery. Like you didn't break out of jail. We'll see about that. Tell it to the judge, boy, tell it to the judge. Let's go."

Junior Thompson's photo in local papers, probably his mug shot.

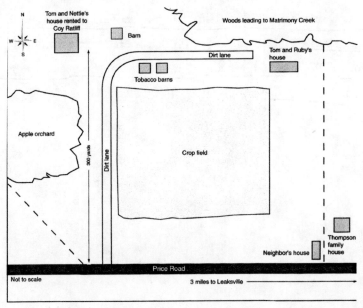

Illustration by Steve Hetzel

Tom Pratt's farm property in relation to the Thompson home on Price Road.
The dirt lane is now known as Mabes Road.

Chapter 2

Tom Pratt

Four years earlier: June 5, 1943

Tom Pratt couldn't believe the turn his life was taking. He felt stunned every time he looked at her, as if it couldn't be real. But it was true: Ruby was driving this car and they were going to get their marriage license. As the car ambled away from Leaksville to the County Courthouse in Wentworth, his thoughts rambled, too. He was 77 years old, this girl was only 32, and he believed she loved him. As she chattered on about her job at the bedspread mill and a dress she wanted to buy, his mind wandered. What would his children say? What would Nettie have said?

He thought back on all the twists and turns that had led up to this, his second chance at life. He had been born in Virginia just after the end of the Civil War. His family soon moved to Rockingham County, North Carolina, where he grew up with ten younger brothers and sisters. Pa's life during the Civil War had been tough, and maybe that's why Pa had been so driven to make money. He had bought up as much land as he could, ending up with about 1,000 acres around Buffalo Island Creek, about eight miles west of Leaksville. Pa had farmed, had a gristmill, a blacksmith shop, and an office. Pa had even loaned money to the richest man in the county, J. Turner Morehead! When Pa died in 1897, Tom inherited his share of the land that was divided between him and his brothers. His sisters inherited $100 each. The old homeplace went to his youngest brother Harvey and his family, who lived there with Ma until she died. Ma had only just died a few years ago, and he was relieved he didn't have to tell her about this marriage.

Ruby had grown quiet while driving, but he hadn't noticed, and he didn't fill in the silence. In general, he was not a big talker. He could talk to his sons, of course, about farming or politics. He had always talked to Nettie about everything under the sun. But around Ruby, well, he sure could get tongue-tied around her. Lots of times he couldn't think of a thing to say to Ruby, his mind completely blank, like a stunned old possum that just fell out of a tree. Glancing sideways at her, he compared himself to her. Like him, she was a hard worker. She had a job in the mill and did a lot of cooking and housekeeping for him—and they weren't even married yet! If he had been slowing down due to his age, she was just getting started—just look at the way she was handling this car! That's what these modern girls did. They spoke their minds and tried new things. He admired that. Feeling a little bolder, he took a longer look at her. Her hair was curly and brown, pinned back at the sides, but it blew around her face by the air blowing in the car window. She had on a dark blue dress with a belt that looked like it had diamonds on the buckle. Nettie wouldn't have worn anything like that! She had the prettiest smile he thought he'd ever seen. "Ruby, you're the sweetest thing I've ever known," he blurted out, reaching out to touch her curls. She giggled. "Well, bless your heart." He didn't feel silly. She never made him feel like an old man, even though on the inside he felt as humble as a housecat. She was the breath of the future; she was life itself.

What did she really see in him? He had come from good, hard-working people. He had been handsome once, he thought, and maybe he was still a little handsome. He wasn't fat and he still had a lot of his hair. His mind was clear and he could still put in a full day's work. In fact, he was quite strong for an old fella and still did everything around his farm that he'd always done. Although his tall frame was stooped, he was healthy, and except for some rheumatism, he had never really been sick. He'd spent his life as a farmer and carpenter. Unlike Pa, he had never gotten rich, but he did have his farm. The farm, all his carpentry work for Drury Moore, and his grown children and his grandchildren—these were the things that a man looked back on with pride, what a man lives his life for. This surely that must be what Ruby loved about him.

With Nettie gone, he had been lonely, but he didn't talk about it. You had to take what comes in life. All he really had to look forward to were the Sunday visits with the young'uns. It was a long lonely week until then. Plenty of time to think out there while planting tobacco, worming tobacco, hoeing tobacco, pulling tobacco, curing tobacco, and selling tobacco at a good price.

Along the country road, they passed a rusty little sign in front of a small church. "Jesus Saves!" it proclaimed. While his father had been a staunch Missionary Baptist, Tom didn't go to church. He knew that Jesus was his Savior and that Heaven and Hell were real places—well everybody but the heathens knew that—but he didn't think beyond it. "What a friend we have in Jesus," the old hymn says. Tom's best friends had been his wife and his family, and they had been more real help to him than the Lord who sometimes took notice of you and sometimes didn't. Nettie hadn't felt that way. She had accepted it when Alma died, trusting the Lord in the midst of her grief. Tom had simply accepted it as an unavoidable fact of life: sometimes we lose the ones we love, but life goes on anyway.

Tom knew that Ruby didn't attend church. It was apparently not that important to her, either. But most of his family and most of the people in this community could be found in a church pew on Sunday morning. A lot of people wouldn't miss it for anything. Churches were everywhere, and if that weren't enough, the itinerant preachers would come through town, set up their tents for a week, and save as many souls as they could before moving on. Nobody could get as worked up about the Lord as some of these traveling evangelists. Faith healing, speaking in tongues—the choice between being saved or going to hell was made very clear. He had to admit that not everybody went in for that sort of thing—not him, and not his own children, certainly—but the undeniable presence of religion was part of life here, same as farming or the mills. Religion filled the air like a mist. You might like it or you might not, but you had to breathe it in anyway.

"You know what I like to do, Ruby, on a Sunday morning? I like to sit with a good hot cup of coffee and read. I catch up with what's going on with President Roosevelt and the war. I can easily spend most of the morning just reading the paper. Then in the afternoon I usually get with my kids. We just sit and talk and eat, and the young 'uns run around. But it's real nice. I really like that."

Ruby didn't answer right away. "Well, I guess that's what we'll do then," she said half-heartedly.

So that was that. Life would go on the way it had been, only now Ruby would be there to keep him company and be a part of his family. In

20

a little while they'd be in Wentworth getting that marriage license. He felt a strange mixture of excitement and self-reproach. It was hard not to think of Nettie, his dear wife of 49 years. He'd known her most of his life. She had been the ninth of ten children in the Morgan family and her family had lived not far from his own. It felt like he was betraying her somehow, though she'd been dead for seven years now. He tried to squelch the guilty feelings. Would Nettie have liked Ruby? Not under these circumstances, no sir, he had to admit she would not have liked it. Nettie'd been as practical as the day is long, and she would have thought his decision wasn't smart. He remembered the look on her face when she didn't like something but didn't say so. Tom knew he had often been serious and a little impulsive, but Nettie had been the opposite: friendly, sensible, with an easy laugh and a kind manner. Her ability to handle a dollar must have come from her father, who had been a licensed whiskey distiller. Nettie had always been Tom's partner in business matters; she had always given him good advice though he hadn't always taken it. He loved Ruby but he still missed Nettie. He somehow felt like he was betraying Nettie by getting married again. But on the other hand, when he thought of Ruby, he felt a little guilty for missing Nettie. It was an odd mix-up of feelings.

Where had their lives gone? He imagined Nettie's face changing over time: first as a girl with freckles on her nose riding her horse into town with her daddy, then as a young bride, then as a mother with children hanging onto her skirts. It's funny how pictures come into your head. He could see her standing in the back door, looking over the garden. She wasn't worried about getting enough rain like he had been. No, she was admiring her flowers, the purple and white dianthus, the pink petunias, the deep red coleus and silver...dang, what was the name of

21

them things? Dusty millers. He'd sort of wondered why she'd spent time putting in flowers when there was squash and butterbeans to plant, something they could eat the next winter. But when he remembered her face, the sun hitting it and the warm summer breeze pushing her wisps of hair across her forehead, he felt, all these years later, the pleasure she had taken in them, the beauty of the earth. Could it really have been seven years since she died?

The car hit a small pothole and he was jolted back to the present. Flowers. Women liked flowers. He'd have to pick something pretty for Ruby. Something red, like her name. But after a minute he allowed himself to be lulled back into his memories. He hadn't wanted to think much about Nettie recently, what with Ruby taking all his attention. But now that he was going through with this marriage it seemed he couldn't stop thinking about Nettie. He somehow felt he owed it to her.

He had married Nettie on January 3, 1887, fifty-six years ago, in her father's parlor, when they were both just 20. Pearl was born the first year they were married. Then came Alma, Jake, Clyde, Jim, Reid, and Betty. Twenty years of having babies! Betty was born in 1907 when Nettie was 41. Then the next year, 1908, Alma got sick and died when she was just 17. While Pearl had always been dependable and constant, it was Alma who had brought laughter and music to the family, playing the dulcimer and livening up the evenings with her sense of fun. Reid, who was five when she died, and Betty, one, would never really remember her. But with five children to provide for under the age of twelve, there was little time to grieve. Pearl had been a tremendous help with the little ones, and he marveled at how much like her mother she was. He had come to rely on her in ways then that lasted to this day. Looking back now though, it always seemed to him that there had been so much work to do, and so little time to play. Alma's music still echoed in his ears, though it was ages ago now, a lifetime ago. It had all happened before Ruby was even born. He looked over at her, momentarily back to the present.

"What was your family like, Ruby, growin' up?"

"Well, you know we lived in different places. Daddy farmed on halves, of course, for different men. You know my brothers, I think, John, Frank, Nathan, Marion and Bill. I've got two younger sisters, Lillie and Lucille. Lillie was named for my mama. Lillie's fifteen and Lucille's twelve. Mama died a few years ago."

Tom had twenty grandchildren, and he even had great-grandchildren, but he was not about to point out this fact. The first grandson, Deed, Pearl's boy, had started calling him "Old Pa" years ago. All the other grandchildren took it up. "Old Pa and Old Mammie"–that's what they'd called Nettie–those were the names they'd been stuck with. Everybody had nicknames, but he wasn't going to tell Ruby his, though no doubt she knew it.

"Looka yonder, Ruby, I built the porch on that house." Ruby looked in the direction of the house as she drove by. "That's real good, Tom," she replied, but she didn't seem to notice all the scrollwork around the top of the porch, the way the lathe had turned the balusters, the way the porch just seemed to invite all who walked by to come and sit. But he didn't mind. She might have her mind on other things, too.

Tom had developed a knack for fine carpentry while growing up and he had made a career of it. Most of his work had been the detailed work on staircases, doors, windows, fireplaces, and moldings that were so popular on the fine houses in these parts. But in spite of the work he'd had, he and Nettie had struggled to get by for years. He had been in and out of debt many times. Local merchants were usually willing to carry him until the crops came in. Not always, though. There was that summer in 1906 when they owed $15.40 to the Leaksville Mercantile Company. They had to mortgage his entire tobacco crop, corn fodder, shucks and his even his red cow until the bill was paid. It was tough to always owe money, but worse was that feeling that you could never have anything just for the fun of it, just to be reckless once in a while. Nettie and the kids had deserved better.

Out of the blue, Tom said, "You think you could teach me how to drive sometime?"

Ruby looked surprised. "I 'spect so. You want to learn to drive?"

"I don't know. Looks like it might be fun. I could get my own car; wouldn't have to borrow yours. I had a car once, did you know that?"

"No, I didn't."

"Well, we were livin' in town by then, and it was harder to get out to see Ma– Betty and Reid were still just little kids and couldn't walk so far. It was a 1915 Model T Ford Touring Car. I'm tellin' you, it was beautiful! It had electric headlights and oil burning sidelights, and inside there was leather seats. To get it to start you had to– "

"But what did you do with it if you couldn't drive?"

"Ah, p'shaw, Ruby, I just wanted it! I got it to surprise Nettie and the boys. I thought I would learn to drive it, but I was just too busy to get to it. Anyway, Jake and Clyde drove it, and Jim, when he got a little older. They picked up how to drive real easy. Jim drives a truck now, you know, for a livin'. Anyway, at first, Nettie wouldn't even get in it. Said we'd all get ourselves killed in it. But the kids just kept beggin' her, 'Come on, Mama, let's take a ride'–and so she did. She got over her fear. She said she felt like a queen going to her castle when we took a ride. Ha! Then, well, the boys 'ould carry me and Nettie anywhere we needed to go if we couldn't walk there."

She laughed. "Well if you want to learn to drive now I suppose I could show you. It's not hard."

"You know I walk everywhere. I don't need a car, Ruby, just thought it might be somethin' I'd like to do. I don't need to ride most times." He wanted to make sure she understood that he didn't need anyone's help, but also that he was interested in keeping up with the times. A nice feeling settled over him because she could see the kind of man he was.

In fact, he had never been afraid to try new things. Sometimes you had to take a risk to see what might happen. Nettie had always been more cautious, keeping him in line when his ideas got a little out of hand. In 1909, not long after Alma died, they decided to move to town. It was Nettie who bought the land on Johnson Street in the new Oakland neighborhood of Leaksville. Fancy that, a woman owning property! His name wasn't even on the deed. But he had built the house on it, a nice place in town where the children could walk to school. Jake started working at the Leaksville Woolen Mill when he was 14. The young people used to go roller skating up there on the third floor of the company store. In town, everything was close by. Yessir, that had been a good move and a good house, and they had lived in it for over twenty years.

"What'd you say, Ruby?" knowing he hadn't been listening at all.

"I was sayin' that you got to get busy on the garden if you're hopin' to have any tomatoes this year. The strawberries are already as big as apples."

"Oh that's so. I 'spect you're right." It was nice to see Ruby so cheerful. But the closer they got to Wentworth, the more lost he became in thought, and he drifted off again. Seems like he had to put it all in order in his mind. Everything that had happened in his life: growing up, work, marriage, children, grandchildren, the farm, Alma's death, Mama and Nettie...where did the years go? As for himself, he knew that he was at an age when some men were looking death square in the face, but not him. It's like he was starting all over. He was 77 years old! How did he get so lucky? He still couldn't take it all in. Sometimes he felt a little foolish, but then again, he was in high spirits. He had to sort it out.

Tom fell silent again, resuming his daydreaming. By 1925 they had been living on Johnson Street for sixteen years. All the children except Reid were grown and married. What had it been about Reid? They had not been able to control him. He was like a wild horse. Reid, though, 22 years old at that point, had given them fits ever since he was a kid. Maybe he had gotten away with too much as the youngest son. Maybe Reid had tried too hard to fit in with his older brothers. For one thing, he sure couldn't handle his liquor. Tom and Nettie never could figure out where they had gone wrong. Strong as an ox, Reid was, and a good worker at the mill, but he would start drinking on Friday night and not get sober again until work time on Monday. Nettie had tried talking to him to no use. Tom didn't see that talk was necessary. Wasn't it obvious how a grown man should act? Oh, there was nobody who could make Tom madder than Reid! The drinking was bad enough, but that was nothing compared to what came next.

Reid was 24 when he approached them one day with a pained look on his face. "Mama, Papa," he had said, standing there with that letter in his hands, squirming like a worm in hot ashes. Reid had said nothing more, just handed Tom the letter to read, with Nettie reading over his shoulder. What was this? It was from a Mr. B. C. Trotter, an attorney, naming Reid as the father of a baby girl. Reid had fathered a baby? When?! Who was this girl? Is this what had been going on when Reid would disappear and not come home like Nettie had asked him to? This letter said the family was suing Reid for $1,000. A thousand dollars! As Tom had read, a knot had settled in his stomach. It was like being kicked by a mule. How was Reid going to come up with that kind of money? Well, from them, obviously! "What'd you do that for?" Tom had demanded. "What'd you go and do that for? How could you do this to us?" Reid's sputtering responses and explanations were hardly heard. And Tom had stomped out of the house, leaving Reid standing there gape-mouthed, and Nettie saying, "Now, Tom, now, Tom–" but he hadn't waited around to hear what she would have said next.

The news had made him feel like he was going crazy. How can you make a boy grow up and be a man? How could you get him to do the right thing? Reid said the girl wouldn't marry him. Tom found that next to impossible to believe, but the fact was, they weren't gonna marry. Tom had had to admit there was nothing he could do about this situation. Thinking about it now brought back the pain, how Nettie had cried, and how he had yelled and cursed. How humiliated they had been by Reid's immorality! But the truth was, he and Reid had always butted heads and probably always would.

Tom and Nettie borrowed the money to pay the baby's mother by mortgaging their house for $1,000. Every five months for a year and a half they paid $200 to the clerk of the court, Hunter K. Penn, in Wentworth, who then paid it to the girl's family. Reid worked, but he didn't have that kind of money. And, Nettie had said, a child out there with no daddy wasn't right. The baby was named Loraine and was raised by her grandmother and uncle. Tom had heard that the mother eventually married someone else. What a mess that had been. Nettie had felt so bad.

The lull of the ride on the warm day kept him lost in his thoughts. By 1930, the Great Depression had come on strong and carpentry and millwork work had dried up. Though they were both 64 years old, there was no thought of retirement as they still needed an income. All the children but Reid had moved out with families of their own. They didn't need that big house on Johnson Street anymore. They'd been happy there for twenty years, but it was time to move again. Tom and Nettie decided he had to go back to farming. He had never liked it much, but what else could he do? Times were hard and they had few choices. Now, where to go?

Everyone in town knew that when Old Man Dump Ivie–a well-known and cracker-jack lawyer–died in 1927, that his tenant farm would be sold. Tom knew that his son Allan, also a lawyer, was administrator of the estate, and Tom began to dicker with Allan about selling it. With about eighty-seven acres backing up to a branch of Matrimony Creek, a house, an apple orchard, plus room for tobacco, corn, rye, a vegetable garden, a chicken lot and two mules, it would be just perfect for Tom and Nettie. It was a big piece of property for two people, but Tom made the investment, knowing he could always sell off a part of it or lease it to sharecroppers if necessary. So Tom and Nettie sold the Johnson Street house and on June 2, 1930, bought the old Dump Ivie Farm for $3,500.

Tom mightn't've wanted to go back to farming, but the Dump Ivie farm was in an ideal location. It was on the north side of Price Road, about three miles west of town. The farm house sat about 300 yards back from the road. Tom and Nettie had both grown up a few miles west of there, on the north side of Old Stoneville Road. His ma, now in her eighties, was still living there with Harvey at the old homeplace. Pearl and her husband Dan Holland also lived within walking distance. Pearl's daughter Edna had married Harold Hoover and they had two children, Becky and Wink. He and Nettie liked Harold so much that the same day they bought this farm, they sold him a piece of it, fifteen acres, for $10. They also sold three smaller parcels of land to raise some cash, so when all was said and done, Tom and Nettie had about sixty-four acres. Moving to the Dump Ivie farm had brought them closer to almost his entire family. It felt right.

Tom and Nettie's closest new neighbor was a colored man named Edd Thompson, whose property was in front of theirs, and closer to the road. Edd had a job at Fieldcrest, mixing batches of starch for the sheets. He had a lot of responsibility—the type of job that a white man would have if he could get it. Edd lived with his wife Reeves and their sons Weldon, Junior Edd and Pete. Edd had been a good neighbor over the years, except for once when Tom threatened to sue him for not keeping his chickens in a pen. But after Tom wrote Edd a note about it, the problem was solved. Sometimes Tom hired Edd to do some of the farm work. Edd's sons would play with his own grandchildren in the orchard, and overall it had worked out just fine.

Tom and Nettie's new house on the farm, built in 1813, was smaller than they'd had on Johnson Street, but comfortable. Tom had remodeled it some after they moved in. Their water came from a dug well, and of course there was a privy outside. They'd used kerosene lamps, as there was no electricity until around 1936. There was a sitting room with a large log-burning fireplace, a kitchen, a dining room, and two bedrooms. There was a screened-in porch that held a large tin-lined wooden icebox. The iceman would come every three to four days.

"Ruby, do you like watermelon?"

"Well, of course I do! Who doesn't like watermelon? Why on earth are you askin' me about watermelons?"

"You know that spring branch that runs down behind the house? I once built a springbox in that branch. Oh, that water was cold as ice! The springbox was about three feet long, 'bout this wide" (he motioned eighteen inches with his hands) "and a foot high. I bored holes on each end, and the water flowed right through the box and down the branch. I covered the whole thing with a hinged lid to keep the animals out. I put my watermelons in there. Kept 'em nice and fresh for sellin'. It was better'n an icebox."

"You think I don't know what a springbox is, Tom?" Honestly, she thought, sometimes he talked to her like she was five years old.

He was a little embarrassed. "Well, everybody's got an icebox these days." He had to remember that though she was young, she wasn't entirely uninformed. Why had he told her anyway? He knew he wanted to impress her with his accomplishments, big and small. He had thought his springbox was clever. But how could he tell her about a life's work, the hours and hours of very hard work, without sounding like he was bragging or looking for sympathy? How could he make her understand what they had gone through to survive?

Although he'd remodeled it some, the house had been livable from the start. But getting the farm into shape, that was another matter. First, he built a barn for the livestock, two tobacco barns, a corncrib and a tobacco packhouse. Then he turned to the land itself. The land had been neglected and overgrown with matted Bermuda grass, so thick that he had had to cut into it with an ax just to get the point of a turning plow to stick into the ground. Working with his two mules, he planted as quickly as he could in hopes of making a crop that first year.

After buying the farm in 1930, he had needed to make some money right away. He bought and operated a sawmill on the backside of the farm. He cut tall pines, oak and poplar trees and dragged the logs to the sawmill. Driven by a large noisy, vertical steam engine, the sawmill required four or five skilled hands to operate. It was rough and tumble work. They kept clean rags and a jug of kerosene handy to daub the cuts and bruises they suffered. He sold lumber, and he sold leftover slabs for stovewood. The mills would buy it from him to sell cheap to their employees. In 1932 he cut ten cords of slabs which were about eight feet long, hauled them into town and sold it to the Carolina Cotton and Woolen Mills Company. He was paid $3.50 and was glad to get it.

His goal for the farm had been to be as self-sufficient as possible: food, water, vegetables, firewood, lumber—all the basic necessities he'd hoped to provide for themselves. Corn was an important cash crop and they were sunk if they didn't get enough rain. They used every bit of an ear of corn. After it was dried, the corn was shucked, then shelled, and ground into corn meal as they needed it. You were careful not to grind up too much at once or it would get wormy before you could use it. Cracked corn fed the chickens. Hogs would eat the corn, cobs and all. Corn fodder was fed to the mules. Corn shucks were fed to cows, and poorer people used shucks for mattresses. Last of all, he could make a good hot fire from the corncobs in the fireplace, though they'd burn up quick. Rats getting into the corncrib were always a nuisance, but a good barn cat or two could see to that. If there was such a thing as a good cat.

There was a large apple orchard in front of his house, between his house and Harold Hoover's. It sure did look pretty in the springtime with its white blossoms, and the fragrance would drift back their way and be real sweet. He had a hand-turned mill to crush the apples to make cider. After a few days, sweet cider would ferment and have a nice bite to it. Fermented cider eventually turned into vinegar, which Nettie used to make pickles.

"I know you like apples," he said, as an afterthought. "We'll have all you want."

"Yes, that'll be good. I'll cook you some real tasty pies when they come in." She winked, and he blushed.

But income from the sawmill, corn crop, and apples were nothing compared to tobacco. If you wanted to make money, you had to grow tobacco. Tobacco was his main crop, his main source of income, and probably his biggest headache. Good night! Growing tobacco, selling tobacco, and worrying about tobacco had been his life now, twelve months out of the year, for over fifteen years. This was not something he needed to explain to Ruby. Her daddy had grown it, too. The first year there, he, Jake and Reid had cut a few acres of pines off the land so he could plant it, and tobacco had preoccupied him ever since.

Five to ten cords of pine were needed to cure the tobacco come fall. After cutting the trees and sawing off the limbs, they cut the trunks to eight to ten feet long. Larger trees they split with a maul and sledge hammer and then hauled it to the tobacco barns to dry out. Their beds sure did feel good after doing hard work like that all day! But cutting and hauling pine logs was just the first step he needed to take. This would be a year-long job.

Some people measured time by the passing seasons or by the ages of their children. He thought of time in terms of the growth cycle of tobacco. In late January or February he sowed the very tiny tobacco seeds in a large bed, maybe twenty-five by fifty feet, and covered it with cheesecloth to keep the birds out and the soil warm. After a month or so, if all went well, the young plants would be about eight or ten inches tall. Then he pulled out the weak-looking plants to thin them out, and the rest kept growing.

Meantime, he'd plow the ground using his turning plow and a couple of mules, and then harrow the ground to break up the large clumps of soil. He lay off the soil in rows about four feet apart with a coulter. He then transplanted the young tobacco plants from the seedbed along the rows about two and a half feet apart with a planting peg. What backbreaking work that was! That peg was just a nine-inch length of hard wood, rounded off for holding against his palm on one end and whittled to a point on the other end. But that piece of wood is what kept him in business. He'd push it into the soil and make a nice hole, add fertilizer and water and the young plant. Each little plant had to be kept watered, the soil pushed against the roots to keep the air out and keep the plant from withering. Great day! It seemed those little plants required more care than all his young'uns! Even so, not all those little plants would survive. After a few days, he'd have to pull out the wilted ones and replace them.

As the tobacco plants began to grow and the weather became warmer, he had to cultivate them every so often to keep out the grass and weeds, first with a coulter and then between the plants with a hoe. He often enlisted his grandchildren and neighbor children to pull the worms off the growing plants. Those worms could get to be three inches long, and if you didn't get them off they'd devour every plant in your crop. You'd kill them by mashing them between two rocks. Then every week or so the plants had to be suckered to remove the smaller leaves so that some of the other leaves could get sunlight. Flowers and seed heads were topped off to make the plant grow larger. Young children could do that work, too. Of course, the best-looking plants were saved for their seeds. He'd save out ten to twenty plants, wrap their heads in cheesecloth, and wait for them to mature. The tiny seeds dried naturally and were saved for the next year's planting.

Finally by August or maybe September the harvesting could start. He'd pull a ground slide slowly between the rows with his trained mule and pull off the lowest leaves and place them neatly on the slide in a burlap bin. The mule pulled the slide between the rows and finally to the tobacco barn. Farm helpers would unload the leaves, string them together a few at a time along either side of a split wooden pole about four feet long and an inch and a half around.

Now it was time to start curing. Each tobacco barn was divided into vertical sections called rooms. Each barn held four to five rooms. Starting at the top of the barn, he and the other hands—sometimes neighbors and sometimes men he'd hired—hung the poles of tobacco in these rooms so that hot air could rise between the leaves. Once the barn was filled, he'd start a small fire in the horizontal rock flue that opened to the outside front of the barn. Slowly the temperature would be raised and the color of the leaves would slowly turn from green to a golden yellow. This dried the leaves, and you could smell tobacco all around. Curing usually took six days, and you couldn't leave it alone. The temperature of the barn had to be kept just right. The curers slept in shifts, but even so, there wasn't much resting either. He had built his barns with sheet metal shelters in case it rained. A cool September rain at night was nothing you'd want to be in, but you couldn't leave, either. Logs had to be fed into the flue to keep the fire going. And if he'd missed chinking any spaces in the log walls in the spring by filling them up with clay, the temperature inside the barn mightn't stay hot enough or steady enough and the leaves wouldn't cure evenly. Then there was always the fear of fire, or of a barn overheating which would reduce the quality of the leaves.

After about six days of this, they'd let the barn would cool down. He'd take out the poles that held the tobacco. The tobacco was brittle and could crumble at this point, so the next step was it had to get some moisture put back into it. He carried the poles of tobacco over to the pack house, which wasn't really a house, but a large hole dug in the hillside covered with a roof and closed at the front with a door. After a few days the tobacco absorbed moisture from the soil and became pliant again. The tobacco would be stored there until the fall. He then took the leaves out, sorted them by size and graded them for quality. It was now ready for sale.

Yessir, growing tobacco was one tough, aggravating, back-breaking, never-ending job. And dirty! The plant was covered with gum that got all over you, your clothes, your skin, under your fingernails and everywhere. The only way to get it off your skin was to wash with kerosene or turpentine. There were only two good things about growing tobacco. One, he enjoyed a good chew. He enjoyed it more knowing what it took him to get it. And two, he could sell it.

Tobacco markets were all in the area. Three he had used over the years were King's Warehouse in Leaksville, Glenn's Warehouse, and Brown's Warehouse in Stoneville. He also sold at warehouses in Martinsville, Virginia, and in Winston-Salem. Farmers from all over the county would haul in their crops, early on by horse-drawn wagons but later in trucks, and it could be quite a sight to see. It was a chance to visit with friends and other farmers, compare the sales figures, talk politics, talk about rabbit and possum hunting and listen to gossip. All the farmers hoped for high prices. The buyers, who worked for tobacco companies, would examine each man's crop, and quickly decide what they'd be willing to bid for it. The buyers really held the farmers' fates in their hands. The auctioneer would rattle off the prices in a sing-song, and the buyers would bid for the best-looking lot, always hoping to keep prices low but knowing they'd have to pay more for good quality tobacco. The whole thing would be over in a matter of a few minutes. Tom would plant up to four acres, and if he was lucky, he could get about $300 for his year's labor.

But that's just the way it was. That's what he had to do just to keep food on the table and keep warm in the winter. The work just kept on, day after day, from sun-up to sundown. They never thought to complain about it. Pretty much everybody was in the same boat.

The advantages of moving back to the country with Nettie were obvious during the Depression. He missed his millwork and carpentry, but nearly every man and a few women wanted tobacco. The cow, chickens, hog and garden sometimes made the difference between being fed or going without. He had planted his vegetable garden for their own use and sold the surplus. They'd have squash, cucumbers, cantaloupes, peppers, snap beans, peas, tomatoes, okra, butter beans, sweet corn, strawberries, and of course, melons. Nettie also canned snap beans, butter beans, apples, peaches, pears, beets, corn, okra, and tomatoes. She put up cucumber pickle, pickle relish, watermelon rind pickle, and made damson, strawberry, blackberry, pear, and dewberry preserves. If it could be put in a jar in the summer they could eat it the next winter.

So that's how life was when he and Nettie had made their life on Price Road. Hard work six days a week, and rest on Sundays with the children and grandchildren. He had been the undisputed head of the family and he savored it. He would sit in the yard, chewing, talking, sharpening his pocketknife and whittling, watching for an occasional passing car that left its cloud of dust from the unpaved road. Nettie and the womenfolk brought out the food they had prepared the day before. In the summer they'd cut a watermelon in the front yard. In the late fall, the grandchildren would search his pockets for wild chinquapins as they climbed all over him like a pack of monkeys. Tom saw them all in his memory during those happy years. Their children, grandchildren and great-grandchildren were the biggest accomplishments in his life. He and Nettie had raised a fine family of good people.

By 1935 Tom and Nettie were 69 years old and Ma was 89. Ma had always been real strong. This year, though, Ma's strength had run out. On July 24, 1935, Bettie Pratt died.

Meanwhile, Nettie, who had diabetes, was often tired and needed rest. Then one cold drizzling day she fell from the porch and broke her hip. It had been hours before anyone found her. Tom felt anguished again as he thought of Nettie lying in the rain, in pain and alone. Finally, Harold Hoover, their grandson-in-law, came across her and they were able to get her inside. They had done everything they could to make her comfortable, but her pain was severe and she was confined to bed.

Tom hired a colored lady, Aunt Caroline, to move in and look after her. She was a large, educated, gray-haired woman, and she waited on Nettie hand and foot. She had no relatives in Leaksville, so he didn't know why she had come all the way there from Chicago. He wondered what had ever become of her. When she had wanted to go to church, his son Clyde had taken her with him, sitting right in the middle of the pew with his whole family. Not one person batted an eye as far as he had ever heard. Everybody knew what a great help that lady had been to Nettie. Some saw her as an answer to prayer.

Tom had seen that Nettie was frustrated at being so helpless. All that time in bed had given her a lot of time to think. Reid was in his thirties and still living with them. It wasn't bad having him there, but Nettie felt he should have been married by now, with a family of his own. He was working at the mill but still drinking heavily on his days off. What would become of him? Nettie was sure that the right wife could straighten him out. So as she lay in her sickbed thinking about Reid, Tom realized she was hatching a plan.

One of Tom's regular customers for eggs was a girl named Custis Talbert. Custis had left her home in the Blue Ridge mountains to find work. She wound up living with a couple named George and Eva Butler, minding their two children while they worked in the mill. As time went on, Custis became friendly with Nettie. Custis, who perhaps missed her own mama, would sit by Nettie's bed and visit with her, bring her news from town or comb her hair. Custis was just as sweet as she could be and Nettie loved her. Tom felt very fond of her, but it was Nettie who had bigger plans for Custis.

"Reid," Nettie had said in a sweet voice one day, "Go help that girl with them eggs." Well, Nettie's plan worked. The next thing you know Reid and Custis were getting married, when Reid was 34 and Custis was 20. Custis knew all about Reid's daughter and accepted it. Nettie was right: the love of a good woman had changed Reid's life. Reid and Custis lived with them for a short while, then they got a home of their own. Reid continued to work at the sheeting mill in Draper, and though he still drank and still fought with Tom now and then over this and that, Reid loved Custis. Nettie finally got to see all of her children settled.

Bedridden for months, Nettie just couldn't seem to get well. She developed pneumonia and died on March 26, 1936, at age 69, three days before Tom's 70th birthday. Ma had just died the previous summer, and now he had lost Nettie. Ma had lived to be 89 and he realized that he just assumed that he and Nettie would do the same.

So that was the end. He guessed he had known all along that she wasn't going to recover. After she died, there was a vast emptiness in his life. So many times he thought of something he wanted to tell her, only to realize with a jolt that she was no longer there. The funeral had been nice. It seemed that neighbors brought more food than he could eat in a lifetime. But the fact was, he hadn't felt much like eating at all. She was buried at the El Bethel Presbyterian Church cemetery, which was just up the road from him. When his time came, he would be buried next to her, in a cemetery on Price Road.

In 1938, Custis gave birth to twin girls, named Nettie Colleen and Edna Earline. Edna Earline died when she was just a new baby. Colleen was good as gold, and Tom had to admit that Reid doted on her and was a good father. Tom realized that Colleen was the only grandchild who had not met Nettie. Maybe that's why she had such a special place in his heart.

These long memories had put him in a somber, reflective mood. What a long life he'd had, long and filled with so many people, so much work, and so many events that no one could have foreseen.

Ruby broke into his thoughts. "Tom?" she said quietly. "We're here. Seems like you left me for a few minutes there. Are you all right?" she asked gently.

Startled to find himself in the courthouse parking lot, he answered, "Yeah, I'm fine. I'm fine. Ruby, I'm right here. I ain't left you, and I ain't ever going to."

She turned to the rear-view mirror. "Goodness, the wind has blown my hair all over the place." She straightened it with her fingers and re-pinned it. "Does it look all right?" She turned to him and smiled.

He reached over and took her hand, looking down for fear that she would see the emotion he felt overwhelming him. Composing himself, he looked at her again, awestruck at her feminine habits as she sat looking at him with a puzzled face. His life had been good so far, filled with such joy and sadness that he could never explain it to a woman this young. You just had to live through it. Goodness, he was planning to marry her! His mind was a jumble of words and emotion, but all he could manage to say was, "I think you look as purty as a picture." Life sure was a mystery. Growing old hadn't given him any new answers.

Tom and Nettie Pratt with Pearl (standing), Alma, and Jake (baby).
Approximate date is 1898.

The house Tom built at what is now 109 Johnson Street, Eden, N.C. The land
was purchased by Nettie, with her name on the deed.

Tom and Nettie Pratt with their children and grand-children, about 1922, in front of the house at 109 Johnson Street, Leaksville (now Eden)

Back row: Dan B. Holland, Dan Holland, Pearl Pratt Holland, Fannie Sue Cox Pratt (wife of Clyde), Clyde Milton Pratt, holding daughter Frances, Evie Collins Pratt (wife of Jim), holding daughter Hovis, James (Jim) Pratt.

Front row: Edna Holland, Robert Reid Pratt, William Thomas Pratt ("Old Pa"), Peck Holland, Nettie Morgan Pratt ("Old Mammie"), Betty Hyler Pratt, Josie Smith Pratt (wife Thomas B.), Thomas B. ("Jake") Pratt.

Tom and Nettie's second child, Alma, died at age 16 in 1908.

42

Tom and Nettie Pratt, photos probably taken in the early 1920s.

Note found in Tom Pratt's papers. It was probably not sent. (Who typed it?)
In spite of its content, grandchildren reported a cordial relationship between
Tom Pratt and Ed Thompson. This note is dated April 28, 1931. Junior
Thompson was born in June 18, 1931 (according to his death certificate.)

BROWN'S WAREHOUSE

FOR THE SALE OF

LEAF TOBACCO

All Errors Promptly Corrected
Insurance and Storage Free

Stoneville, N. C. _1-2-4_ 194_7_

Sale Made For _Pratt & Ratliff_

No._____ Gross_____

No.	POUNDS	PRICE		AMOUNT	
211	184	1		404	
	120	29		348 0	
	304			55 0	
LESS: WAREHOUSE CHARGES		30		2.18	
AUCTION FEES		50			
COMMISSION 2½ PER CENT			3.6		
ADVANCES				53.86	
FREIGHT AND DRAYAGE					
NET PROCEEDS					

A bill of sale for tobacco from Brown's Warehouse, Stoneville, N.C., written to Tom Pratt and Coy Ratliff. They sold 304 pounds and made $309.89 after paying warehouse charges, auction fees, and a commission. It is dated January 24, 1947, eight months prior to Tom's murder.

44

Chapter 3

Tom and Ruby

June 5, 1943

Ruby finished combing her hair, added some lipstick, and looked at Tom for his approval. Then she said brightly, "Well, let's go then!"

Tom took his eyes from Ruby and looked at the red brick Rockingham County Courthouse. It had been built in 1907 after fire destroyed the previous building. Three stories tall, it housed the county courtroom, judges' chambers, and the county government offices. The jail was across the street. Coming here reminded him of all that trouble with Reid and that girl, having to send money to the clerk of the court. It was humiliating. Well, that had been over fifteen years ago. Time to let it go. He turned to grin at Ruby. "Ruby, you never can tell what life will bring!" He scooted out of the car to open her door for her. "I still can't believe it," he added. Ruby agreed. "Neither can I!" She smiled and took his arm.

They walked in, unsure of where to go. Two large staircases with massive oak banisters curved up on the left and right walls of the foyer to the second floor courtroom. Green and white mosaic tile floors led to an array of offices straight ahead. They followed the signs that directed them to the Registrar's Office. The gold lettering on the door announced the right office, and Tom opened the door for Ruby.

They approached the counter. A clerk looked up at them expectantly.

"We're here to get a marriage license," Tom said. He timidly put his arm around Ruby's shoulder and noticed her blush. He wanted there to be no mistake that this was his bride, not his daughter.

"I see," said the clerk. "I need to fill out the license, and we'll get you on your way." Smiling, she walked back to her desk to retrieve a pen and whispered something to a co-worker. Tom felt a little steamed having to be waited on by that snickering woman in her fancy office. Well, let them think what they wanted.

Tom gave his information while Ruby's eyes darted around the room. The clerk filled in the form with her fine script.

Wentworth, N.C.   June 5, 1943

State of North Carolina, County of Rockingham

Order of Register of Deeds

No. 6471

To any Ordained Minister of any Religion Denomination or any Justice of the Peace of said County.

W. Tom Pratt having applied to me for a LICENSE for the marriage of himself of Leaksville R-1 and Ruby Edwards, Leaksville.

For Tom's part, the clerk filled in: Age 78 years; COLOR White, the son of W. F. Pratt and Elizabeth Pratt, the father now Dead, the mother Dead, resident of _____ (she left this blank).

For Ruby's side, the clerk wrote: Age 32; COLOR White, the daughter of Ruffin Edwards and

Lillie Edwards, the father now Living, the mother Dead, resident of Leaksville N.C.

And there being no legal impediment to such marriage known to me, you are hereby authorized, at any time within sixty days from the date hereof, to celebrate the proposed marriage at any place within the said County. You are required, within sixty days after you shall have celebrated such marriage, to return this License to me, at my office, with your signature subscribed to the Certificate under this License, and with the blanks therein filled according to the facts, under penalty of forfeiting $200.00 to the use of any person who shall sue for the same.

It was signed by the Register of Deeds, R. E. Wall.

Next, the clerk took a large book from the shelf, the Marriage Register for Rockingham County, and filled in their names. Well that was it, then. They had sixty days to get married. He again held the door for her as they stepped out into the warm June day and went to the car. It hadn't taken twenty minutes.

Getting the license had emboldened him. "Well, honey, we done it. We're gonna to get married! Are you happy?" Tom asked.

"I sure am! Tom, we're going to have a nice life. It'll work out just fine!" Tom wanted to kiss her as they headed to the car but didn't. A tug-of-war went on inside him whenever they were off the farm and people could see them together. He knew he shouldn't feel ashamed because everything was proper, but he was still aware of feeling foolish at looking so old next to her. He tried not to let on. They settled back into the car and she started the motor.

A somersault of emotion was going through him. Goodness gracious, getting married again! Something nagged at him though. Was this really the right thing to do? He stared at the folded paper in his hands, the license that proved he was about to start a new life. He thought about Nettie again, and again felt a tug of guilt.

He had been so lonely after she died. He'd sometimes go to Pearl's to eat, but it wasn't the same as eating at home with Nettie. She had died in 1936, still in the middle of the Depression, and he had to admit that he was 70 years old with no wife to help him and a lot of land to tend. He started thinking that if he had a smaller house, he could rent the one he and Nettie had lived in to some tenant farmers. The tenant farmer could help him with his crops and have his own plot, too. The thought had cheered him, and planning it helped bring him out of his deep sadness over Ma's and Nettie's deaths. It would be good to have something to do. So he had gone down to the cow pasture, beyond the tobacco barns, and built a small log house. It felt good to wield a hammer again, to the amazement of his children and grandchildren who thought he was just an old man, Old Pa. He rented the larger house to tenant farmers, Coy and Vera Ratliff, and he was content in his new place built with his own hands. That's the house he'd be living in with Ruby. Coy and Vera lived in the big house now, and besides, he didn't want to bring Ruby into the house he had shared with Nettie.

Ruby Edwards! Though he had tried to fix in his own mind why she was marrying him, the truth was, he really didn't know why this girl had shown any interest in him. He was now 77 years old; she was 32, younger than Betty, his baby girl. At first Ruby had started coming to help him around the house. She was friendly with Coy and Vera, and they probably told her he could use a cook. But she'd come, and she'd worked hard, too. Cooked for him, cleaned, helped with some lighter farm work. She had a job at Fieldcrest's bedspread mill, working the second shift, from 3 to 11. She would come by in the late morning, straighten the house and fix him some dinner and clean up, all before going to work. He had told her she could quit that job once they were married, but Ruby wanted to hang onto it. She said it would be good to have a little cushion. He reckoned that was all right by him if that's what she wanted to do. It proved to him just what a hard worker she was.

At first Ruby just came a couple of days a week, but then it was more and more often. It seemed like she tried to make a little bit of cheery conversation, or brighten up the house a little bit. He realized that he had started to look forward to her visits. He'd put on a clean shirt, shave, and run a comb over his head before she arrived. It started to occur to him that she might make a pretty good wife. She was already getting to be an old maid, over 30 and not married, and no woman wanted that. But, no, it was still a crazy notion, wasn't it? What could she possibly want with him? That's when he started to notice the little things, like bringing him a cake or giving him a sweet smile. One day she'd said, "Mr. Pratt, do you mind if I call you 'Tom?'" Then she gave him dinner and put her hand on his shoulder, left it there for just a second. His heart about jumped into his throat. Yes, he was old, but he was strong and surely she could see that. She made him feel like a man of 20 again! He thought that she wouldn't be coming around so much if she weren't interested. She wasn't old, but she wasn't young, either. She needed a husband, and he needed a wife. He made up his mind to ask her to marry him. But first he would ask his oldest children what they thought. Maybe he shouldn't have.

"No, Papa, no sir, I don't think that's a good idea," Jake had said flatly. Tom couldn't quite make out the look on Jake's face. Stunned, he supposed. Well he reckoned it came as a surprise, but he felt like it shouldn't have been. Couldn't all his children see how happy he had been in the last few months?

"Why not? She helps me out a lot and she likes me, too. I could use another pair of hands around the place, and she's nice, she's a good cook, she's good-looking, and she works hard. She's got her own car, and she'll keep her job, too—even though I'll tell her she can quit," he added hastily. He could not let anyone think that a woman was supporting him. He tried to think of anything else to add to this list to make his case. He was not about to try to explain the feeling he got just looking at her, or what it did to him when she took his hand. And he didn't want to tell Jake of his crushing fear of dying alone out there on the farm, where maybe nobody would find him. He never got over feeling guilty about Nettie's fall from the porch, hurt and in the rain for hours. He was terrified that something like that could happen to him. But he would never utter this to a single soul.

"We just don't think she's a good match for you, Papa. How in the world are you goin' to keep up with a young woman like that?"

"Don't have to, she knows my ways. She's been comin' by to see me for a while now. I think it might be good for both of us."

Jake struggled to ask his last question, which came out sounding like a challenge. "Well, do you love her?" It wasn't his mama's memory that caused his discomfort; it was the bald discussion of emotion that was simply never done between them.

Tom was equally uncomfortable with having to answer and he started to get mad. What kind of question was that? Did his son think he'd get married to someone he didn't love? "Of course I love her!" Jake saw that the discussion was closed.

"Seems like your mind is pretty well made up."

"Yes, it is. I'm gonna ask her and I hope y'all will be nice to her. She's going to be a good wife." He slowly stood to go.

" 'Course we will, Papa."

"All right then. I'll let y'all know when we get married." There would be no church wedding; that wasn't necessary. He'd married Nettie in her father's home. Everybody had been so pleased then, but nobody would be pleased now. Ruby's mother was dead; Ruby's father probably wouldn't be happy about it. He assumed they would go to a justice of the peace to make it official.

"Well, good luck to you, then. Make the best of it." Jake had said the right thing but had not been pleased. The conversations with Clyde, Jim, and Pearl didn't go any better than this one. They all seemed to think this was a bad idea. In his mind, Betty and Reid were still the babies. He'd tell them about it later.

Tom was pretty certain that Ruby would say "yes." Why had she been coming to his house all this time if she weren't angling for a husband? Why else would she have been doing all that housework and all that cooking? More than that, he was sure she loved him. She always said something to make him laugh. She listened to his stories and she teased him good-naturedly about things and she treated him like a man– not an old man, but a man. One day as she was about to leave for work, he walked her to the door. He was determined to get a little closer to her, and he did. Rather than reach for the door, he reached for her, pulled her into a squeeze, and quickly kissed her cheek. His face reddened while waiting for her reaction.

"Why, I declare, Tom! You old scoundrel!" But she was smiling as she said it. And she leaned in and gave him a short kiss on the mouth. "I've got to go," she said. "You know if I'm late for work I'll get fired. I'll see you tomorrow!" He tried to give her another kiss but she ducked him, and off she went.

Things changed between them after that, as he had hoped. She was more like a lady-friend than a housekeeper now. He couldn't ever stop thinking about the kisses. He spent his days and nights dreaming about the next one. Sometimes she allowed it. Other times she'd say something like, "We haven't got time for that now, Sugar. If I don't get this cornbread in the oven you'll never have your dinner." Shoot! What did he care about cornbread? He'd rather starve. But she was firm about it. After she'd leave for work he sure missed her until the next time she came. More and more he started to feel heartsick–full of spirit when she would arrive, and lonesome and blue when she'd go. He didn't want her leaving anymore. That's when he decided he loved her and had to marry her. And once his mind was made up about something, that's always what he did.

One morning he was up extra early. He hurried through his morning work, cleaned himself up and walked into Leaksville. The little bell at Albert Rogers jewelers on Washington Street tinkled when he opened the door. He felt like a fish out of water in there, but he knew what he wanted–a gold wedding ring. He picked out the prettiest one he could find, paid for it, and got out of there as quickly as he could. His stomach was turning flip flops the whole time, but he didn't regret it. How would he propose? He wasn't a smooth talker. What if she turned him down?

She arrived that day as she usually did, stopping in before work. This time he made her sit down with him on the sofa. "Ruby, I got somethin' I want to talk to you about." She sat with him, his hand over hers, and looked at him quizzically and waited.

"Well, now, honey, you know that I...I mean, you've been comin' here and it means a whole lot to me. I look forward to it every day and...and...I was sort of hopin' that we could make it permanent."

"Permanent?"

"Yeah, uh." He took a deep breath. "Ruby, I love you and I want you to be my wife. If you'll have me." Before she could say anything, he took the ring from his pocket. "I got you this ring here, and I'd be honored if you'd wear it when you're my wife." There, he had gotten it all out. Now what would she say?

"Well, Tom, I...I suppose..." She looked at his hopeful face. He had wanted so much to please her. Now that he'd asked her, was she really so surprised? "Yes, Tom, I will marry you." Relief flooded through him, and joy, and love, and excitement. She said yes! He hugged her and kissed her. "You won't be sorry, Ruby. I'll make you the happiest woman in the world!" She hugged him too, with little tears in her eyes. He could never have imagined feeling this happy again. He couldn't wait until they were married! And what a relief it was, too, to know he wasn't going to spend his last days alone! Everything was working out. Thank the Lord.

It was no surprise that people didn't share in their happiness. Tom had heard the gossip back from town. His own children had said, "If Ruby wants to marry an old man, she's gettin' the short end of the stick." But the children didn't confront him about it. If his mind was set on it, they would go along. They treated her properly, the few times they came to visit. The problem was, they were all sheepish and uncomfortable around each other. Conversations about the weather couldn't smooth over the uneasiness. Even Tom wasn't sure how to act with Ruby in front of his children. It was different when they were alone, but in front of his children, who were all older than Ruby, and with the memory of Nettie so strong among them...well, he just didn't know which way to look. So in the end it was just easier to avoid getting together, and that's what they did. Sunday dinners on the farm came to an end. Pearl invited the family to her place and though Ruby was invited, Tom went there alone.

Tom knew that Ruby hadn't had the easiest life growing up, but he didn't feel sorry for her. She made her way as well as most, and look at her now: she had a job, she had a car, and she was going to marry him with this big farm. She'd done all right. He knew that she was married before, something he didn't want anyone to know about. He had asked her, and she had admitted it. "Yes, it's true. I was very young, Tom. I was only 16, and it wasn't good. We were like children running away from home. We got divorced and I just think of it like I was never married." Never married. That suited him better. Divorce was not something decent people did. Once you got married, you stayed married.

But he hadn't been completely satisfied with her answer. He felt flushed. Doubt crept into his mind for a second. "I know you'll never divorce me!" he said abruptly, and probably a little too harshly.

"Now, Sugar, why on earth are you worryin' about something like that?" She smiled, patted his face, and looked at him with those big eyes, waiting for him to speak.

Embarrassed now, he tried to defend himself. "Divorce's a sin, that's all. 'What God has brought together let no man put asunder.'" As much as he feared dying alone, or being sick with no one to care for him, the humiliation he would have to endure if she left him was the thing he feared the most.

She sighed and smiled, patted his hand. "It'll be all right," she said, and he had come to believe that it would. ⑩

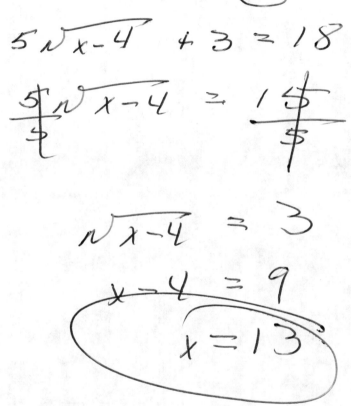

$$5\sqrt{x-4} + 3 = 18$$

$$\frac{5\sqrt{x-4}}{5} = \frac{15}{5}$$

$$\sqrt{x-4} = 3$$

$$x-4 = 9$$

$$x = 13$$

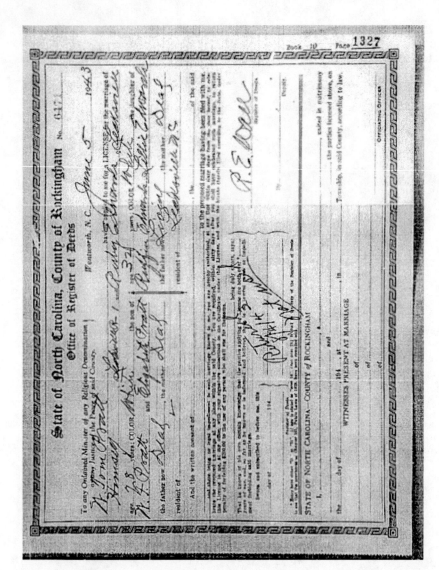

Tom and Ruby's marriage license, dated June 5, 1943, but returned not used on August 4, 1943.

It was found in the marriage register in the Office of the Register of Deeds, Wentworth, Rockingham County, N.C., Book 10, page 1327.

56

Chapter 4

Ruby

Four years later: June, 1947

Ruby rolled over and pulled the pillow over her pounding head. The sun—and Tom—had already been up for hours. It was almost 8:00; she'd have to get up soon. Working the second shift allowed her to sleep late, but she still had a lot to do before leaving for work at 2:15. Tom would be long asleep by the time she got home at night, so she rarely had to fool with him. At the moment, she wasn't thinking about him at all.

She struggled to get out of bed. She put on her bathrobe and went down to boil some water for coffee. Tom had already had his breakfast (she'd found the empty coffee cup and the leavings from fried eggs and biscuit on a plate) but he would expect her to make his dinner and so she had to get moving. The biscuits had to be made, and she could snap some beans and boil the collard greens. By now, Tom had already seen to the animals and would be out in the fields. She'd need to bring in some stove wood, bring in some water from the well for cooking, washing dishes, and her own washing up before work. She'd fill the washtub outside and wring out a few clothes to hang up to dry, and iron a dress to wear to work. After she went to work, Tom would make up his own supper of leftover cornbread, pinto beans, and maybe a slice of ham.

She was moving too slow to have much time for straightening the house before work. It was a small place, with a parlor and anteroom, a tiny kitchen in the back where they ate, and a bedroom upstairs. They had electric lights, which were a great improvement over the kerosene lamps she had grown up with. Their parlor was presentable. The nicest thing they had was their Karastan rug. There were a few decent pieces of upholstered furniture and side tables, which she decorated with potted plants and doilies she had tatted, and little figurines. She was certainly not embarrassed if her friends came by, except for one thing: the tiny room off the side of the living room just big enough for Tom's single bed. The stairs up to her room went through there. She slept upstairs; he slept downstairs. Her friends teased her about that bed and those stairs, a visible reminder of her married life to an old man. But it was certainly practical for lots of other reasons. He was down here nearer to the outside privy. He was in bed early and up early; for her it was just the opposite. She could tiptoe in at night and he never stirred. But most of all, she didn't want to sleep with him. He was not only old enough to be her father, he was old enough to be her grandfather! She had made sure the sleeping arrangements became their habit early on.

The morning dragged by, filled with all the things that needed to get done. In a way she was grateful to have things to do because they passed the time. Another hour closer to going to work, which meant another hour closer to the end of the day. She finished up her morning work and looked around with a little satisfaction. Everything was done. No matter how miserable she felt, she always did what she had to do. She got herself dressed for work, grabbed her car keys, and headed down to the mill. It was overcast today, the clouds outside matching the clouds in her head.

She had taken her first job in the mill in 1930, when she was 19. Now she was 36 and still there, currently running a cone winding machine at the bedspread mill. Though she'd been in a bad frame of mind lately, she liked her job and was grateful for a reason to get out of the house. But even if she hadn't been stuck in the awful marriage to Tom, she'd have liked her job. The mill gave her the chance to do something besides working in the garden. Everybody vied for jobs at the mill. The wages were good and the pay was steady, not like farming where everything depended on the sun, the rain, and the bugs, and you never knew from year to year how you were gonna survive. Being able to work year-round, indoors, with good pay—well all that was a blessing, and it was the reason people moved to Leaksville from Virginia and other places out in the county, just to have a chance to work at the mill.

She pulled into the parking lot exactly at 2:40, as planned, and walked over to the mill gate and went inside. Her foreman, Mr. Tolbert, always kept an eye on his workers, and if anyone were late, they'd be reprimanded. She made sure she was never late.

"Hey, Ruby!" a friend yelled over the noisy machinery.

"Hey, Earline!" she yelled back.

"Looks like we might get some rain this evenin'."

"It sure does."

There, she told herself, you're feeling better already. There was just enough time to say "hello" to the other women and get to her machine. As the first shift people were leaving, she took the place of the woman who had been at that machine just before her. She checked the production sheets. There was a little contest in her head to see how many cones her co-worker had filled. She liked to think she could do a little better than the woman before her. Trying hard to look forward to her day, she began to put spin bobbins on the holders, and doff off the cones as needed. Everyone around her was doing the same thing.

The department she worked in was just for coning yarn for bedspreads. There were maybe fifteen coning machines in this area, and each machine was perhaps thirty feet long, with twenty-five winding positions on each side of the machine, so that one operator worked on each side. The machines made a continuous droning noise, like if you were an ant in a beehive that's what you'd hear. New operators could learn how to hear over the noise and you could carry on a conversation as long as you didn't mind speaking up a bit and talking right into the other person's ear.

Each operator was always assigned to the same machine and while you were working, it was like you owned that machine. You were responsible for everything that happened with it. It started with the spin bobbin, which was a small tube about eight to ten inches long and about one inch around. It held about three ounces of cotton yarn. Her job was to transfer yarn off of the spin bobbins and to wind it onto large cones, tying broken ends together as necessary. This would make large cones of yarn that would be woven into bedspreads. When one of the yarns broke, the winding position stopped automatically so that she could tie the two ends together. She used her left hand to pull the two ends of the yarn–the yarn on the spin bobbin and the yarn on the cone–through a little W-shaped gadget on the knotter that she wore on her right hand, squeezed the trigger on it, and that tied the knot. It was really clever how it worked. She then started the winding position up again. The machine whirred into action, winding the yarn rapidly and tightly from the bobbin to the cone. When the cone filled up the position would stop and she'd remove it, and put it on a rack on the top of the machine. Her job was also to inspect the yarn for defects or breakage by patrolling the length of the machine. If a yarn broke, the winding position would stop by itself. She'd take her knotter and tie it up again, and then restart the position. She monitored yarn all day long. If a machine developed a problem she'd report it to the fixer. At the end of her shift someone else stepped in to do exactly what she'd been doing for the last eight hours. She liked to check how many cones she'd filled each day because that's how she was paid: by the number of cones. If all went well, she could generally produce about 300 cones a day, depending on the size of the yarn.

Once she got the hang of it, she could do this job and hardly even think about it. It was just you and your machine, hour after hour, following the same routine. Sometimes she felt like she didn't know where her fingers left off and the knotter and the bobbins and the cones began. When she first took this job, her movements were clumsy and she was slow. But now her hands knew what to do all on their own: pull the ends together, thread, squeeze, restart, pull the ends together, thread, squeeze, restart. Her feet, too, knew what they were doing without requiring her to direct them: move back and forth, right to left, left to right alongside the machine, all day long, wearing a hole in the floor. Her eyes, too, told her, "go on, we can handle this job," as they constantly checked the bobbins, the cones, the yarn, and the equipment. So Ruby worked on, her body a dance partner with this machine, while her mind could be off anywhere: at a picnic, dancing at the Palomar, laughing inwardly at a joke she had heard, thinking about the latest picture with Gary Cooper. The women around her were sharing gossip while they worked. They kept busy, though. Mr. Tolbert's desk was on a raised platform right in the middle of their production floor, and if he thought someone wasn't pulling her weight, he'd let you know it. Ruby wasn't afraid of Mr. Tolbert, but she wasn't in the mood to gossip today. She kept her head on her work.

She glanced up at the clock; it was 6:55. The dope wagon would be coming through soon. The company had a nice cafeteria but nobody but the managers, supervisors and foremen ate there. Ruby had brought a cold supper from home–an apple and a peanut butter sandwich. She ran over to the dope wagon and bought a Coca-Cola. She walked back to her machine with some other women.

"Hey, did y'all see in the *Leaksville News* that Fieldcrest is going to put on a pageant? It's going to be in the fall."

"Oh, really? What are they doing?"

"They're going to have a play and some music about the history of Leaksville and the mills and all. The paper said 300 people from town can be in the play."

"Three hundred people? Well, who's going to be left to be in the audience?"

"I don't know; I reckon I will be. I don't want to be in no play."

Ruby was enjoying the thrust of this conversation. It was mindless town news, nothing personal. Suddenly, it shifted to her.

"Ruby, how's Mr. Pratt gettin' along?"

"Oh, he's just fine. We're lookin' forward to summer. And how's your husband?" As the chatter continued, Ruby had to force herself to smile. She wasn't about to admit to any troubles at home. These were not the friends she'd be meeting on Friday night who knew all about Tom and the bed in the tiny room. These ladies, well, nobody was better than anybody else at the mill, but this group might have thought so. Luckily, they all needed to get back to work, so this conversation had to end.

"Well, you tell Mr. Pratt I said 'hey.'"

"I sure will."

The conversation had made her feel bluer than ever. Those women didn't struggle with their husbands the way she did. It was so embarrassing to be married to him! She wondered what they said behind her back about it. Ah, she had half a shift to go. It was a good night when the lights blinked to signal the end of the shift while she was lost in a daydream. It was a bad night if she kept glancing at her watch, as if her eyes could push the minute hand along to quitting time.

If she caught up with some of her friends, even for a few minutes, it kept her sane. Sometimes, maybe on a Friday night, they'd find a place to have a beer or two, or sit in somebody's parlor and play cards. It was the only time these days she felt alive. Sometimes Tom knew she was gone; sometimes he didn't. She would only have a few hours before she'd have to go home and get some sleep before she'd have to do it all over again.

Mama had warned her, "You make your bed and you're going to lie in it." She refused to feel sorry for herself and give satisfaction to her mama's words. She had spent her life chasing happiness and never seemed to find it. Her large family was not much different from anyone else's. She was eight when Nathan was born, and she had had a lot of responsibility looking after him and Marion. Sometimes she had felt like their second mother. They were still quite young when she left home, and Lillie and Lucille were still home with Daddy. Like almost everybody she knew, she had grown up with farming. Like everyone she knew, she went to the mills to make better pay and try to get ahead. No one she knew had had an easy life, but many people had happy lives nonetheless. Why hadn't she found the happiness she had looked for? Why hadn't things worked out better for her? What had Mama seen that she couldn't?

Twice she had married for love. Ruby had fallen in love with Carl Meeks the way any fifteen-year old girl does, with his handsome smile and strong arms, and the way he made her feel all grown up. Mama and Daddy had been so busy in those days they didn't notice her much, didn't see how much she was changing. They just expected her to be the same little girl she had always been, and she wasn't! She had been just itching for some kind of excitement in her life, something to get her off the farm. She dreamed of being Carl's wife, so sure she could be happy once she was married and away from home. They married on April 8, 1926. They had been happy as she set up their little home. Eventually, though, keeping the garden and the house with Carl wasn't much better than living at home had been. The excitement of being a married woman wore off. They had waited for a baby that had not come. They decided that she would get a job at the mill, and then quit it when she got pregnant. As it turned out, she liked the job, and as it turned out, no baby came.

Time went by, and life with Carl became achingly dull. It wasn't too long before they both realized what a mistake they had made; the fighting was a constant drumbeat and the fun was long gone. They split up. She still felt like a kid, not a person who has to think about grown-up things. After a while it felt like she had never been married at all. She kept her job at the mill and finally turned 21—well wasn't that the legal grown-up age? And that's when she met Charlie Corum. All of a sudden it was like she woke up. She spent all day trying to catch a glimpse of him at work, and when he noticed her looking at him, he started looking back. At first, she convinced herself that there was no harm in a little flirting. She never got this kind of attention from Carl, who had been as ordinary as an old mule. Charlie was a real man, sure of himself, clever, and funny. There was something a little dangerous about him, which she found very exciting. One smile from him made her feel like she was the center of the universe. She could not stop thinking about him. Now *this* was love! Once he had offered her a ride up to The Boulevard to go to Milner's five and dime, and he had taken her on a little side trip out in the country. He had offered her a drink–well, why not? Everybody did it–and it was there that they first kissed in his car. She spent every waking moment from that day on trying to meet up with him. She didn't tell Charlie about Carl. When he met her, she was living at home, and there was no reason to upset him with that. Carl was a thing of the past. But being in love with Charlie was like a person needing a stiff drink. She was mad with desire for him, and he wanted to marry her. She went to Carl, asking him to file for a divorce so she could marry again, and he said he would. Their divorce was filed on September 22, 1933. Six weeks later, on November 4, she married Charlie Corum. She reasoned that Charlie never needed to find out about Carl.

She had told Tom about Carl, though she made it sound like their seven-year marriage had lasted just a few months. Well, it wasn't as if they had lived together seven years. But she hadn't known what to say about Charlie. Charlie had been the love of her life, if there was such a thing. They set up house and continued working at the mill. But unlike the time with Carl that felt like a restless sleep, her years with Charlie were like living every night on the Fourth of July. At first, every day was more exciting than the one before. Even going to work, even just eating supper, everything about him was like lightning. And when they fought about stupid things that shouldn't have mattered, they would make up with the intensity of their first nights together. As time went by, though, the fights got uglier, louder and meaner. Both became stubborn and refused to be the first one to make up. What could she do? She couldn't contemplate being twice divorced, so she stayed on. Then one day he said to her, "What's this I hear about you being married to some feller named Carl Meeks?" There was controlled rage in his voice, but he was waiting for an explanation.

"Who told you that?" she demanded.

"Never you mind. I heard it on good authority. Is it true? Is it true, Ruby, that you were married to somebody else before me?"

He already knew the answer. What could she say? Oh, damn, how had he found out? She had no choice but to admit it, and though she tried to reason with him and explain, his fury would hear no reason. "How could you not tell me sumpthin' like that? Get out!" he had screamed. "Get out! Get out, get out!" It was done. Although she tried to talk to him some more, this was the final straw, and they both knew it. In 1939 she was 28 years old and going home to live with Mama and Daddy.

They allowed her back, hoping she'd learned some lessons about life, and she had. She had learned that she had no clue what love was all about, and that the happiness that she had sought would not be found in the arms of good-looking man. She had made a mess of her life. Now she'd go back home, try to slow down, start over, and give herself time to think. Lucille, the youngest, was only 9 years old and Ruby made herself useful. When Mama took sick, Ruby did all that she could to make Mama comfortable and take care of the girls. She kept her job at the mill, helped with the expenses, and tried very hard to be good.

Things changed after Mama died. It frightened her to think that she'd spend the rest of her life taking care of Daddy like some old maid.

Ruby ventured out with friends again, trying to feel like an adult though she was living at home. Daddy was miserable, always complaining and criticizing. He just never would leave her alone about anything! He raised a fuss every time she went out. She was well past 30 years old and he treated her like a child. It dawned on Ruby that she had to get herself some kind of a plan to get out of there. Where was a divorced woman supposed to go? Then Coy and Vera Ratliff told her they'd rented a house on Mr. Pratt's farm. At first she thought, well maybe there would be a place for her, too. And then this whole thing just seemed to take off of its own accord.

Funny how she put this plan into motion and felt like a spider caught in her own web. The Pratt farm was a fine piece of land, it sure was, with everything a person could need. She'd grown up doing farm work; she was no stranger to hard country work like some town girl might be. She knew how to do any kind of work with animals or crops that might need to be done, and she was not lazy. Yes, she could see herself right here, and she could help him out. But how? Maybe she could be a live-in nurse. Hadn't they had a live-in nurse for his wife when she was sick? Of course, that was a colored woman. She'd expect some better arrangement than that, though she didn't know quite what. But if she could stay there, she could have her freedom and she could probably live like she wanted to. Her brother and Jim Pratt were friends. Maybe Jim could tell Mr. Pratt she was all right.

Coy told her Mr. Pratt could use some help with the meals. He did, too. Poor old skinny thing, he didn't appear to be eating at all until she showed up. She thought maybe she could work up to the nurse idea. The problem was, even in his seventies, Mr. Pratt hadn't needed a nurse. No, he was a strong old man, did everything that was needed around the place, and never seemed to get sick. There was no way he would have let her live with him, even as a border, unless they were married. It would look indecent. So her plan had to change a little bit. She thought and she thought, but she couldn't figure any other way around it. There was only one solution. She'd have to marry him. That was the only way she was going to get to live here. She had married for love twice already and look where that had gotten her! This time she'd be smart about it. She knew she'd have to sweeten up old Mr. Pratt, somehow make him think this was his idea. Having been married twice had taught her a thing or two about men, young or old, it didn't matter. They were all the same. So she started working on it and it didn't take long. Flattery, smiles, making herself useful to him; it all came out as she wanted.

When her friends figured out what she was up to, she defended herself quite well. "He needs me," she had said, "he can't get along on that big place all by hisself. He's not getting any younger. Was eating like a bird until I came along." By the time she had convinced him of his desire to marry her, she had just about convinced herself that it was a perfectly natural thing to do.

She had been controlling the situation very well. He had fallen in love with her; of that she was certain. And she was fond enough of him at first, the way you might be of a sweet old man that you didn't have to see every day. She could manage him. Things were moving along just as she'd wanted. So, why, when he proposed, did she feel so surprised? Why did it seem like her world had just turned upside down? She'd had to control herself at that moment to keep from running out the door. She reminded herself that this was what she had hoped to accomplish, and that she had to say yes. So she did.

68

She remembered the butterflies in her stomach the day they went to Wentworth to get the license. He had seemed distant, far off somewhere. She was afraid he was changing his mind, so she had tried to be as pleasant as a spring day. She decided that he was just nervous, perhaps as nervous as she was. She'd like to have died of embarrassment in the registrar's office, but there was no other way.

Maybe she should have listened to that still, small voice in her head. If she had, she wouldn't be in this miserable situation today. Almost the day after they got the marriage license that June she and Tom started fighting like cats and dogs. It was getting too close, too real. Was she really going through with this? Her conflict over marrying him almost ruined her plan. On the one hand she couldn't imagine spending her life with this old man. On the other hand she longed for the independence and security she would feel at owning this farm. Yet the more she thought about being this old man's wife, the more she knew she needed to be with young people and have fun. She got careless about going out—he had seen her honky-tonkin' with her friends, speeding down the Price Road just as he happened to be walking back to the farm. It had embarrassed and humiliated him. The marriage license had been good for sixty days. The summer passed without a wedding. By August, yet another blow-up between them had ended in a threat that he would never marry her. To prove his point, he had mailed the license back to the Court Registrar. Oh Lord! She had pushed him too far. The summer had come and gone, and then the fall. This was taking too long! She just had to move away from Daddy. She swallowed her pride once more to get back in his good graces. Lord, this was harder than she thought! She was jealous of the carefree life of her friends, but when she thought about Carl and Charlie, it became plain. Don't be a fool: marry this old man and worry about getting along with him later.

Which was what she did. Begging forgiveness, acting contrite, and promising to be a good wife softened him up again. By December she was back in his good graces. She didn't wait until their next fight for him to change his mind again. Lots of folks went to Martinsville to get a quick marriage. There wasn't much to the ceremony. They went to the justice of the peace office and the whole thing was done in ten minutes. There were other couples there, waiting to get married, mostly young kids. She glanced furtively around at them in the waiting room, trying to keep her dignity about her, her dress smoothed and her hat on straight. Would anybody think that she really wanted to marry this old man? She was still young and attractive, and lots of men friends enjoyed her company. She just wouldn't have them. Men who sweet-talked you before marriage changed after. And with what she had been through so far in her life with young men, well she was through with that. No more taking orders from somebody and having to do what he said no matter what–she wasn't going to live like that ever again! Tom might have his problems, but she could control him. So she held her head high and got through the brief ceremony as best she could. At least she didn't have a swollen belly like some of the young girls she saw. Their fate was sealed. She felt sorry for them. She was controlling her own fate now. So on Monday, December 13, 1943, they were married by Dr. J. P. McCabe at the courthouse. Dr. McCabe was pastor of the First Baptist Church in Martinsville, and sometimes he came over to the courthouse to marry folks. As for her, she put her other husbands out of her mind and moved on. She was Ruby Pratt now.

She could see Tom was real happy, and that was good. What she was doing wasn't so bad if he could be that happy. The fact that she didn't love him was truly beside the point. The point was, he was happy and she could stay right here on the farm, keep her job, keep her friends, have a good place to live, and be free of Daddy and any other man who wanted to tell her what to do. In return she would keep the place clean and keep him well-fed. And if he died, well…well she didn't know what would happen if Tom died, but she felt entitled to this land. They were married, after all. And wasn't she working night and day to care for him and hold a job at the bedspread mill, too?

But that was then. That was in 1943, when she thought she had all this figured out. Now it was 1947, four years that had gone from barely tolerable to intolerable. He wasn't any worse than any other man and was better than some. But Lord! Things had not worked out for her the way she had thought they would.

It had started out all right, all things considered. He had not asked her to stop working at the mill like some men might have. She had work to do with the animals and in the garden and the kitchen and the house, but he did not ask her to help in the fields. He rarely insisted that she share his bed, and if she did, it was a duty that was over with quick enough. She could easily claim female trouble, or fear of becoming pregnant. He didn't want that any more than she did. She did not have to suffer the embarrassment of going to church with him, since he didn't go anyway. He did not ask her to cook family dinners or to go with him to his children's. She could have gone but didn't. She thought they looked at her in an odd way. They didn't trust her. No one seemed to know what to say to her, or she to them. She could feel that as well as see it.

At first her time with Tom was spent doing the odds and ends that always need to get done—mending clothes or peeling apples or embroidering bed linens. They might sit on the little porch together in the evenings when she wasn't working, making small talk. The problem was, he talked about crops and tobacco and rainfall and the tobacco prices he might get at the auction. She wanted to talk about the mill gossip, which she could not. He didn't know half her friends and didn't approve of the other half. She could never tell him some of the jokes she heard, for example, or what stories were being told. He wouldn't have approved. He wasn't interested in movie stars or the latest song being played on the new radio station, WLOE. So she kept all that to herself.

She was happy to run errands in her car, which got her into town, where she might arrange to run into one of her friends. If she was really lucky, she might take in a picture show on The Boulevard or at the Balmar on Washington Street. She started feeling suffocated in this marriage to Tom, Old Pa, feeling old herself though she was only in her thirties. She started looking for anything that could relieve the deadening, unending boredom of life with an old man on a farm. She spent less and less time with him, avoiding being with him as much as she could. But it seemed like the more she tried to keep away from him, the more he was asking her to sit with him, or take a ride, or get into her bed. And if she refused, he got mad, and then she'd get mad back. Wasn't it enough that she did all these things for him—cooking, cleaning, mending? He wanted her all to himself, and no sir, he couldn't have it that way. She thought she was going to suffocate.

Eventually, slowly, she started taking chances again. For if she didn't, surely she would die like a caged animal. She visited Nathan and Marion. She started seeing friends after work, which would be quite late of course. They'd sit in her car and share a drink. They'd go to the Palomar over on Draper Road. They'd go out to somebody's house and just talk and laugh almost till day-break. She had a nice crowd of friends, funny, lively, made her feel like a person when she was with them instead of like a nobody. They accepted her, even the ones who knew about her past husbands. No one judged her. No one worried about who was respectable or went to church or had a drink. No one looked down at her for being out while her husband was home. They understood how hard she worked to take care of him, and how cranky he could be in spite of her efforts. They just had fun. She could get home and slip in and he never really knew where she had been or what time she got home.

It was bound to happen that some men would take more than a passing interest in her. She didn't talk about her marriage and they didn't ask. It was bound to happen that she started taking a few more chances, and started not to care if Tom found out or not. What was he going to do about it anyway? Yes, he found out all right, or thought he did, when she would come in so late with a little alcohol on her breath, or when she would take off in the middle of a Saturday afternoon and not come home until midnight, or when friends would drive up and she would leave with them. He'd demand to know what was going on. Oh, he'd carry on and holler and get mad and *forbid*, yes, *forbid* her from going out. He got downright mean, calling her a gadabout and said she was shaming him and every other mean thing he could think of. Sometimes he even tried to block her in the doorway, but she'd go out anyway, even more determined not to be controlled. He was now treating her just like her Daddy did, and just like every other married man. What gave these men the right?

She wasn't above provoking him so that he would leave. There were times when he would get so mad that he would yell, "I'm going to

73

Pearl's!" and off he'd go, slamming the door, to her great relief. Thank heaven, he was out of her hair. He'd often spend the night over there and she could unwind on her own. One night, after a particularly ugly fight, Marion and Nathan and some friends drove up and she invited them in, not expecting Tom back until the next day. Surely her brothers were allowed to visit her in her own house! They were having a fine time when Tom suddenly came in, after having cooled off at Pearl's. What a row there had been that night! Her brothers tried to stand up for her but it hadn't mattered. Tempers flared, words passed across them all, and she felt a combination of anger, guilt, and embarrassment in front of her friends and brothers. Oooo, he made her so mad! She told everyone good night, stormed upstairs, and locked herself in the bedroom. She'd go to sleep and maybe Tom would be gone in the morning.

Scenes like this became more frequent as time went by. Sometimes she felt like she must be living somebody else's life, because this had not been the plan. Hadn't she lived like this with Charlie and vowed never to live like this again? Why shouldn't she have friends, and how did he have the right to talk to her like she was a child? She worked hard, helped with expenses, had bought that hog with him out there in the pen, kept food on his table, kept his clothes clean and his home neat, and this is the thanks she got! She never asked for anything! And she wouldn't be spoken to like this!

The blinking lights pulled her out of her thoughts and signaled the end of the shift at 11 p.m. The third shift workers were starting to arrive and she hadn't even noticed them. The mill ran these machines twenty-four hours a day, stopping only on Sundays. She could now feel how tired she was. Her hands, feet, eyes and ears were now ready for a rest. There was lint in her hair. She sometimes had that curious feeling of

74

$$x + 9 = 16$$
$$x = 7$$

being bone tired in her body and yet her mind was racing ten paces ahead. She'd been winding all day; now she wanted to unwind herself! But how was she going to do that—go home to Tom's snoring and sit up in her bedroom and stare out the window at the moon?

She was trapped and she knew it. Three times divorced? She'd be the laughingstock of Rockingham County. No home, no man, nowhere to go. Sometimes she dreamed of just running away, but it was a fantasy and she knew it. Where would she go? Greensboro? Too close. New York City? She was not about to go live among the Yankees. Atlanta? Charleston? Richmond? She didn't know a soul in those places, and was frightened of even thinking of trying to survive alone in the city. At least here she had a job and her brothers and sisters and her friends. For all the hard times she suffered in life, Leaksville was still home. She'd just have to stay right here, stay clear of him as much as she could, and make the best of it. She could survive. She always had, and she always would.

$$\sqrt{x-3} + \sqrt{x+9} = 6$$

$$\sqrt{x-3} = 6 - \sqrt{x+9}$$

$$x - 3 = (6 - \sqrt{x+9})(6 - \sqrt{x+9})$$

$$x - 3 = 36 - 6\sqrt{x+9} - 6\sqrt{x+9} + x + 9$$

$$x - 3 = 45 - 12\sqrt{x+9}$$

$$48 = 12\sqrt{x+9}$$

$$\frac{-48}{-12} = \frac{-12\sqrt{x+9}}{-12}$$

$$4 = \sqrt{x+9}$$

$|12-5i|$

$$\sqrt{144+25} = \sqrt{169} = 13$$

$$|a+bi| = \sqrt{a^2+b^2}$$

$$= \sqrt{12^2+(-5)^2}$$

$$\sqrt{144+25}$$

$$\sqrt{169} = 13$$

$\sqrt{x} + x = 20$

$\sqrt{x} = 20 - x$

$x = (20-x)(20-x)$

$x = 400 - 20x - 20x + x^2$

$0 = x^2 - 41x + 400$

$0 = (x-16)(x-25)$

$x=16 \qquad x=25$

answer

extraneous root

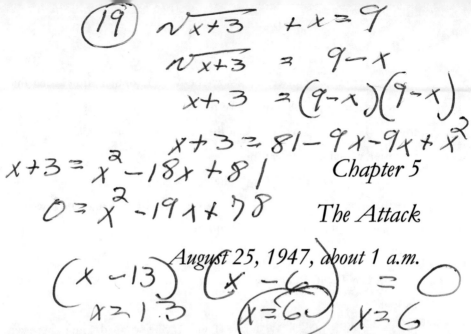

$$\boxed{19} \quad \sqrt{x+3} + x = 9$$
$$\sqrt{x+3} = 9-x$$
$$x+3 = (9-x)(9-x)$$
$$x+3 = 81 - 9x - 9x + x^2$$
$$x+3 = x^2 - 18x + 81$$
$$0 = x^2 - 19x + 78$$
$$(x-13)(x-6) = 0$$
$$x = 13 \qquad x = 6 \qquad x = 6$$

Chapter 5

The Attack

August 25, 1947, about 1 a.m.

"AAAAAGGHH! OOOHHH!" Ruby hurried down the steps and rushed to Tom's side. He was on the floor, bleeding from the head, blood was everywhere, good Lord, what to do? What was she to do? She didn't know whether to approach him or run away. She grabbed a towel from the kitchen, tried to dab his head–

"Aaaagghh!" he cried out. "Ruby! Ruby!" His left eye was barely visible, caking with blood; he was rocking from side to side on the floor, hand to his head, clearly helpless. She recoiled at him–at the blood, at the sight of this pitiful old man. How did this happen? How could this be? Panic filled her heart and mind. What if he died? How would she explain this? This wasn't supposed to happen. Tears rolled down her own sobbing face. All alone here, all alone!

"Tom, I've got to get help. Don't try and move." She didn't know whether he could understand her. She pulled open the kitchen door, hesitated, gave a quick look around. It was black as pitch out there. Looking to the spot under the kitchen window, she made out the overturned butter churn. She was going to have to run out into this dark night to get to Coy's place, but knew she had to go. She ran, cursing that this jerkwater town still didn't have telephone lines out in that part of the country. How was anyone to call the police if nobody had a telephone? Someone would have to get them.

"Coy! Vera! Coy! Coy!" She ran toward their house up the lane, past the tobacco barns, screaming their names. In a second she saw their lights cut on. She didn't know whether to run closer or run back, and her feet suddenly seemed glued to the ground.

Coy Ratliff flung open his door. "Ruby, what's the matter? What's wrong?"

"Come, please Coy, come! Tom's—" She stopped. She didn't even know what to say to describe it. "Tom's on the floor and bleeding. Just come!"

Coy grabbed a flashlight from a peg on the wall and ran with Ruby back to the house. "Good God A'mighty, Ruby, what happened here?" Coy immediately went to Tom's side on the floor. He knew Tom was accustomed to sleeping here in the front room. Tom was wearing his long underwear and a blue work shirt, now covered with blood. Coy grabbed the towel that Ruby had left beside him, and tried to staunch the bleeding. Poor old Tom was in a bad way. "Get some clean towels. What happened?" he more demanded than asked.

"I—I—just—what do I do? Somebody came in here to rob us. Tom must've tried to stop him."

"Did you see him?"

"Yes, yes, I—Coy I'm scared to death, what do I do?"

"Who's that?" Tom demanded, without opening his eyes.

"It's me, Coy Ratliff. Mr. Pratt, I got to get you some help." Turning to Ruby, Coy said, "You stay by his side. Hold the towel on his head. I'll go down to Harold and Edna's. Gotta get an ambulance. Lock the door."

Ruby stayed by Tom's side as she'd been told to do. Leaning over him now, she trembled at the sight of him, repulsed by the injury and terrified of what might happen next. She gulped air as she fought back tears. "Now Tom," she said, "stay still, Coy's gone to get Harold. Just stay quiet now." Her mind raced. She had to compose herself. They would be asking her a hundred questions. What would she say? She'd been upstairs of course, sleeping, when she heard the commotion. The man had come in through the kitchen window. She'd seen the butter churn he used to climb in on. She'd come down the steps to see a big man with a flashlight and a knife who didn't expect to see her. Tom had been dragged out of his bed, onto the floor, trying to fight. The man was big, menacing, coming after her too, so she had run back upstairs...

A pounding at the door startled her. It was Harold and Edna Hoover and their son Wink. Edna was Tom's granddaughter, and she went right to his side. Harold and Wink were both carrying shotguns. Ruby paced the room. Harold knelt by Tom, quickly seeing that this was no wound that they could mend without a doctor. Fifteen-year-old Wink was wide-eyed, trying to find a way to be helpful and at the same time, stay out of the way. He clutched his shotgun, wary of the sounds of the night.

"Ruby, what on earth happened here?"

"I was sleeping upstairs and I heard a commotion. I come downstairs, outside the stairwell here, and I was face-to-face with this big nigger man."

"Did you get a good look at him?"

"Yes, I—he was as big as you, Mr. Hoover! He was yellow-skinned, had a light in one hand and a knife in the other. Liked to scare me to death. I run back up the stairs and into my room, and I guess he done run out the door."

Wink looked at his dad. His dad was five feet ten and one-half inches tall and 248 pounds. That was a big man indeed. No wonder she'd a'been scared like that.

"Where's that dog y'all keep?"

"He run off sometime today. He's bound to be 'round here somewhere. I sure could have used him here tonight."

"Wink," said his father, "I got to go get the sheriff and the ambulance. You stay here with Ruby and Mr. Pratt and make sure nothing happens. Son, don't be afraid to use that gun if you have to." Coy and Harold together left in a hurry.

Wink accepted this responsibility, as he had no choice in the matter, though he didn't feel too good about it. It was August, and although the crops were laid by, it was black as pitch out there. That thief could be anywhere.

They sat awkwardly, Ruby going over it again: who broke in, what he looked like.

"Well how'd he get in here, Ruby?"

"I reckon he climbed in the kitchen window. He got my churn, set it up outside my kitchen window and climbed through there. Do you want to go see?"

"Naw, I don't want to go see! We're staying right here until somebody gets back!" But Wink did take a walk into the tiny kitchen. The oven door was propped closed as usual, with the hickory stick Old Pa used to brace it shut pushed between the oven door and the opposite wall, with space only big enough to stand in. Wink tried to picture a 248-pound man coming into the window and climbing past that stick without knocking it over. Maybe if the man had had a flashlight he could maneuver it; still it would be hard for a big man to fit through that little space without knocking down the stick.

Eventually Coy and Harold returned with the ambulance, Deputy Sheriff Curtis Land showed up, and other people came up to the house. With the ambulance finally there, the men gently lifted Tom onto a stretcher. Harold stood right next to the stretcher, Wink beside his daddy. Tom opened his good eye, looked at Harold and bellowed, "Harold! Where y'all carryin' me to?"

Harold responded gently, "Mr. Pratt, you've been hurt. We're carryin' you to the hospital." Hesitating for just a second, Harold decided to ask, "Who did this to you?"

Tom closed his eyes and didn't say a word. Harold, who had just been called by his own name, felt for sure that Mr. Pratt could have given them a name or some type of description if he'd wanted to. Poor old soul was just wrung out. Maybe they could get the name later.

① $\sqrt{12} + \sqrt{75} = 7\sqrt{3}$

② 30 (1)

③ $i^{66} = -1$ (1.)

$\quad i^2 = -1$

$\quad i^3 = -i$

$\quad i^4 = 1$

④ $5 - 2i$ (4)

⑤ $x^2 - 6x + 34 = 0$

$\quad ax^2 + bx + c = 0$

$\quad a = 1, \ b = -6, \ c = 34$

$$x = \frac{-b \pm \sqrt{b^2 - 4ac}}{2a}$$

$$x = \frac{6 \pm \sqrt{36 - 4(34)}}{2}$$

$$x = \frac{6 \pm \sqrt{36 - 136}}{2}$$

$$x = \frac{6 \pm \sqrt{-100}}{2}$$

$$x = \frac{6 \pm 10i}{2} \quad (!)$$

$$x = 3 \pm 5i$$

Chapter 6

Death of Old Pa

Monday, August 25, 1947, 2:00 a.m.

It was one of those hot and humid North Carolina summer nights, where no breeze comes to take away the thick air that blankets the town. Jake and Josie locked the screen doors and otherwise left the house open just to keep from suffocating in the heat. When they and their 21-year old son Herbert had gone to bed, the heat had been the only thing to disturb them.

Herbert suddenly awoke to the pounding at the front door screen. "Jake! Jake! Wake up! Wake up! Old Pa's been hurt! Old Pa's been hurt!" Harold Hoover, his cousin Edna's husband, frantically called into the house, rousing the three occupants into action. Herbert's room was the closest to the front door, and he let Harold in. Rushing into the hallway, Jake and Josie saw their distraught nephew.

"Harold, what is it? What happened?" demanded Jake.

"Somebody hit Mr. Pratt in the head and the police and ambulance came to take him to the hospital. Coy Ratliff came for me. There's twenty men are up there now, looking through the woods."

"What? When? How did they…? How bad is it?"

"It's real bad, Jake, don't know if he's going to make it. Looks like his head is split open. He could talk, though, that's a good sign."

"What's he saying? Did he see who did it?"

"No, he didn't see nobody. He's sorta in and out, like, knowed we was there but not what happened to him."

"Where's Ruby?"

"She's with Mr. Pratt at the hospital. She mighta seen who did it. Thinks it was a robbery."

Throwing on his clothes, Jake ran to get in the car with Harold. They sped off to the hospital, not knowing what on earth to expect next. This left Josie and Herbert to sit and wait for news, as they had no telephone and no car. Josie cried and did as she always did in times of trouble, which was to open her Bible and pray. A thousand questions went through their minds, but no answers would be available until Old Pa could talk to them. They'd just have to wait. Herbert tried to doze off but found sleep difficult. He still needed to get to work the next day at Fieldcrest and he just hoped that Old Pa would recover. His dad would be back when he could.

Custis Pratt couldn't sleep. The heat wouldn't let her. It was Sunday night and Colleen, her 10-year-old daughter, had cuddled up with Reid that night to sleep. Custis stayed up alone, in the quiet, thinking about her life, her marriage and daughter, how far she'd come from the country girl living in the mountains with eleven younger brothers and sisters, to this life in Leaksville with her husband and one daughter. She remembered Edna Earline, Colleen's twin, who had died as a baby. Custis and Reid had had plenty of rough times, as his drinking had been the source of a lot of problems. Custis was no stranger to the problems of alcohol. Her own daddy had been killed when she was four in an accident that took the lives of three men. Everybody had gone up on the mountain for a picnic, and late in the day the men got to drinking and shooting at each other for fun, and three of them got killed. Her mama had been expecting her third child when it happened. My, my times were rough then. There was nobody to help out, no government agency or Social Security in those days. Mama later married another real good man, and nine more children came. As the oldest, Custis had had a lot of responsibility with the little ones. When she got to be a teenager she came to town to live with the Butlers and care for their children while they worked at the mill. Long about in there was when she met Reid. Old Mammie had made sure of it.

She knew about Reid's other daughter before she married him. She even met Laraine, who was about 10 years old by the time they married. That little girl had had a hard life and she felt sorry for her. Custis was a forgiving person. She felt that Reid had made mistakes, but had become a better man. She loved him and agreed to marry him. This had made Old Mammie very happy, even as she lay in the bed dying from pneumonia. Colleen had been born not long after Old Mammie had died.

In spite of his drinking, one thing was for sure: little Colleen loved her daddy and he loved her. Lots of times Reid wouldn't come home on a Sunday, having spent every minute from Friday night after work until late Sunday evening with the friends and the liquor. Everybody had been after Reid to quit drinking, and oh my, the fights that had gone on between Reid and Old Pa had torn her apart. Her father-in-law took a little drink now and again himself, but he would not tolerate drunkenness.

Today, being a Sunday, Reid had gone to church with them at the Osborne Baptist Mission, and they had sat in the yard drinking iced tea to cool down in the evening. They ate supper, and about 8:00 Reid went to bed. Maybe it was the heat. Custis sat peering out the window, trying to find a breeze, as her husband and child slept. Staring aimlessly out the window she noticed headlights. She saw that a car was creeping down their road, slowing as it came to her house, and then turn around and come back on by. "Now I wonder who on earth that is at this time of night?" But she didn't recognize the car and it moved on. Custis finally made her way to bed in spite of the heat.

She wasn't asleep long before there was a loud knocking at the door. Reid and Custis, sleeping in separate rooms that night, both jumped to answer the door. Robert Barnes was at the door. Seeing a police officer in the middle of the night would make anyone's blood run cold. "I've got bad news for you folks. Reid, your daddy has been badly hurt and is in the hospital. Someone hit him in the head. Mrs. Pratt says she got a look at him, a big black man, and thinks she might know him if she sees him again."

"What? Where is he? What happened?"

"Taken to Leaksville Hospital. Harold Hoover came to get the ambulance. Mr. Pratt's still alive but it's serious."

"But who done this? What happened? "

"Somebody hit him in the head. He was talkin' a little but couldn't say who did it."

"Who does Ruby think did it?"

"Don't know. She says this man came in to rob the place but didn't know she was there. He ran out the front door when he saw her. She's scared to death. You folks been in all evening?"

"Yes, we been right here. Had no idea."

"Well you might want to get over and see him, but he's hurt real bad. I've got to go."

As Deputy Sheriff Barnes left, shock and grief overtook Reid and the 44-year old man started crying like a baby. "I can't believe it. It's not possible. I shouldn't-a been fighting with him so much."

Custis tried to keep a calm head. "Now Reid, you get yourself together and get over to the hospital right now and see your daddy."

"I'll go in the morning; I'm too shook up to go now. He don't want to see me like this."

"You'll go right now. You mightn't have another chance."

So Reid did as his wife suggested and drove to the hospital. It wasn't until days later that Custis thought about that car driving slowly past their house in the dead of night. She never did learn who that was.

Colleen Pratt had cried and cried all morning after waking up and learning the news that her beloved grandpa had been attacked and taken to the hospital. When her daddy had come home that morning, she begged and pleaded with him to take her to see him. Reid was exhausted from the heat, the trouble, the loss of sleep. Just seeing your father in that condition was enough to wear a man out. Old Pa hadn't said anything, had come in and out of consciousness. The doctor didn't seem to think he could do much. He was bleeding in his brain and it was just a matter of time. Now here was little Colleen going on and on. Why, sometimes he thought she loved Old Pa better'n he did. Never having refused his daughter too much of what she really wanted, he agreed to take her down there.

Ruby was at the hospital when they arrived. Colleen stifled a gasp when she saw her grandfather and fought back her tears again. Her grandpa looked awful. His right eye was bandaged tight. Half his face was turned purple from the injury, with bandages wrapped all over his head. He lay limp in the bed, almost unrecognizable from the quiet old man she'd always known. She went to his side, took his hand, watched his left eye flutter a bit. She didn't speak, but looked to Ruby with the question in her eyes. "He ain't said much," said Ruby. "He don't know what's goin' on, poor thing." But it did seem to Colleen that her grandpa did know they were there, and who they were.

Colleen kept quiet around the bustle of grown-ups in and out of the room. Her Aunt Pearl, Uncle Jake, Uncle Clyde, Uncle Jim, Aunt Betty—all of them were there or had been at the hospital, either in the room or waiting outside. Nurses were hushing them. "Hospital ain't no place for a little girl," one of them had said to her daddy, but he ignored her. Colleen stood quietly in the corner and watched. Dr. Harris looked very grim. Her daddy looked very, very sad. "Who done this to you, Papa? Who done this to you?" Old Pa made no answer. It wasn't clear to Colleen that he had heard, or understood, what Daddy was asking. Ruby was moving nervously around the room, straightening the pillow in a side chair. "Who done this to you, Papa?" Reid again asked. Old Pa stirred, opened his mouth, only to call out, "Oh Lord."

Ruby, standing in front of the chair with the straightened pillow, made a slight moan, swooned and seemed to faint into the chair. A nurse came rushing to Ruby's side. "There, there, honey, just take it easy now," she said, patting Ruby's hand. "This is all just too much for her," she said to no one in particular. Ruby opened her eyes and smiled sweetly. "I just don't know what came over me," she said.

Colleen noticed that Ruby never left anyone alone with Old Pa. She knew that as a child she wasn't supposed to ask the questions about Ruby that she'd like to ask, but she could hear the grown-ups talking from time to time and knew that there was something funny about that lady. Why, she was younger than Aunt Betty! Daddy had been real mad about Old Pa marrying her, and Uncle Jake had said, "Papa's lost his mind." "I'm only 10," thought Colleen, "but I know what I'm seeing."

Hazel Estes, Jim's daughter, arrived around 4 p.m. With babies to watch at home, it was hard for her to get away, but she'd made it. She found Old Pa all alone, didn't see anyone around at all. Old Pa looked real bad, appeared to be unconscious. Hazel said goodbye to him then, fairly certain that it would take a miracle for him to recover.

Tom Pratt died at 6:30 p.m. on August 25, 1947, less than twenty-four hours after the attack. Because the death occurred within twenty-four hours of the attack, the criminal charge would be murder.

An old postcard of Leaksville Hospital, now an apartment building.

$$\frac{27^{x+1}}{\sqrt{3}} = 9^{2x-3}$$

$$\frac{3^{3x+3}}{3^{1/2}} = 3^{4x-6}$$

$$3^{3x+3-(1/2)} = 3^{4x-6}$$

$$3^{3x+2\frac{1}{2}} = 3^{4x-6}$$

$$3x + \frac{5}{2} = 4x-6$$

NORTH CAROLINA STATE BOARD OF HEALTH
BUREAU OF VITAL STATISTICS

CERTIFICATE OF DEATH

130

Registration Dist. No. **79-50**   Certificate No. **48**

1. PLACE OF DEATH:
   (a) County **Rockingham**
   (b) Township _____ (If in town limits, leave blank)
   (c) City or town **Leaksville** (If outside city or town limits, write RURAL)
   (d) Street, hospital or institution **Hospital**
   (e) Length of stay in hospital or institution **- 48 hrs.** (Yrs., mos., or days)
   In this community _____ (Yrs., mos., or days)

2. HOME (USUAL RESIDENCE) OF DECEASED:
   (a) State **N.C.**   (b) County **Rock.**
   (c) City or town **Leaksvill-**
   (d) Street or R.F.D. **I**
   (e) Is place of residence in corporate limits? _____
   (f) If foreign born, how long in U.S.A.? _____ years.

3(a) FULL NAME **Tom W. Pratt**
3(b) If veteran, name war _____   3(c) Social Security No. _____
4. Sex **Male**   5. Color or Race **White**   6(a) Single, married, widowed, or divorced. **Married**
6(b) Name of husband or wife **Ruby Edwards Pratt**
   (c) Age of husband or wife if alive **35** years.
7. Birth date of deceased **3/29/66** (month, day and year)
8. AGE: Years **81**   Months _____   Days _____   If less than one day _____ hrs. _____ mins.
9. Birthplace **Va.** (City, town, or county) (State or foreign country)
10. Usual occupation **Farmer**
11. Industry or business _____

FATHER
12. Name **Fred Pratt**
13. Birthplace **Va.**

MOTHER
14. Maiden Name **Bettie Martin**
15. Birthplace **Va.**

16(a) Informant's Signature **Tom W. Pratt Jr.**
   (b) Address **Leaksville, N.C.**
17(a) **Burial** (Burial, cremation, or removal)   (b) Date thereof **8/28/47** (Month, day, year)
   (c) Cemetery **El Bethel**
   (d) Location **Leaksville, N.C.**
18(a) Funeral director **L - S Fun. Home**
   (b) Address **Leaksville, N.C.**
19(a) **9/11** 19**47** (b) **Mrs. Ruby I. Jenkins**
   Filed   Registrar

MEDICAL CERTIFICATION

20. Date of death **8/26** 19**47**, at **In the P**
21. I certify that death occurred on the date above stated; that I attended deceased from **8/25** 19**47** to **8/26/47** 19___ and that I last saw h__ alive on **8/26/47** 19___
Immediate cause of death **Frac. of skull**   Duration
Intracranial injury
subdural hemotona
Due to _____
Due to _____

Other conditions (Include pregnancy within 3 months of death) _____
Major findings: Of operations _____
Of autopsy: _____

Physician
Underline the cause to which death should be charged statistically.

22. If death was due to external causes, fill in the following:
   (a) Accident, suicide, or homicide (specify) _____
   (b) Date of occurrence _____
   (c) Where did injury occur? _____ (City or town) (County) (State)
   (d) Did injury occur about home, on farm, in industrial place, in a public place? _____ (Specify type of place)
   While at work? _____
   (e) Means of injury _____

23. Signature **R. P. Harris**   M.D.
   Address **Leaksville, N** date signed

(left margin, vertical) Please write the ... s of death clearly and legibly.

Tom Pratt's death certificate contains many errors, including the wrong date of death, which was August 25, not August 26. His name was William Thomas Pratt, not Tom W. Pratt. The length of stay was about 16 hours, not 48. The burial was August 27, not August 28. The "informant" was Thomas B. Pratt, not "Tom W. Pratt, Jr." The doctor's signature is typed, not signed.

$$4x - 6 = 3x + \frac{5}{2}$$

$$x = 8\frac{1}{2}$$

$$x = \frac{17}{2}$$

Tom Pratt ("Old Pa") and granddaughter Colleen Pratt (daughter of Reid and Custis), taken about 1940.

Chapter 7

Sheriff Munsey Hodges

Tuesday, August 26, 1947

Sheriff Munsey Hodges fell into his chair at the police station and let go a heavy sigh. It was 11 p.m., and he'd spent the entire day going over the crime scene, interviewing witnesses, making phone calls to the State Bureau of Investigation, and speaking to reporters. He was exhausted, but he couldn't go home yet. People had been at him all day, everyone from Mayor John Smith to his deputies to the victim's family, everyone wanting to know facts and details that he himself did not yet know, everyone pushing for an arrest before he could even gather everyone's statements. He had closed the door to his office, trying to settle his thoughts. A little fan on the file cabinet pushed the hot air around. His desk was littered with half-filled cups of cold coffee, overflowing ashtrays, and notepads full of statements. He pushed everything to one side, put his tired head in his hand, and tried to think.

Here he was, just weeks before the September meeting of the Rockingham County Commissioners, and he suddenly had this vicious murder to solve. It was no surprise that old Mr. Pratt had died last night after that beating he took. But here it was: there was no murder weapon, no suspects, and no obvious motive. He had hoped to go into that meeting with great news of all his improvements to the County Police force. Now all the news would pale in comparison to this crime and he would have to spend a lot of time answering questions all about it. Already the county commissioners had out a $100 reward for information leading to the arrest of the assailant, and a Leaksville businessman had put up another $100. He wondered who that was. He'd have to ask Mayor Smith. Well, he could still hope that something would break in the case before then. He had a couple weeks to work on it

He'd been elected to the Sheriff's office last November, beating the Republican candidate J. S. Wilson, Jr. by 1,984 votes of 8,220 votes cast. It was a sizable win. His career had taken many turns up to this point. Born in a log cabin in 1894 in Pittsylvania County, Virginia, and moved to Rockingham County when he was eight years old, he'd grown up in this county, worked here, married Zell, and was raising his family. He had run a grocery store on The Boulevard, sold insurance, had been a deputy sheriff and the county tax collector. He reckoned those jobs meant he knew almost everyone in the county, and that helped get him elected. Besides, he was a Democrat, and the South votes Democrat. Always did, always would.

He had been elected as a reformer, and that was what he had intended to be. The last sheriff had been rumored to be in cahoots with the bootleggers—he even ordered the police car fenders painted white. Shoot! How were you going to sneak up on bootleggers in a black and white car? It had been the laughingstock of the state. So when he took office last December 2, he immediately went to work updating the police cars, equipment, and communications. He had two-way radios installed on seven of the county's eight automobiles. A broadcast short wave radio station at Spray and another one at Reidsville were now operating on a 24-hour basis.

Drinking and gambling, that's what many people did to pass the time here, and it often led to violence. It was the constant war against those vices that kept the people of this county safe from their own foolishness. Those old timers were still out there making their moonshine, but he would find them. Sure, some of the real rascally ones would just move their stills across the state line into Virginia, but the police would get them, too, eventually. In the last seven months, they'd located and captured thirty-four stills and seven cars loaded with bootleg whiskey. They'd destroyed 5,700 gallons of mash and 1,100 gallons of whiskey. They'd seized and destroyed eight illegal slot machines. They'd seized three truckloads of bottled-in-bond whiskey and sold it to the ABC stores in other counties, giving the proceeds of $12,770 to the county school fund.

Also noted in the report, the force had patrolled 119,267 miles of unincorporated territory including escorts for seventy-two funerals. There had been 1,549 arrests made with 682 deputy officers assisting. Munsey's deputies had served twenty execution notices, thirty-five claims and deliveries, eleven tax suits, fifty-seven notices, 228 summonses, and 375 subpoenas. Deputies spent sixty-six days in Superior court. Revenue of $2,865 was added to the county treasury from the sale of confiscated property. Fifty-six investigations and forty-seven search warrants resulted in the recovery of $7,180 of stolen property. They'd traveled 8,443 miles conveying 252 prisoners and 298 miles carrying two lunatics to asylums.

It was an impressive report. He had been poised to make quite a splash at the commissioner's meeting. He had a lot of friends who would be rooting for him. His first eight months in office had been a stellar success. It was bad timing for him that this murder had to take place now, though he supposed it was far worse timing for Mr. Pratt. Everyone in town knew somebody in the Pratt family. Even Josie Pratt was one of Zell's good friends. People were locking their doors at night and worried about who this person might be that would attack a poor defenseless old man in his own bed. All anybody could talk about was this murder. Feelings were running high. Rumors were getting started; everybody was talking about Ruby and her carrying on. People would be looking to him to make an arrest quickly. Of course, he wanted it to be the right person. He would have to get this person behind bars, and he hoped, be able to report it to the county commissioners in less than three weeks' time.

The press had been after him for statements all day and it was part of his job to give them something. He wanted to calm people down so he said the right, reassuring things. He said they had several suspects and that they hoped to make an arrest very soon. He gave them the official account of the attack, that an intruder had placed an old churn under the window, raised the screen and entered the house. He suggested that Mr. Pratt had turned on a light and recognized his attacker. In truth, there was no way to know if the old man had recognized his attacker. If he saw him, he never said who the attacker was. But Munsey was hoping to suggest that there was a personal motive for this crime, rather than a random event. People needed some reassurance now. And he needed to solve this crime. He hadn't wasted any time contacting the State Bureau of Investigation, which was on board by Monday evening. He had been assigned Robert Allen, a Reidsville native, from the Bureau. That was good. Reidsville was just 12 miles from Leaksville. Mr. Allen would know these people and these roads and these woods much better than most people.

Munsey lit up another stale-tasting cigarette and thought again, for the thousandth time today, who might have done this crime. It probably was a random robbery, as Ruby claimed. Lots of times these old folks kept money stashed in their houses, especially since the banks had failed in the Depression. An old man might attract somebody who thought he could get some cash. But nothing was missing that anybody knew about but a chop ax. As for a stranger, trouble is, no one had reported seeing any strangers hanging around this week. One thing about a small community, strangers are noticed. If a stranger did it, he had slipped in and out completely unnoticed.

Another thought did cross his mind. He wondered about the fights between Mr. Pratt and his son Reid. But he had sent Deputy Sheriff Robert Barnes to Reid's house himself that night just to assess the situation. Getting a suspect's first reaction to the news was important. Barnes thought Reid had seemed too shocked and upset to have known about it. It was also clear that he had been sleeping. And what's more, Ruby herself had said she saw the man, a big Negro with long slick hair. Reid Pratt was big around the belly, but he wasn't no Negro.

His mind turned again to Ruby. Ruby's robbery story didn't quite add up, now did it? A random person she'd never seen beating her husband to death. A big man who had climbed on a butter churn, opened the kitchen screen, climbed in and got past that little stick that propped up the oven door, and then attempted a robbery. Then, instead of robbery, he commits murder. The man runs out the door, into the woods, and gets away without any of that gang of twenty men finding him. It just didn't make sense. Blast it! If there was any truth to it, he needed bloodhounds. He needed those bloodhounds and he needed them right now!

He stubbed out the cigarette. Lord, this was one headache he did not need. Munsey knew he had lost control of the investigation before it had even started. Modern investigation techniques have you separate the witnesses, get statements, and keep everyone out of the crime scene to look for clues left behind. Before he could even get to the crime scene, Coy Ratliff, Harold Hoover and others had gone for help. But it wasn't just the police and ambulance they called. Word of the attack spread like wildfire throughout the night. Men and their shotguns poured in to start searching the woods. Ruby was talking a mile a minute to whoever would listen. People were in and out of that house and all over the area all night. The crime scene was totally contaminated now, by people involved with the case or not involved, all wanting to help out or just be a part of the action.

His deputy Curtis Land had been the first officer to arrive on the crime scene. Ruby had told anyone who would listen–and they all did–that the intruder was as big as Curtis Land. Since Curtis Land (and his whole family for that matter) were well-known to be some of the largest people in the county, that would indeed be one big fella. That's who the men went searching for in the woods, but never found.

Who else could have done this thing? Could Ruby have been lying about what she saw? If she was, he had no way of knowing if she didn't change her story. Ruby said she saw a big black man do it, and that's the theory he was going to work under for now.

The clock on the wall said 12:23. He'd had enough for one day. He'd question Ruby again tomorrow and try to get more details from her. He put out his last cigarette, took his hat from the coat rack and put it on. Leaving his office, he let the door go with a slam.

Chapter 8
Munsey and Ruby
Wednesday, August 27, 1947

"Now Ruby, you got to know what you saw that night." Sheriff Hodges sat with Ruby on the settee at the house on Price Road, just a few feet away from where Tom Pratt had been attacked. Munsey's big frame didn't feel quite comfortable in this delicate furniture. She had fixed him some tea but he wasn't drinking it. He was trying with all his might to make Ruby remember anything that could help him solve this case. She was real nervous, sometimes crying, sometimes composed. Her little dog was sitting at her feet.

"I just don't know, Munsey." She went on, slowly and deliberately, as if she were repeating this for a child. "I told you, I was sleepin'. I heard a commotion downstairs that woke me up. I opened my door and came down the steps. He was standin' over Tom. He was a big nigger, with long slicked-back hair. I'd never seen him before. He was standing over Tom and hitting him, and I come down the steps and surprised him. He come toward me and I screamed. I ran back up the stairs and locked myself in the room. I didn't stop to look at him good." She twisted a wet handkerchief in her hands and fought back the tears.

"Ok, Ruby, now just take it easy. How did you happen to see this feller if it was one o'clock in the morning?"

"Tom has that pull-string hitched to the bedpost that cuts on the light overhead. He can cut the lights on and off from his bed without getting up. The light was on. He musta heard a noise and cut on the light."

"So you saw this person with that light, even though the rest of the house was dark."

"That's right."

"What else?"

"I showed you where he come in the window at the back of the house, standing on the churn."

"Yes, but how could a man as big as what you said come in that little window?"

"Well I don't know how he done it, but he done it!" She sounded exasperated. The task of having to explain her story again seemed too much for her. "I been over it and over it. You know I had the funeral this morning. I had to face all them people that don't like me. They think this is all my fault." Her nerves were starting to catch up to her and she started sobbing again. Munsey ran his hand through his graying hair and waited a moment before resuming. He handed her a fresh handkerchief from his back pocket, which she took wordlessly, dabbing her eyes and blowing her nose.

"But you came down again."

"What?"

"You came down the steps again after you saw the man and ran upstairs."

"That's right. Tom was calling me and I peeked out. I saw that the man was gone and the front door was wide open. So I came down, locked the door, and tried to help Tom, but I couldn't. He was bleeding too bad. So I ran out for Coy, calling for him. I guess I'm lucky that he heard me. I sure didn't want to be out with that person running loose."

"Now a stranger comes into your house in the middle of the night and your little dog here didn't make a sound?"

"No, that sure was bad luck. I don't know what happened to Collie that day. He had run off earlier in the day. I didn't know where he got to, but he knows his way back. He's done it before."

"So this dog made no noise before or after the intruder came in."

"No, Munsey, he couldn't make a noise if he was nowhere 'round here. He coulda been anywhere, chasing a rabbit through the woods or anything. Collie wasn't here."

"All right, now, Ruby. Now let's think this through one last time. A man come in your house while you were upstairs. You hear a commotion and come down the steps. The light is on and you see him hitting your husband. Do you think you'd know this man if you saw him again? A picture of him?"

"I don't know. I guess so. Yes, I think so."

"Ruby, this is a terrible crime that's been committed. This is real important. The people here are real upset about it, and the faster we can find a suspect, the better off everybody will be." He put a special emphasis on "everybody" hoping she'd understand that he meant her, too. She nodded her agreement but looked worried.

"I didn't have anything to do with it!" she blurted out.

He ignored that last statement. Every tongue in town was wagging about Ruby and she knew it. Of course he had to ask himself what she had to gain from Tom Pratt's death, and the answer was "plenty." Sixty-four acres of land, two houses, and whatever money he had stashed away. If the there was a will, most of his property would surely go to his children, though Mr. Pratt undoubtedly would have provided for her, too. If there wasn't a will, he reckoned she'd get an even share of it with the children.

Still, he had to ponder whether she was capable of such a thing. The Pratt children didn't like her, that was true, but none of them had accused her. No one even hinted at that. They'd been more embarrassed about this marriage than anything. They thought that she wouldn't make him happy, and she hadn't. Mr. Pratt probably thought that Ruby would obey him like another one of his children. Ruby probably thought she could have her own way most of the time. Everyone knew Mr. Pratt and Ruby fought all the time. And the family didn't like Ruby's reputation for parties with her friends. In fact, he himself had been among her friends. Hell, he knew everybody in the county. It was just his way of keeping his eye on people, including her. People made more of that than what it was, and the truth was, they didn't really know anything. 'Course now, he wished he hadn't of seen her. He was uncomfortable on this settee, uncomfortable drinking her tea, uncomfortable with some of his memories, uncomfortable with having to conduct a murder investigation with her as a suspect. He was too close to all of it, felt tainted by the past. But he couldn't let thinking about his own feelings cloud his judgment; nor could he let people start to speculate that there had been something between him and Ruby. His career and reputation both would be ruined. Zell wouldn't forgive him. There's no telling what would happen if rumors got out. Which is all they were.

No, the bottom line was, Ruby wasn't capable of murder, even if she did learn the hard way that being married to an old man wasn't so easy. He was sure of that. She might have figured on inheriting a lot some day and being able to take it easy, but that wasn't a crime. And besides, there was no evidence that it had been her. No bloodstained clothes, no murder weapon. Tom Pratt was old, but he had been a strong old man. He could have fought her off. Nope, best to put that idea out of his mind. Ruby didn't do it.

He started another tack. "You know there's a fellow right down the road here, Junior Thompson, escaped from a road gang last year. You know him?"

She hesitated. "I suppose so. I've seen him."

"Describe him to me."

"He's a big yellow-skinned nigger boy."

"What a minute, now, Ruby. Junior Thompson isn't so big. That's his brothers that're big, but not him. Are you sure you know Junior Thompson?"

"Well..."

"If you saw a picture of him, would that help you remember? Because Junior Thompson's got to go back to jail; I've got to round him up. Just hasn't been a priority. Now I regret that I didn't do it sooner, might've spared all of this. Boy like that escapes from a road gang, no telling what he's capable of. He ever get Tom mad?"

"Why, I don't know. Did you say you have a picture of him?"

"Tell you what. Tomorrow we'll go down to the station; you look at all the pictures we've got of known suspects. You can tell me what you think."

"Do I have to?" All of a sudden she sounded as meek as a kitten.

"Good Lord, Ruby, of course you have to! You're the only witness! This whole case rests on what you saw." He stood up. "I'll come by and pick you up in the morning." Munsey's patience for Ruby's tears had just about run out. Didn't she realize what was at stake here?

She walked him to the door, resigning herself to this most unpleasant task. "I thank you, Munsey–, uh, Sheriff Hodges. I'm sorry to be so much trouble. I'll be ready first thing."

Sheriff Munsey Hodges, from a 1946 article printed in *The Leaskville News*. Used with permission from *The Eden News*.

Chapter 9

The Line-up

Thursday, September 4, 1947

Only two weeks ago, her husband had been alive and they had miserably kept out of each other's way as much as possible, or they had fought when he had been so stubbornly mean to her about her friends. Ten days ago he had been murdered. Eight days ago his children buried him next to his first wife. Seven days ago she identified Junior Thompson from photographs at the sheriff's office. Yesterday a posse had caught up with Junior and arrested him. And today Ruby found herself at the Guilford County jail over in Greensboro, about to identify him as the one who she saw murder her husband. This was a nightmare from which she could not wake up. In a few minutes, she'd have to look at that boy again. It still wouldn't be over though. She'd have to testify at the trial, and she'd have to figure out, once again, once again, once again, where her life was going next. She was 36; she had had three husbands. She would have to move again, and she was wrung out.

Part of her hoped she'd get to keep the farm, but part of her couldn't wait to get away from there. She couldn't forget how Tom had lain on the floor, bleeding and broken, moaning and in pain. She'd see his face when she tried to go to sleep at night, and again in the quiet moments of morning when she was out there feeding the chickens or bringing in the stove wood—doing the work he had done. How would she have the strength to stay on there alone? She was embarrassed and humiliated. It was one thing to be the center of attention among your friends, quite another to see your name in the paper every week associated with a murder. She didn't like the notoriety. It was low class. The worst of it was that nobody outside her close circle seemed to believe her version of events. The Pratts had been cool and distant from her. The community wasn't on her side. She had come to despise her husband, yes, she admitted it. In the past when she had anticipated the death of her old husband, she had never imagined feeling so guilty and helpless. If she had never married him, would this have happened? Was she accountable? Somehow she'd have to hold her head up in this town just to move on with her life.

Munsey had carried her down here to the jail in his patrol car. Far from feeling like a celebrity, she had hoped to God that no one saw her as they pulled onto Highway 14. His two-way radio squawked from time to time. Under other circumstances she might have found that interesting, but not today. Today she wished she was anywhere else, doing anything else, but riding with Munsey Hodges in his patrol car. Munsey had said, "Sheriff Walters will be meeting us" and "this won't take too long" and "hope we get back before dinnertime." He hadn't said anything about his belief in her, that she was a good person, that he admired how she was holding up, or that he sympathized for her trouble. It was obvious to her that he was a man doing his job, and that was it. She felt like she didn't know him at all.

The dull heat of September had drained her of her nervous energy during the ride, but entering the jail made it all return. It all felt so strange. She felt weak and as though she were in danger, though she knew she was not. Now she sat on the hard wooden bench in the lobby while Munsey went off in search of Sheriff Walters. Presently he came back. "Come on this way," Munsey said, escorting her down a hall, through a locked door to another hall, to a small, darkened room. Sheriff John E. Walters from the Greensboro police greeted her. Agent Allen was also there. She had met him when they had gone over the photographs. On the other side of the room was a large window, through which could be seen a lit room. "Mrs. Pratt," Sheriff Walters began. "Eight suspects will be entering that room over yonder. They won't be able to see or hear you, but you can see them." At that moment a buzzer sounded, causing Ruby to jump. She tried to act as if nothing had happened. As if going to the county jail to look at murderers was something she did every day of the week. At that moment a door opened and eight Negro men entered, each holding a cardboard number.

Sheriff Walters spoke gently to her. "Mrs. Pratt, I need you to take a close look at each of these men and tell me if the man you saw attacking your husband on August 25th is here." His manner was slow and easy, and he seemed prepared to wait all day if necessary. He was being kind to her, but she still wished she could disappear.

She looked at each man briefly, but didn't take any time to study them. She didn't want to look at their horrible black faces. They were dressed in shabby everyday clothes, not in prison garb. All of them had the same grim, worn look of defeat, with dull eyes and faces that made young men look old. She didn't want to be a part of this, not part of this world where bad people lived behind bars and good people had to look at them. She felt dirtied by it. She wanted nothing more than get away from here, to get back home. And though she felt like crying, she didn't. She would try to keep some shred of dignity about herself. So she looked, as asked, but she didn't need any time. Without further hesitation she said flatly, "That's him. Number 4." Of course she could identify Junior Thompson. He'd been living 300 yards from her house for the last year.

"Are you sure? Take a good look. Take your time."

"Yes, I'm sure."

"Well, that's fine then. Please just wait a minute and we're going to do this again." Sheriff Walters disappeared through a door. Shortly afterwards the men on the other side of the glass also left the room. They returned in a different order; this time Junior was Number 6. Sheriff Walters returned and asked the same question, "Can you identify the man you saw attacking your husband on the night of August 25?"

"Yessir, Number 6."

"Please wait another moment." The sheriff exited again, the men left the room, and the men returned in yet a third order. This time some of the clothing had been changed; some men had traded their shirts. Sheriff Walters returned. "Mrs. Pratt, can you now please identify the man who you saw attacking your husband on the night of August 25th?"

"Number 2."

Sheriff Walters lifted a microphone from the wall. "Number 2, step forward." Junior, his face expressionless except for weariness, stepped forward.

"Are you sure, Ma'am?"

"Yessir."

"Thank you. Now, Mrs. Pratt, I know this is difficult. Please bear with us. We need to be sure." Again Sheriff Walters left her standing there with Munsey and Agent Allen, while he exited the room and the suspects also filed out. She couldn't have felt more tense if she'd been in that line of suspects herself. She was struggling to keep her composure, and a panicky feeling that made her want to run out of the room was rising up in her belly. She looked at Munsey hoping for some reassurance, or some words of kindness, or anything that would make this ordeal stop. He was dressed in his uniform, of course, with his hat in his left hand. He stood there, with all his weight on his right leg, leaning with his right hand on the molding of the glass. How could he be so relaxed? He kept his eyes on the window to the observation room, saying nothing. "Munsey, I–"

"Hush now, Ruby. I'm not supposed to say anything to you while you're lookin' at the suspects." Feeling mildly rebuked, she drew in a deep breath, pulled herself up to her tallest posture, pushed down the nausea that was creeping into her throat, swallowed hard, and looked away from him, back to the observation window, just as he was doing.

For a fourth time, the men filed into the observation room. This time Junior was wearing the blue work shirt that another man had had on the last time. Sheriff Walters returned. "Mrs. Pratt, can you please identify the man you saw beating your husband on the night of August 25th?"

"Number 8."

"Take all the time you need, Mrs. Pratt. Are you quite sure?"

She had had enough, and though she was a lady she was starting to feel angry. Why on earth were they putting her through this? Hadn't she told them three times already? She had no choice but to remain polite, so she kept her voice even and low. "That's him, absolutely, Number 8. That's Junior Thompson that killed my husband."

$$e^{2x} \cdot e^{3x} = e^{5x}$$

$$e^{15x^2} / e^{3x} = e^{15x^2 - 3x}$$

$$e^2 \cdot e^4 + 2\left(3e^3\right)^2$$

$$e^6 + 2\left(9e^6\right)$$

$$e^6 + 18e^6 = \boxed{19e^6}$$

$$\frac{e^{-2} \sqrt{e^8}}{\left(e \cdot e^2\right)^2} =$$

$$= \frac{e^{-2} e^4}{e^6}$$

$$= \frac{e^2}{e^6} = \frac{1}{e^4}$$

$$= e^{-4}$$

(16)

$$4^{x+3} = 2^{3x-3}$$

$$2^{2x+6}$$

$$3x - 3 = 2x + 6$$

$$x = 9$$

$$4^{12} = 8^8$$

$$16,777,216 = 16,777,216$$

The evenings were cooler now. The crops were laid by, the summer flowers were fading, but the trees were still lush with green. The crickets began singing as evening fell, though they, too, would soon fall silent for the winter. The kitchen windows were open in the alcove that held the kitchen table, and Jake and Clyde sat over peach cobbler while Josie poured the coffee. "Josie, this is mighty good." Josie thanked Clyde, her brother-in-law, and moved out of the way. They had passed half an hour with small talk of families, what was happening at church, but she knew the men wanted to talk alone. This business with Mr. Pratt's murder had taken over everyone's minds. Even when they weren't discussing it, they were thinking about it, and she could tell that Jake was coming to a decision about something. She had listened to Jake's opinions but he'd have to work this out with Clyde. She had heard the same rumors that everyone else had heard, but she wasn't a gossip herself. She tried not to think ill of anybody; she would not pass judgment. Therefore, she wouldn't be the one to speculate about who had killed her father-in-law, nor to give her husband advice about how to proceed. She was sure her father-in-law was now with the Lord. As for the killer, she shuddered at the thought of what would become of his soul, and more immediately, whether this person was still on the prowl looking for somebody else.

Josie cleared off the kitchen table while the brothers got down to serious conversation. Clyde broke the ice. "Jake, I've been over that house with a fine tooth comb. Are you sure Papa had a will?"

"I thought he had one, but I never asked him about it, but I am sure he had one. Grandpa had one; and you know Papa would have had one, too. But I can't find it anywhere. Maybe he didn't have one after all." Jake gazed absentmindedly into his coffee cup as if it could tell him where to find that will.

"Maybe he thought he'd change the will after he married Ruby. Maybe he just couldn't decide how to do it and kept putting it off. Still, where's the old will?"

"I don't know. And if we don't find it, Ruby's going to end up with the farm. Though if she thought he was rich, she's got another thought comin'. Somethin' else– the police ain't telling us what we really need to know. Munsey's got Junior Thompson locked up but I just don't see why he'd do it. Do you?"

"Nah." Clyde picked at a few crumbs with his fork. "They said it was a robbery, but I don't know. Papa certainly didn't have anything valuable."

"Just the land. Whatever happened to that chop ax on the back porch? That blade was sharp enough to shave you. I picked it up and looked at it not that long ago. You would never catch Papa using a dull ax–"

112

"–That's right–"

"–But now I can't find it anywhere. Munsey even sent Well-Digger Jones down into the well to look for it, but he didn't find it."

"Doctor Harris said Papa had been hit by a blunt object, maybe a rock. There was dirt all in the wound."

Jake sighed with resignation. "Anyway, no telling where that ax got to. My guess is that it was used one way or another."

"You think that Junior could've killed him with that ax?"

"Might could. Nothin' was missin' from the house but the ax— and maybe his will. It doesn't add up to me. Junior knew that Papa was at home. Why would he take a chance like that? What do you think, Clyde?"

Clyde paused and looked at his older brother. For all the teasing they'd done between them about Papa marrying this young woman, they had never thought it would end like this. Papa was 81; no one had thought he'd live forever. But certainly not to end up like this, brutally murdered in his own home, for no apparent reason. Seemed like Munsey got an easy target, that boy who had escaped from jail, but he couldn't figure why Junior would kill Papa. Only one person he knew of could have had a motive. Clyde decided to offer his opinion.

"Jake, I've heard things and so have you, about Ruby. She was married to a Corum for awhile. I even heard there was somebody else before him. Seems to me like that girl's been all over. If Papa doesn't have a will, she's going to get everything he had. I don't know anything, really, about Papa's gettin' married. He said they did, but I don't know. Do you?"

"No. I don't. I think they went up to Martinsville to get married, but I don't know. She's been callin' herself 'Mrs. Pratt' several years now, and she wears a weddin' ring. You know anything about Papa buyin' that ring?"

"Nope."

"Me, neither. But one thing I do know, and I'm telling you the truth, she's just not our kind of people."

"You can sure say that again. Well, I think we ought to look into the marriage. All that land and everything is gonna go to her, and we don't even know if they was really married."

"Papa wouldn't have lived with her without bein' married. He did some crazy things but he wouldn't've gone that far. They both acted like they was married. She says they were. Well, they both did."

"Well she sure will be ridin' high if there's no will!"

Jake thought back to five years ago and the conversation he'd had with Papa about getting married. Papa had been bound and determined to do it, and there was to be no talking him out of it. "Do you remember when he was so happy about her?"

"Yeah, I thought he was losing his mind! Sure seems like a long time ago."

"I don't know if I ever told you this, Clyde, but after Mama died, Papa would come over to visit us. You know that big picture of Mama we have in the bedroom? Whenever he was getting ready to go, he'd say, 'I want to go see Nettie,' and he'd go in the bedroom and stare at that picture on the wall for a long time, all by himself in there. Wouldn't say anything, but when he was ready, he'd come out and go on home. I reckon he was lonelier than any of us really thought about."

"Yeah, I reckon so. Still, to take up with Ruby, of all people! What on earth was he thinkin'?"

"She keeps a clean house." Jake had to allow that Ruby did keep a clean house. But he felt sure that *that* hadn't been what Papa had been thinking. Papa had been thinking that he felt like a young man again. His excitement had been barely contained. They hadn't wanted to take that away from him, and they had respected him enough not to try too hard to talk him out of marrying Ruby. Besides, only Mama could talk Papa out of anything once he'd put his mind to it. They came to regret it, and they were sure Papa had, too, though he'd never admitted it outright.

Jake and Clyde had been the middle children, a few years younger than Pearl and Alma; a few years older than Jim, Reid, and Betty. They had always been close. Their wives, Josie and Fannie Sue, were good friends, too. They went to the First Christian Church together in Spray. But this was a difficult conversation. Each lost in his own thoughts, sipping coffee and staring at their empty plates, struggling for what sort of direction to take. Jake got up and put the plates in the sink. He took a toothpick from the metal holder on the table, sat back down and crossed his long legs, poking the toothpick in his mouth. His mind was turning every which way.

"I'll tell you what, Clyde, I think Munsey's got the wrong boy. I don't think Junior did it. Do you?"

"No. I've thought long and hard on it, but I don't think so, either. But I think he's gonna go to prison for it."

"Yeah. Me too."

"There's something else. You've heard people talk about her and Munsey."

"Yeah. But I have no way of knowing if there's any truth to them rumors. People will make up stories out of anything. It's not like we can ask him. If they're not true, they'll ruin his reputation. If they are true—"

"—If they are true then he's helpin' her cover it up! What if she did it with somebody and he's helpin' her lie about it?!"

Jake jumped up and began to pace the kitchen floor. "Then there's not a blessed thing we can do about it! I think we have to forget about rumors. Munsey's still the sheriff, even if he's got the wrong fellow behind bars. Besides, even if the rumors are true, I don't think Munsey would cover up a crime. We've all known him for years. He seems like a good ol' boy to me."

"Well, I hope you're right. Do you really reckon Ruby...?" Clyde didn't finish the question. Over his life, Papa had had business schemes that failed, had often said things without thinking, had lost his temper time and again, and had been heart sick with Reid for his trouble with that girl from North Spray, but marrying Ruby had been the stupidest, stubbornist, most foolhardy thing Papa had ever done.

Jake answered Clyde's unfinished question. "No, no, not her directly. I don't think so. Oh I just don't know. Maybe some friends of hers, her brothers or somebody. Her friends were the worst bunch of people! Always comin' up to the farm, looking for her to fix them something to eat, always bringin' a bottle. That's what Papa said." He just couldn't decide how deeply Ruby was involved in this, or whether she was involved at all. Like most men, Jake liked knowing the facts. Not knowing the facts was driving him crazy. If they'd been outside, he might have spit.

"I know. They'd sit around all day on a Saturday like there was nothing to do. Those friends of hers was so lazy they wouldn't work in a pie factory. No wonder Papa was mad all the time."

"You know, she marries an old man and thinks it'll only be a year or two before he dies and she gets everything. Why else on earth would she marry him? And they fought like cats and dogs all the time. Pearl said she never knew when Papa was just going to show up at her place, madder than a wet hen. Maybe Ruby just couldn't stand waitin' anymore.

But I still don't think she did it herself. I heard that Ruby's brother went to the Leaksville Bank and Trust Company the very next day, the very next day! – asking how much money Papa had in his bank account!"

"Yeah, I heard that, too. They didn't let the man be buried before wondering about what he mighta left behind."

"Where was that dog of hers that night? I think they mighta tied him up somewhere so he'd be outta the way."

"You mean they tied up the dog before somebody came over to kill Papa? That would mean the whole thing was planned! No, now that would be premeditated murder. Would Ruby stoop that low? I'd sure hate to think that!" This idea was too far-fetched for Jake. Premeditated murder? Good night! He'd have to dismiss thoughts like that and just hope that Munsey would investigate the case thoroughly, and let the evidence speak for itself.

Then Jake continued. "You know what I think? I think it all happened by accident. I think one of her men-friends showed up drunk that night and got into a row with Papa. Papa probably tried to kick him out, and the man grabbed something and slugged him with it, and Papa's head cracked open like a watermelon. Well, they didn't know what to do; they panicked. So they cooked up the idea of the robbery and the nigger comin' in through the kitchen window. They turned over the butter churn under the window. Then I think Ruby let the man get far away before she called for help. That's why there's all that talk about whether his blood was dry, and whether her bed had been slept in. If she'd let him lay there for awhile while this man ran away, the blood might of clotted up. And then she needed someone to blame, and somebody gave her the idea of Junior, so she blamed Junior. That's what I think happened. I just think the whole thing was done before they knew what happened. One, two, three, and it's all done."

"But if you're right, who was it?"

"I have no earthly idea."

Jake got a disgusted look on his face. This discussion was creating that sickening feeling in his gut he'd felt ever since the night Harold had pounded on his door. "You're probably right. It probably was like that. But it's still murder, and helping to cover it up is a crime, too. But if Ruby knows who done it, she's not saying. She declared it was a big fat nigger that night—everybody heard her say so—and then two days later she goes and says it was definitely Junior Thompson, the skinniest little runt on Price Road."

"Well, he's been in trouble before. It was robbery then, too. You know, the Greensboro paper said Papa had testified against Junior at a trial, but I just don't recall ever hearing anything about that. Did you?"

"No, I don't know who told that. All kinds of stories wind up in the newspaper, and they never even asked us about it. Papa never testified anywhere that I ever heard about. Well, guilty or not, Junior's gonna pay for it, just the same."

"I think so, too. No lawyer's gonna to touch this case with a colored boy's word against Ruby. And that'll be the end of Junior for sure."

Jake was exasperated at the facts that they'd already been over a thousand times. "I know, but the person she described sure didn't sound a bit like Junior."

This time it was Clyde's turn to get up. Helping himself to a glass of water, he took a drink before answering. It seemed like they were going in circles. No wonder, this whole case was going in circles. Nothing fit.

118

Clyde tried to think clearly. What should they be doing? Clyde said, "Jake, what about Ruby marrying Papa? Do you reckon we can find out if it's legal?"

"I 'spect so, but we will need a lawyer for that." Jake paused a minute before commenting. An idea had been forming in his head and he didn't know how it would be received. But the time was ripe to ask it. "What do you think about us hiring a lawyer to defend Junior?"

Clyde looked slightly taken aback. "You reckon we could do that? I mean, I believe the boy's innocent, but..." He pondered it. Hiring a lawyer for Junior would be hardly different than accusing Ruby of murder. Were they ready to make such a public statement about their feelings on the case? But maybe Jake was right. Unless they acted, this whole affair would come to a close and the killer would never be found. There was one thing for sure. "It wouldn't be right to send Junior to jail for murder. He might even get the gas chamber. I couldn't live with that if he didn't do it."

"Me, neither." Jake presented his plan to Clyde. "Well here's what I think we should do. Let's find out about this marriage first. I don't think we can just assume they were married. Papa thought so, but maybe they weren't. Let's look into it."

"All right."

"We have to talk to Pearl and the others, but I want to let Edd Thompson know we're standing behind his boy. I can send Herbert over to the finishing mill to find him and he can pass the message. You sure you agree we should pay for a lawyer to defend Junior? I've got some money saved. Maybe this is the time to use it."

"That's gonna to seem mighty strange to most folks; just think about it. Us paying for a lawyer to defend the boy accused of killin' Papa.

A colored boy at that." They both fell silent for a while, chewing on the idea. Finally Clyde said, "But I have to agree, I think it's the right thing to do."

Would there be repercussions for hiring Junior's lawyer? Jake figured they had to think of that. Junior being colored was something that had to be considered. Clyde had taken Mama's nurse, Aunt Caroline, to church with his family and sat her right there with them, and no one said a word. That was a Christian act, but a temporary one. People might not have felt the same if the church was going to get integrated on a permanent basis. For the most part, people kept to their own kind and took care of their own. There were the white schools and the colored schools, different churches, jobs that white people had that the colored men didn't get. Even the prisons were segregated! Marrying across racial lines was illegal, of course, and no decent person, white or colored, would want to do that. On the other hand, they had all grown up as neighbors, and relations between the races were pretty good in this town as long as everybody played by the rules. The Ku Klux Klan had not made any noises around here for ages; Jake didn't give a hoot about that anyway. What about anybody else in town? What if other people said something? He decided he really didn't give a hoot about that, either. A person's life was at stake. He could stand a little gossip if he felt he was doing the right thing. Wasn't he one of only a few hundred Republicans in this whole county of Democrats? Everybody knew it and he didn't care. Shoot! That's how he felt. Well, Jake and Clyde reckoned that people who knew them would stand by them, and people who didn't, well, that would be just too bad.

Would Edd Thompson even take the money for his boy? He would have to rely on a court appointed lawyer without their help, and what chance would he have then? They figured they could offer him the money in a way that wasn't insulting to his pride.

Jake got up and closed the window. It was long past dark now, pushing 10 o'clock. The decision to stand behind Junior seemed to come from out of the blue, yet when they spoke it out loud, each man felt the integrity of it. They firmly believed that Junior was innocent, and whether colored or white, an innocent man should not go to jail for murder. A white man might stand a fighting chance with a jury. A black boy, a little no-account kid like Junior, didn't stand a chance at all. The word of a white woman over a colored boy would be believed no matter what. Junior's only shot for getting off was their involvement; that much was crystal clear. No court-appointed lawyer was going get Junior off.

But taking a stand for Junior was going to come at a price, and Ruby was going to have to pay it. In short, it would humiliate her. Once she heard that they were hiring a lawyer for Junior, well, the whole town would know it, wouldn't they? What would people say about the Pratt family not supporting Ruby's story? If tongues had been wagging before, there would be no other topic of conversation now. If anyone had ever questioned whether the Pratt family approved of Ruby before, now there would be no doubt. Hiring a lawyer for Junior was a slap in her face. Ever since she had started seeing Papa, the Pratt family had privately admitted to feeling something between uneasiness and hard feelings toward Ruby. Instead of bringing him happiness in his last years, she had brought him misery. Of course, Papa had been foolish enough to marry her, so he bore some of the blame. Publicly they had kept quiet about their opinions. Papa's marriage was nobody's business. But murder changes things. Everything would change now. Without ever saying anything about Ruby, the whole town would know the Pratts didn't believe her story, they questioned her motives, they disapproved of her reputation, and they virtually held her responsible. Fact was, this action said the same about Munsey, that he'd arrested the wrong man. But Munsey hadn't been there the night of the murder. Ruby had been. And they didn't believe her story.

Energized by their decision, the two brothers continued to discuss the details until close to midnight. They'd get answers on the marriage first, then hire a criminal attorney. One thing they agreed on was that they didn't want any mistakes. If they were to do this, they'd have to do it right. That would mean getting the best lawyers that could be had. Jake grabbed the *Tri-City Directory* from the shelf in the sitting room and they looked through the short list of attorneys. Any lawyer could probably find out about the marriages, but they wanted to have total confidence in the answers. The best law firm around was only about twelve miles away, in Reidsville.

"What about Sharp and Sharp?" asked Jake. "They're the best." Giving Clyde a way out, he added, "We might get the daughter, though."

"People say she's as good as he is. Must be a right smart girl, going to law school and all that. She's been working with her father for nearly twenty years now, into all sorts of things. Politics and such."

"Not married," Jake answered flatly, as if this explained everything. "Most men wouldn't want to be married to woman lawyer. Might find themselves sleepin' out on the back porch!"

"Yeah, or locked up in jail! I guess I'm lucky Fannie Sue didn't take to becomin' a lawyer! She'd win every argument!" While the image of Clyde's wife becoming a lawyer caused a momentary chuckle, they were not unaccustomed to the idea of women being good in business. Mama advised Papa on his business ideas all along, from the gristmill to turning to carpentry for a living. Her money bought the land on Johnson Street. It was her name on the mortgage for the farm on Price Road. How they wished her good counsel could have kept him from marrying Ruby!

"Well," Jake offered, "I hear Miss Sharp is real good."

"I heard a colored man walked into her office one day and said, 'Are you the woman lawyer I've been hearin' about?'"

"Yeah," Jake jumped in, "and she said, 'Indeed I am! Now what can I do for you?' And he said, 'Nothin'. I just wanted to come up and see what you looked like.'"

"Yeah," Clyde carried it on, "He musta thought she'd be as ugly as a mud fence!" They liked retelling the local stories that both of them already knew. Everybody had a story, and the stories got bigger each time. But what was said about Miss Sharp, well, that was true. And though they poked fun at the colored man who couldn't imagine a woman lawyer, they harbored a few reservations themselves.

After a moment, Clyde continued, "But I guess I'd rather have Mr. Sharp just the same. Might be easier to talk to a man. Just to be sure."

They agreed that they would retain Jim Sharp to look into Ruby's marriages. Without a will, they had to decide whether to lay a claim to Papa's estate. Currently Ruby, as the wife, was the executrix. If Papa and Ruby were indeed married, she would inherit it all.

Once settling on Mr. Sharp, the discussion moved on to the criminal case. There was no question about who they wanted for the defense attorney, as there was one top dog in the criminal field, and everybody knew who that was. Leaksville attorney J. Hampton Price and his partner D. Floyd Osborne kept a thriving law practice and a big office up on The Boulevard, just a few blocks from Jake's house.

Clyde wondered, "You reckon Hamp Price will take this case?"

"Why not?"

"Well, he's a state senator, and this being a colored boy and all."

"Aw, hello! Wouldn't we be paying him? He'll do it."

"He is the best there is, for sure. They say you could shoot somebody in the back and Hamp will declare you're innocent–and get a jury to think so, too."

"Yeah, boy, he's got quite a reputation. He knows every politician in Rockingham County, every judge on every court, and half the folks in Raleigh. He could go anywhere, but he keeps his practice right here. I like that."

"Big fish in a small pond, I guess."

"Let's go up to The Boulevard this week and see if we can hire him."

Jake and Clyde were not wrong in their assessment of J. Hampton Price. He was a State Senator, an excellent attorney and the consummate politician. You could have asked anyone in the whole county: if there were a way to get Junior off, Hamp Price would be the one to find it.

J. Hampton Price, from a *Leaksville News* photo in 1944.

The law practice of Price and Osborne was on the second floor of this building on The Boulevard of Leaksville, N.C.

125

Pascal's Triangle

$$1$$
$$1 \quad 1$$
$$1 \quad 2 \quad 1$$
$$1 \quad 3 \quad 3 \quad 1$$
$$1 \quad 4 \quad 6 \quad 4 \quad 1$$
$$1 , 5 , 10 , 10 , 5 , 1$$
$$1 , 6 , 15 , 20 , 15 , 6 , 1$$

$$\binom{9}{4} = \frac{9!}{5! \, 4!}$$

$$\frac{3 \cdot 2 \cdot 3}{9 \cdot 8 \cdot 7 \cdot 6} \frac{}{4 \cdot 3 \cdot 2 \cdot 1} $$

$$= 126$$

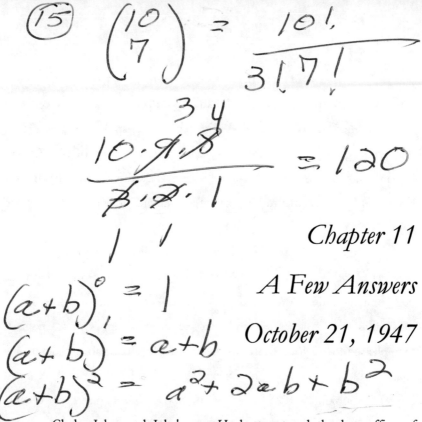

$$\text{(15)} \quad \binom{10}{7} = \frac{10!}{3!\,7!}$$

$$\frac{10 \cdot 9 \cdot 8}{3 \cdot 2 \cdot 1} = 120$$

$$(a+b)^0 = 1$$
$$(a+b)^1 = a+b$$
$$(a+b)^2 = a^2 + 2ab + b^2$$

Chapter 11

A Few Answers

October 21, 1947

Clyde, Jake, and Jake's son Herbert entered the law office of Sharp and Sharp–James Merritt Sharp and his daughter Susie Sharp–wearing their Sunday clothes, hats in hand. A secretary had asked them to wait for Mr. Sharp when a pleasant woman about 40 years old stopped to greet them. "Good afternoon, gentlemen. I'm Susie Sharp," she said, shaking their hands. "I presume you are waiting to see my father."

"That's right, Ma'am," replied Jake.

"He'll be along directly. Y'all have a pleasant day."

"Thank you, Ma'am," said Clyde, as she disappeared behind an office door.

The three of them exchanged looks, but said nothing that could be overheard by the secretary. They grinned a little sheepishly to each other. She hadn't looked so bad. No way you could tell she wasn't an ordinary woman.

Jake had asked Herbert to come along. He wanted Herbert to take notes at the meeting so that he and Clyde could concentrate on what Mr. Sharp had to say. There had also been the unspoken understanding that a college graduate might be able to decipher some of Mr. Sharp's explanations in case they didn't quite understand. Mostly, though, Herbert knew that his place was to keep quiet and let the older men conduct the conversation.

The secretary ushered them into Mr. Sharp's office. "Mr. Pratt, Mr. Pratt, and Mr. Pratt!" said Mr. Sharp, moving out from behind his desk, smiling and shaking hands all around. The spectacled, white-haired Mr. Sharp was 70 years old and had a courteous, unassuming manner. "I'm pleased to see you. Please do sit down." Mr. Sharp moved back to his chair. The three men took chairs opposite Mr. Sharp's large desk in an impressive-looking office filled with books. Herbert's eyes quickly scanned the titles of the law books. So much knowledge! He took out his notebook and a pencil from the breast pocket of his coat and got ready to write.

Mr. Sharp wasted no time on idle conversation. "You gentlemen asked me to look into a few items for you, and I have some information that I think you'll find useful. First of all, I understand you haven't been able to find a will among your father's papers. If he wrote one and if it was recorded, you can get the will on record in the county courthouse in Wentworth. If you do eventually find the will, you will have seven years to probate it, or it will be void."

"That means it wouldn't be any good?" Jake asked.

"That's correct. It would be the same as not having a will."

"Who is the executor if there is no will? Would his wife be the executor?" asked Clyde.

"An executor would be appointed by the court, and of course, you can petition the court to be the executor. There's a hearing in which the court decides how the property shall be distributed. There's no law that says how soon that hearing has to take place, but it's supposed to be speedy, so that people can settle their affairs."

"What if we find a will at his house, but it wasn't filed at the courthouse?"

"A will does not have to be recorded before the man's death. If it's not recorded, it can still be a valid document if it's signed and a judge deems it is legitimate."

"What if we think there is a will and somebody else has a-hold of it?"

"In that case, and what may be of particular interest to you, if you can prove there is a will and it is not produced, the holder can be kept in jail for the rest of his natural life."

Jake and Clyde drew in breaths and Herbert scribbled furiously. "Did you say that if there's a will and the person holding it won't give it to us, that person can go to jail *for life?*" Clyde had asked the question, but none of them could believe their ears.

"Yes sir, that's quite correct, but you'd have to be able to prove it. The State of North Carolina takes property rights very seriously. Of course, it would be very difficult to prove if someone is hiding a will that has never been filed at the courthouse. Have you gentlemen ever seen it?"

"No sir, we haven't. We always thought he had one, as our grandfather did. We assumed he did, too."

"And your father never discussed it with you?"

"We always assumed he'd divide everything six ways among his children, but with his marriage we didn't know what he was plannin'."

"I see. That brings us to the next matter. You inquired about Mrs. Pratt's prior marriages. The Pratt men leaned forward a bit more. This is what they'd been waiting for.

"Ruby Edwards married Carl Meeks on April 8, 1926." Herbert did a quick calculation in his head. Twenty-one years ago, Ruby was just a young teenager. Mr. Sharp continued, "Mr. Meeks sued for divorce on September 22, 1933." Herbert again did the arithmetic; they'd been married seven years. "And then," Mr. Sharp went on, "she married Charlie Corum on November 4, 1933. They lived together just over five years, before starting a divorce proceeding in September, 1939."

"What a minute," Jake interrupted. "You said she divorced her first husband in 1933, and she got married again that same year?"

"Yes, that's almost right. Divorce proceedings from Mr. Meeks started on September 22 and she married Mr. Corum on November 4th, about six weeks later."

"Good night!" Jake exclaimed, while Clyde let out a louder chuckle than usual. Temporarily forgetting that they were sitting in the law office of an esteemed attorney, all of them were thinking the same thing, and they looked at each other with astonishment. Every suspicion they had held about Ruby seemed to be coming true. Nobody minded a second marriage if the first husband had died, but a divorce was just wrong. Divorce might be forgiven if the husband beat her or drank up all their money, but a wife is supposed to stick by her husband for better or worse. It was always to be done as a last resort. They all knew women who had suffered in bad marriages, but what would the world come to if every one of them just up and left? Many a long-suffering woman tolerated bad times, and these were upright women who lived respectably regardless of how hard it got. A woman's reputation was worth her weight in gold.

Now, what was clear to them all, was that Ruby had taken up with another man while still married to her first. Good women did not smoke, did not drink, did not dance, did not play face cards, did not swear, did not take the Lord's name in vain, and did not take up with someone who was not their husband. They did not marry second husbands before the first husband's bags were hardly packed. They had known, of course, that Ruby was not a church-going religious woman. But this new information revealed without a shadow of a doubt that she was most surely the opposite kind. She was the kind of woman with loose morals that would marry twice, divorce twice, and marry an old man for his money. Jake could scarcely believe it. "Great day in heaven," he declared.

Mr. Sharp had allowed them a minute to absorb the information he had just presented them. Then he continued. "There's something more you should know." He certainly held their rapt attention. What else could he tell them now?

"I said you were 'almost' right about marrying Mr. Corum. Mr. Meeks, her first husband, brought suit for divorce, paying all costs for one, as I said, in 1933. When Mr. Corum brought suit, they were granted an annulment instead of a divorce for reasons of bigamy."

"How's that again?" Clyde asked. "Bigamy?"

"Yes, sir. For some reason the first divorce from Mr. Meeks was never completed. Therefore, she was still legally married to Mr. Meeks when she married Mr. Corum. They couldn't be granted a divorce because there was not a legal marriage. Instead they were given an annulment."

"And that means…" said Jake, as he was trying to piece this together.

"That means, Mr. Pratt, that the marriage to your father is also invalid. She is still, legally, married to Mr. Meeks."

"And Papa's farm?"

"Unless there is a will that names her as a beneficiary, she is not entitled to any of his estate."

They gazed at him in stunned silence, waiting for further explanation. Mr. Sharp removed his eyeglasses and leaned back in his chair. "In plain English, gentlemen, you may rest easy. She was not your father's wife. She won't inherit a thing."

$$(a - 2b)^4$$

$$a^4 + 4a^3 \qquad\qquad\qquad +16b^4$$

$$(a)^3 (-2b)' \quad \binom{4}{1}$$

$$a^4 - 8a^3b + 12a^2b^2 - 32ab^3 + 16b^4$$

$$\binom{4}{2} \quad (a^2)(-2b)^2$$

$$+12a^2b^2$$

$$6a^2(4b^2)$$

$+24a^2b^2$

Father and daughter legal team Susie and Jim Sharp of Reidsville, as they appeared in a newspaper article in 1949. The article burst with hometown pride as Susie Sharp had just become North Carolina's first female judge.

$$\left(\begin{array}{c}4\\3\end{array}\right)$$

$$4a\left(-2b\right)^3$$

$$4a\left(-8b^3\right)$$

$$-32ab^3$$

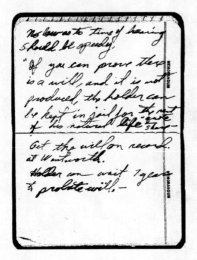
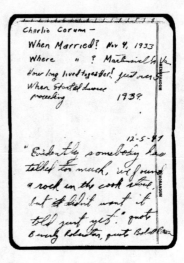

Herbert T. Pratt's notes from the meeting he attended with his father Jake, his
uncle Clyde, and the attorney Jim Sharp. The second note, dated Dec. 5, indicates
that they went back for a follow-up appointment. This note says that Beverly
Robertson, reporter for the *Leaksville News*, had spoken to S.B.I. Agent Bob
Allen, who told her that they had found a rock in the cook stove. This note is
dated after the trial had ended– but apparently the speculation had not

Chapter 12

Jury Selection

Monday, November 3, 1947

Five-year old Douglas Taylor didn't really understand the importance of what he was being asked to do, but he did know that for the simple task of pulling pieces of paper out of a box he was going to be paid five dollars. He understood that this was not playtime, and that he must act very grown-up. Having done this same thing a few days ago, he knew just what to do. His daddy was Captain Taylor, the warden of the state prison near here, and he wanted to make him proud.

Placing his hand into the big box full of rolled up slips of paper, he chose one and handed it to the man in standing at the big table. That man handed it to the man at the big desk, who opened it up and read it aloud, while another lady wrote something down.

"Good Lord above," thought Munsey, observing these proceedings with trepidation. "There's got to be a better way to do this." Could all his hard work go up in smoke because a child was selecting the jury? Using a child was considered to be the most impartial method of selecting a jury, since he was innocent to the ways of the world and unable to read the names he pulled. No one is going to accuse a child of cheating. But still, after Junior had gotten away that night, after it took four days to get bloodhounds from the prison camp in the Fifth District, after bringing Junior in from Virginia and locking him up in Greensboro, after going all over creation to round up this jury pool, it all comes down to a five-year old. He hoped Providence was guiding that boy's hand. It seemed unwise to him, but it wasn't his place to question it. Well, he'd done his job. Let the others do theirs.

Yes, he'd be glad to be done with this case, and maybe they were finally getting to the end. Only through his determination had they caught this nigger, but things hadn't exactly gone well from the get-go. The crime scene had been a disaster. People arriving before Curtis Land even got there, Ruby telling everybody not to touch anything, but of course they had, and that band of men with their guns running off into the woods to trail their quarry. Junior–or whoever'd done this, though he thought it was Junior–had sure been lucky to get away. If they'd found him, they'd have lynched him.

But the biggest problem with all those well-meaning people up at the house was this: they hadn't all seen the same things. Well, of course they *had* all seen the same things, but everybody had a different interpretation of it, didn't they? And didn't he now have to deliver subpoenas to all these people to testify to what they saw? And Ruby's description of the attacker got bigger with every re-telling. Sure would be easier to make this case if it had just been Ruby's word to go by. These little towns were just now starting to put in telephone poles out in the country, but somehow gossip spreads like wildfire anyway. Since that night, all the folks that had been there had buzzed like bees to everyone

136

they knew, and the result was that this whole county had become firmly divided into two camps: those who sided with Ruby, and those who didn't. An impartial jury? Highly doubtful.

Munsey took some comfort in the fact that since catching Junior, every care had been taken to avoid any legal loopholes that might let this rascal go free. They had used eight men in the line-up and Ruby had identified Junior four times. Judge Bobbitt had ordered a special venire to enlarge the jury pool. It had taken Munsey and his deputies most of last week to issue the jury summonses. They had driven from Mayo, to Williamsburg, to Stoneville, to Reidsville, to Leaksville, Spray, and Draper, to Wentworth, Simpsonville, to Ruffin, and to Madison to deliver twenty-four summonses. And at the end of the day, last Wednesday, Judge Bobbitt had said it wasn't enough, too many people had to be excused from serving, so he ordered an additional seventy-five names to be selected by special venire (putting little Douglas Taylor to work), and didn't Munsey and his men have to comb the county again to track down this new pool? And didn't he have to explain to half the women who had not yet heard of the new law that, yes, they and not their husbands, were being called to serve? And didn't he have to tell some of the husbands that, no, they couldn't serve in their wife's place? Didn't he have to hear excuses from most of them that they were too busy, they couldn't get a ride, didn't understand what to do in a court? And didn't he have to tell them to show up or be fined $20? But he was glad to do it. There could be no mistakes; no silly reason to have a mistrial.

So they were all here, those who hadn't been excused earlier this morning when the attorneys asked their questions—eighty-nine potential jurors sitting in the courtroom waiting to see if a five-year old would pull their names. All had come prepared to stay—this jury was being sequestered—and no doubt each one who got to go home today would be relieved. Nevertheless, they all eyed Ralph Scott, the solicitor, and Hampton Price, the defense attorney, with interest. Munsey quietly sighed. Hampton Price! Well no one could ever say this nigger didn't have adequate representation. He only had the best that money could buy. Apparently the Pratt family had seen to that. At least that's what he'd heard, and it was the only explanation that made any sense. The Thompson family wouldn't have had the kind of money you'd need to pay for Hamp Price. He was a state senator, for crying out loud.

Judge Bobbitt was taking a scroll from the clerk, he unrolled it, and announced, "Mrs. A. R. Williams." Mrs. Williams fairly jumped when she heard her name called, but she dutifully made her way to the aisle, walked to the jury box clutching her handbag, and took her seat in the first chair.

"J. C. Thacker." Mr. Thacker looked like he'd just lost at cards, but he rose and walked to the second seat in the jury box.

"Russell Searce." Searce let out a little nervous laugh and quickly jumped to his feet.

Once twelve people were in the jury box, Mr. Scott and Mr. Price took turns questioning them, with Judge Bobbitt asking a question here and there as well. Did any of the jurors know anyone involved in this case, or any of the attorneys? Did anyone feel that serving on the jury would present too much of a hardship for them? Did anyone feel he could not be impartial for any reason? Did any of the ladies feel that the details of a murder might be too distressing for them to discuss? Did anyone feel that they could not work with the other jury members to reach a verdict? The attorneys made notes, asking more follow-up questions, nodding at some

138

jurors, dismissing others. And so the morning dragged on, until both attorneys seemed satisfied with the twelve sitting in the jury box.

J. C. Thacker. Mrs. W. L. Patterson. C. L. Combs. Mrs. A. R. Williams. Russell Searce. J. F. Burgess. Bennie Williams. Russell Draper. Walter Gillespie. H. J. Frye. M. B. Newman. Clyde Comer. Twelve names were called, and the jury box filled up. The rest of the audience, having waited patiently throughout the day's tedious proceedings, was starting to shuffle. They'd been here since 10 o'clock and it was getting on towards 1. They were hungry. Judge Bobbitt ignored them while he turned his attention to newly selected members of the jury.

"Gentlemen—and ladies—of the jury, it is now time for you to be sworn in as jurors. This means that you take an oath that you will follow the instructions that I will give you, that will listen to the evidence as it is presented, and that you will deliver a verdict to the best of your ability. Members of the jury, you will rise, hold up your right hands, and be sworn to try this case."

Looking a bit awkward and nervous, the jury stood.

Judge Bobbitt continued. "Ladies and gentlemen, do you now swear or affirm to try all matters that come before you and render a true verdict according to the evidence?"

"I do."

The clerk boomed, "Members of the jury, you have all been severally sworn or affirmed. Stand together and hear the evidence." The jurors looked uncertain about what to do next. "Be seated," said the clerk.

If the potential jurors thought that they might at last be released, they were wrong. Judge Bobbitt continued, "We now have our jury of twelve, but given the severity of the charges, I think it is likely that this trial will be protracted. I am therefore ordering an alternate juror to be selected and sworn in." The clerk picked up his box of jury names.

Those who had breathed a sigh of relief drew it in again. One more name had to be chosen. Douglas Taylor had been sitting in the front row swinging his short legs. He was given a quick little push by his mother as she whispered in his ear. He suddenly looked alert, walked to the clerk, and chose one last name.

"Mrs. Marion Caudle." Mrs. Caudle looked stunned—of all these people still here, she was called? But she, too, made her way to the jury box and was sworn in like the others. Judge Bobbitt then finally said the words they had been waiting to hear. "Ladies and gentlemen, we will take a recess for lunch. We will reconvene at 2:15. Ladies and gentlemen of the jury pool who were not chosen, the Court wishes to thank you for your service. You are excused." Well, Munsey thought, this was all taking a long time, but the wheels of justice grind slowly, so they say.

When court resumed at 2:15, Judge Bobbitt addressed the jury, giving them the general instructions that he gave all juries—not to speak with anyone about the case, not to discuss the case with other jurors before the deliberation phase, not to read any newspapers. Then he added, "Ladies and gentlemen, you have been summoned here to decide the guilt or innocence of Junior Edd Thompson, who has been charged with burglary in the first degree and murder in first degree. Murder in the first degree is a capital offense, which could result in the death penalty. You must not bear the penalty in mind when you are deliberating the case, but listen to the evidence. You will be hearing testimony starting tomorrow that you must carefully consider when making your decision. Now, to my knowledge, this is the first mixed jury on any capital case in the state of North Carolina. The state has recognized that, as in voting, men and women have equal rights and obligations of citizenship, which includes serving on juries. Each of you has an independent mind and voice in this decision process. Ladies on this jury are to be accorded as much respect in their views as the gentlemen, and I do hope that in the deliberation phase that all of you will listen respectfully and attentively to each of your fellow jurors." With that, Justice Bobbitt tapped his gavel. It was 3 p.m. "Court is adjourned until tomorrow at 9:30 a.m."

Munsey was tired, but he still had to attend a funeral today, which is why the judge let them all leave early. The dean of the county bar, H. R. Scott, had died yesterday, and they were all headed to the funeral. Munsey watched as his two deputies led the jury out. The men were placed in the custody of Deputy Sheriff Bernard Young and the women in the custody of Mrs. Lee Early, one of his women deputies. The jury was headed over to the Belvedere Hotel in Reidsville where they'd be given a good dinner, a good bed, and hopefully would have a good night's rest. Come tomorrow, they'd need it.

The Belvedere Hotel in Reidsville, N.C., where the jury was sequestered.

141

```
NORTH CAROLINA     )                    IN THE SUPERIOR COURT
ROCKINGHAM COUNTY  )  No. 776           OCTOBER CRIMINAL TERM 1947

S T A T E          )

      VS           )          SPECIAL VENIRE DRAWN IN THE CASE OF
                   )          STATE VS. JUNIOR EDD THOMPSON
JUNIOR EDD THOMPSON )
```

1.	N. L. Case	Madison
2.	John M. Jones	Reidsville
3.	Joe Ben Hodges	Reidsville
4.	W. R. Barnes	Reidsville
5.	A. E. Gunn	Wentworth
6.	Joe F. Baughn	Mayo
7.	Mrs. Marion Caudle	Mayo
8.	Mrs. H. W. Stanfield	Williamsburg
9.	Mrs. G. H. Miller	Reidsville
10.	C. L. Combs	Draper
11.	Ben Aiken, Col.	Leaksville
12.	Marvin H. McMichael	Draper
13.	E. H. Jones	Reidsville, R-5
14.	Robert Dalton, Col.	Mayo
15.	Orien Knight	Madison
16.	J. F. Burgess	Draper
17.	Mrs. Hunter Carter	Simpsonville
18.	E. P. Rothrock	Leaksville
19.	Bennie Williams	Williamsburg
20.	Mrs. E. V. Stephenson	Madison
21.	Mrs. Senola Neal, Col.	Reidsville
22.	Joseph Brown	Draper
23.	Monroe Pinnix, Col.	Williamsburg
24.	Mrs. P. G. Beville	Simpsonville
25.	T. J. Fargis	Reidsville
26.	W. J. Crowder	Ruffin
27.	Monroe Alley	Mayo
28.	H. J. Frye	Mayo

Judge Bobbitt ordered a Special Venire (widening of the jury pool) in the case against Junior Edd Thompson. This document, which has been edited for size, was obtained from the State of North Carolina. Note that women are denoted as "Mrs." with husband's name unless there is no husband (Senola Neal). Race was noted as well: "Col." means "colored." The full list of names appears in the chapter notes.

Chapter 13

The Trial, Day 1

Tuesday, November 4, 1947

Mutt Burton arrived early at Rockingham Superior Court in Wentworth on Tuesday morning. Rockingham County was his beat and he had been covering this story for the *Greensboro Daily News* since August. His readers loved this story for all its juicy elements. And he was just as curious as anyone about what would happen today. It had all the makings of great drama—the violence, the old victim and his young wife, the escaped con, the state senator defending the young colored ruffian, the victim's family siding with the defense—and if that weren't enough, women on the jury. All he needed now was an ending.

Mutt lit up a Lucky Strike and puffed casually outside his car while waiting for the courthouse doors to open. Cars had arrived bringing the jurors from their hotel, and sure enough three women got out of them with the men. Male and female deputies led them in. He surveyed the rest of people arriving with his reporter's eye. Some were witnesses, some were family members or friends, and some were just the curious with nothing else to do that day. And he knew that most of them, before ever hearing a word of testimony, had already made up their minds about Junior Thompson's guilt or innocence. He hoped the jurors, at least, would strive to keep an open mind.

Funny that Wentworth was the county seat. There was nothing here except the courthouse, the jail, a post office, Wright Tavern, the Methodist church, the Presbyterian church, a few houses and a cemetery. If you drove down Highway 65 and blinked, you'd miss it. If you lived in Wentworth you were probably associated with the court. There was no hotel, no restaurant, no stores, but you could get dinner at Mrs. Irving's home.

Mutt had been born and raised in Reidsville, a town supported largely by the American Tobacco Company. With its population around 12,000, Reidsville was a metropolis by comparison to Wentworth. Mutt loved Reidsville and had no plans to leave. It's not that he'd never been anywhere else; in fact, he had been stationed in India during his three years of military service during the war. But it sure was great to be back home. Mutt had started his career with the newspaper in 1936 before the war, and they took him back when he returned. Living here allowed him to combine the two things he loved the best: journalism and theatre. Mutt just loved the theatre; he loved literature and drama, he loved acting in local plays, and he loved writing theatre columns for the *News*. Being a reporter had taught Mutt how to get and report the facts, how to dig a little deeper for the story behind the story, and how to carefully observe little details that others might have missed. And his love of the theatre had taught him the same thing–to see as well as to look, to taste and to swallow, not to take things for granted. He was 40 years old, in the prime of his life, and he knew it: a marriage and new baby daughter, abundant

144

friends, a successful newspaper career, and time for involvement in the theatre. Some people suggested that his talent could take him to Washington or New York. As he looked around at all the local folk milling around the courthouse, he was reminded again how much he loved small town life. He wasn't leaving. He was grateful for being there.

The courthouse doors opened and he entered, making his way up the stairs to the second floor courtroom along with some of his fellow reporters from the local press: *The Leaksville News, The Madison Messenger,* even *The Reidsville Review. The Leaksville News* and *Madison Messenger* were weeklies, and by the time those stories were printed sometime next week, this trial would be old news. Mutt's articles would be printed the next day by the *Greensboro Daily News,* the largest local newspaper in these parts, where most people got their news of the region.

The courtroom was located on the second floor in the front of the building. If you looked out the window of the courtroom, you'd see the jail across the street, a stark reminder of your fate if you were the one on trial. Mutt entered the courtroom and angled to get a good seat up front.

Attending court, really, was not that different from attending theatre. There was a setting, a cast of characters and a plot. The play was in two acts: the prosecution and the defense arguments. In court, however, the script was made up as the drama unfolded. You never knew what a witness was going to say, or what twists and turns would appear in the storyline. And like good drama, the trial would rise to a climax at the end when the jury returned the verdict. He wanted his reporting to reflect more than the facts and events of this trial, but the mood as well. This audience would surely leave here with a range of emotions–excited, stunned, angry, relieved—and they could talk about it for days. If he wrote well, that's exactly what his readers would do, too.

The air of anticipation was high as the audience filled every wooden seat in the courtroom and waited for the trial to begin. It was packed, but the people were quietly respectful of the aura of the court, as if they were in church. Many people had turned out and not everyone could get a seat. The courtroom was segregated, of course, with the Negroes sitting up in the balcony. Negroes could serve on a jury (though there were none on this one) but they weren't permitted a seat downstairs in the courtroom to watch a trial. And today so many white people had turned out that most of the colored people would have to wait outside. Well, times were changing, and sooner or later that would change, too.

Once Mutt was settled, he started looking around the courtroom to see what was what. The state solicitor, Ralph James Scott, sat at one of the front tables reviewing his notes. He's rehearsing his lines, Mutt thought, getting ready for Act One. A native of Stokes County, Mr. Scott was 42 and looked all business. Mutt knew about him; he had been making a name for himself. His education had started in a one-room, one teacher schoolhouse and ended with a law degree in 1930 from Wake Forest College. Bright and motivated, he had worked his way through college by tobacco farming and washing dishes at the boarding house where he had lived. He had become involved in the Stokes County Democratic Executive Committee in the 1930's, rising to chairman in 1937. He was elected solicitor of the 21st Judicial District in 1938 and had just won his third re-election to the post last year. His role as solicitor covered Surry, Stokes, Rockingham, and Caswell counties, and Mutt had seen him in action in other trials. He knew his way around a courtroom, even though his esteemed opponent for this trial would be no less than a

146

state senator. Mutt thought that Mr. Scott looked confident. Surely he thought this case was winnable. The victim's wife had seen and identified the attacker. Really, Mutt thought, it was open and shut. Mr. Scott should have one more victory under his belt in a few days.

At the opposite table was Senator J. Hampton Price, Junior Edd Thompson's defense attorney. Mr. Price was as gregarious and sociable as Mr. Scott was serious and formal. The 47-year old Mr. Price had moved to Leaksville in 1924 and had a solo law practice until 1941, when he was joined by his partners D. Floyd Osborne and J. C. Johnson Jr. As state senator, he had been elected president pro tem of the 1943 Senate, which was quite an honor. Hamp had quite a knack with people, that was for sure. Fellow politicians, lawyers and judges respected him and ordinary people were never put off by him. A corpulent man who smoked cigars and generally wore a rolled up hat, he had an animated personality and could have made friends with the devil. In this trial, the evidence appeared to be on Mr. Scott's side, but the jury would warm up to Hamp Price in a heartbeat. He was likable, smart, and politically savvy—a worthy opponent for Mr. Scott.

Junior Edd Thompson had been waiting for this trial to begin in the county jail across the street from the courthouse. Everyone in the courtroom craned their necks to get a good look at him as he made his entrance in handcuffs, was released, and took his seat next to Mr. Price at the front table. For someone accused of so vicious a crime, he sure looked meek now. And look at how he was dressed! Mutt chuckled to himself. "Good costuming, Mr. Price," he thought, as Junior had on a suit that emphasized his small stature and made him look like he'd just dropped by the court on his way home from Sunday school. Mr. Price whispered a few things to him and Junior nodded without expression. One thing was certain: the boisterous Hamp Price looked as confident as a rich man driving a Cadillac. If Mr. Price thought the odds were against him, he sure didn't show it.

The jury filed in and sat in the jury box. History was being made right in front of his eyes, thought Mutt, as this was the first mixed jury on a capital case in the state of North Carolina. Up until then, women had served on juries of lesser crimes. In Leaksville Mrs. R. D. Pulliam had served on a jury that had found a man not guilty of public drunkenness. But some people wondered whether women had the fortitude to deal with the grisly details of murder. Mutt thought they did—just look at Susie Sharp and what she'd gone through as a woman lawyer, yet she'd handled herself just fine. Sometimes she was the only woman in the courtroom. Well, now she'd have some company, whether the women liked it or not. And indeed, many women did not want the responsibility. In Guilford County, like here, women started getting summoned in August, and the court clerk was flooded with calls asking to be excused. It's not that they thought women in general shouldn't serve, but that they themselves had to get out of it. Ladies, if you wanted equal rights, you've got them. Welcome to a man's world.

Promptly at 9:30 a.m. the bailiff entered. "All rise," he bellowed, "The Honorable Judge William H. Bobbitt presiding." You could have heard a pin drop. Mutt thought, the curtain is rising, and the play is about to begin.

The 47-year old Judge Bobbitt entered the courtroom evincing an air of authority that would have been respected in any court in the land. He had been elected judge on the democratic ticket in the 14th Judicial District in 1938. Though young at the time, he had earned his reputation as an eloquent scholar who had been educated at the University of North

Carolina in Chapel Hill. Taking his seat, he called for an official reading of the charges against Junior Edd Thompson.

The clerk of the court came forward. "Defendant will please rise." Junior and Mr. Price both stood. Mutt wondered if the boy knew how lucky he was to have Hampton Price representing him.

The clerk read, "Criminal Docket number 9428, the State of North Carolina versus Junior Edd Thompson. The charges are as follows: did break and enter the dwelling house of Tom Pratt on the 25th day of August, A. D., 1947, in the night time, where two people were sleeping, with the intent to commit a felony; and did with deliberation, premeditation, and malice aforethought, assault, beat, and murder Tom Pratt."

Judge Bobbitt asked, "Does your client understand the charges against him?"

"Yes sir."

"How do you plead?"

Mr. Price answered for him. "The defendant pleads not guilty, Your Honor."

The clerk continued, "Criminal Docket number 9428, the State of North Carolina versus Junior Edd Thompson. The charges are as follows: did break and enter the dwelling house of Tom Pratt on the 25th day of August, A. D., 1947, did feloniously and burglariously did break and enter, with intent, the goods and chattels of the said Tom Pratt in the said dwelling house and then and there being, then and there feloniously and burglariously to steal, take and carry away, against the peace and dignity of the State."

Judge Bobbitt again asked, "Does your client understand the charges against him?"

149

"He does, Your Honor."

"How do you plead?"

"Not guilty."

"Be seated."

State solicitor Ralph Scott now rose to make his opening statements. Mutt knew that every person in the courtroom, and especially the jury, was giving him their full attention.

"Ladies and gentlemen of the jury, good morning. We are here today to weigh the evidence in a brutal crime that was committed against one of our citizens, the 81-year-old Tom Pratt. A man who worked hard all his life. A man who was in the safety and security of own his home with his wife, sleeping after another day's work. A man who might have gone on to enjoy many more years of life, surrounded by the love of his wife, children, grandchildren, and great-grandchildren, had not a terrible thing happened. But that was not to be. On the night of August 25th, an intruder violated Mr. Pratt's security and safety. We will hear testimony today that that intruder beat Mr. Pratt so badly that he was blinded in one eye. Beat him so badly that his skull was crushed. Beat him so badly that his brain began to bleed, from which he could not recover. Then that intruder left Mr. Pratt for dead. But that intruder did not count on one thing: a witness. Mr. Pratt's wife witnessed the attack, and she will present testimony today about who that person was. You will hear evidence that the intruder was the man sitting before you today, Junior Edd Thompson, a neighbor, a child who had grown up playing with Mr. Pratt's own grandchildren. A man who has been in trouble before. A man with so little regard for the law or the sanctity of human life that he would take another person's life without remorse. A man who then ran away, hoping to avoid the long arm of the law. But he is sitting here now, ladies and gentlemen, to answer for the crimes he has committed.

"I know, ladies and gentlemen of the jury, that there has been a lot of talk about this case in the last months. You may have heard things that made you inclined to form an opinion prior to arriving today. But I ask you to put out of your minds anything you may have heard about this case before you arrived today. You must consider the evidence as presented, without letting prior rumors or gossip interfere with your clear thinking.

"There was one witness to this crime, the victim's wife. Mrs. Pratt was the only one who saw what went on during that attack. Other witnesses will express things they heard or saw that night, but bear in mind that Mrs. Pratt was the only person to see the man brutally attacking her husband that terrible night. I ask you to listen only to the evidence as presented, to keep your minds open only to the facts. When you do, I trust that you will return with the only possible verdict that can be applied: a verdict of guilty. Thank you."

Mr. Scott was seated, looking serious and yet satisfied with himself. Mr. Price now took his place in front of the jury box. "Ladies and gentlemen, good morning. You have heard Mr. Scott tell you about the life so tragically taken from Tom Pratt. His life was taken from him with barely a struggle. You have heard Mr. Scott say that Mrs. Pratt was the sole witness to the crime that night, and he is correct. She, and only she, really knows what happened to her husband that night. And I do want you to listen carefully to what Mrs. Pratt says. I want you to carefully consider her words while you are looking at the defendant. I want you to weigh the all evidence and all consider the facts as presented. When you do, I am sure that you will return with your verdict of 'not guilty.' "

Mr. Scott stood up. "The state calls its first witness, Your Honor, Mrs. Ruby Pratt." All eyes were on Ruby as she made her way to the witness box. Mutt noticed the women jurors looking her over, head to toe. Were they sympathetic? He couldn't tell. To Mutt's eye Ruby didn't look terribly nervous, perhaps because she was confident in what she had to say. Ruby placed her hand on the Bible, was sworn in, and sat down.

Mr. Scott began his questioning. "Mrs. Pratt, can you please tell us what happened on the night of August 24th?"

"I had a brief conversation with my husband and retired to bed shortly after 9 o'clock. I was sleeping when I heard him calling out to me, calling my name, around 1:30 in the morning. I rushed down the flight of stairs that leads to his bedroom and I saw a Negro man at the foot of the stairs. He made a start towards me, and I ran quick as I could back up the stairs, but just then I heard a door slam downstairs and I reckoned the man ran out. Tom was calling me again and I went back down to him."

"Was the attacker holding a weapon?"

"He had a knife in one hand a flashlight in the other."

"How did you see the attacker? Wasn't it dark?"

"No sir, the light was on. Tom must have cut the light on. I could see all right."

"After the attacker left and you returned to Mr. Pratt, how did he appear to you?"

"He was lying on the floor. He was beat up real bad over the eye and on the head and bleeding. I called for help from the neighbors, the Ratliffs, and they came."

"What happened after Mr. and Mrs. Ratliff arrived?"

"They tried to give some first aid, but we knew we needed a doctor. So then they went and got Harold Hoover, who had a car. Mr.

Hoover notified the police and called for an ambulance. The ambulance took him to Leaksville Hospital, but he died that evening."

"Mrs. Pratt, were you able to identify your husband's attacker?"

"Yes sir, I was."

"Can you tell us how you did that?"

"Sheriff Hodges showed me some photographs in a book and I picked him out. The next week I went down to Greensboro and picked him out of a line-up."

"And is the man you saw sitting in this courtroom today?"

"Yes, sir, it is."

"Can you point to him?"

Ruby, who had avoided looking in Junior's direction so far, now looked straight at him. Pointing her finger she said, "That's him there."

"Are you absolutely certain, Mrs. Pratt, that the defendant is the man you saw attacking your husband?"

"Yes sir, I am positive."

"Thank you, Mrs. Pratt. I have no further questions."

Hampton Price now rose for cross-examination, walked leisurely toward the witness stand with his hands in his pockets, and looked at Ruby Pratt in a kindly way like he was her best friend in the world. Her testimony had been very confident. Mutt wondered how he would shake her.

"Mrs. Pratt, I am sorry for your loss."

She looked a little taken aback. "Thank you."

"Ma'am, you have testified that you identified Junior Thompson through photographs and through a police line-up."

"Yes sir."

"Mr. Thompson and his family have lived in the El Bethel

community for many years. In fact, their property adjoins yours. Did you know Junior Thompson on sight before the night of the attack?"

"No sir, I didn't. I had seen him once, many years ago, that was all."

"So your testimony is that even though you were neighbors, you did not know Junior Thompson, and that you were able to identify him only through photographs and the line-up as the man who attacked your husband."

"Yes sir, that is correct."

"Mrs. Pratt, you have testified that when you heard your husband scream you came down the steps to assist him, only to find a menacing man standing over him, who then turned toward you."

"Yessir."

"Why did the man not attack you?"

"He didn't get close enough. I ran back up the stairs and that's when he ran out the door."

"Had you come all the way down the stairs?"

"No sir. Only about half way. Soon as I saw him I ran back up."

"And yet you were close enough to identify him?"

"Yes sir."

"Junior Edd Thompson, as you can see here, is five feet, eleven inches tall and weighs 145 pounds. When the neighbors came to assist you after the attack, did you not describe the attacker as a 'heavy-set Negro with slicked back hair?' "

"No, I did not."

"Mrs. Pratt, how old are you?"

"Thirty-nine."

"And how old was Mr. Pratt at the time of his death?"

"Eighty-two."

"And how long have you and Mr. Pratt been married?"

"About five years now."

"Were you happily married?"

Mutt saw the color start to rise in Ruby's face. "We were," she said, though the tight-lipped reply and flash in her eyes conveyed, "We weren't."

"And were you married before you married Mr. Pratt?"

"Yes sir."

"How many times?"

She looked to her lap, dropping her voice. "Twice."

"Excuse me?"

A little louder, she said, "I was married twice before."

"What was the name of your first husband?"

"Carl Meeks."

"And why did Mr. Meeks seek a divorce?"

"We were very young when we married and it just wasn't a good match."

"Who was your second husband?"

"Charlie Corum."

"Why did the marriage with Mr. Corum not succeed?"

"After he found out I had been married before, he wanted a divorce."

"Do you mean to say that he didn't know you had been married to Mr. Meeks?"

"My marriage to Mr. Meeks only lasted a short while. We had been separated for years. It never felt like a real marriage. When I wanted to marry again, I asked him–Mr. Meeks, that is–about the divorce and he took care of it."

"And do you have a record of divorce from Mr. Meeks?"

"No sir, I don't."

"He never gave you any papers?"

"No sir. He said he was taking care of the divorce. He didn't give me any papers."

"Didn't your second husband, Mr. Corum, attain an annulment of marriage after he found out that you were still married to your first husband?"

Ruby seemed confused by the question, and hesitated. "An annulment? I'm not sure what you mean. I thought we got divorced."

"An annulment, Mrs. Pratt, because you were still married to your first husband. Your second husband had to attain an annulment because a divorce wasn't possible. You were still married to Mr. Meeks."

The courtroom was dead silent, with Price's last words swirling in the air. If Mr. Price was asking her a question here, she couldn't seem to make out what it was, and she said nothing.

"Mrs. Pratt, were you legally free to marry Mr. Pratt?"

"I thought I was, yes."

"But you can provide no record of divorce from either husband."

"No sir."

"Because, in fact, you were legally married to Mr. Meeks when you married Mr. Corum, and you were still legally married to Mr. Meeks when you married Mr. Pratt."

"I didn't know it." It was almost painful to watch. She had been eaten alive by Hamp Price.

"No further questions, Your Honor."

Ruby left the witness stand looking like a wilted flower, with her face as red as her name. She made her way quickly to her seat. Mr. Scott, now having to do damage control to his primary witness, quickly called Mr. R. L. Tolbert to the stand. Mr. Tolbert, wearing a look of duty, was sworn in and took his place in the witness box.

Mr. Scott asked, "Mr. Tolbert, would you please tell us where you are employed and your position there?"

"I am a foreman at the Fieldcrest Mills."

"Do you know Mrs. Ruby Pratt?"

"Yes, she is a cone winder under my supervision at the mill."

"How long has she been in your employ?"

"About seven years now."

"What type of worker is Mrs. Pratt?"

"She's very good. She's always on time and puts in a full day."

"Have you ever had to reprimand her for any reason?"

"No."

"And does she get along well with her co-workers?"

"Yes, very well. She's a good employee. I wish I had more like her."

"Thank you, Mr. Tolbert. No further questions."

Mr. Price knew not to go after this one. "No questions, Your Honor."

Mr. Scott stood. "The state calls Dr. R. P. Harris." Dr. Harris, who was well-known and respected in Leaksville, Spray, Draper, was wearing a three-piece suit with a watch chain. He was sworn in and took the witness stand.

"Dr. Harris, did you treat the victim, Mr. Pratt, on the morning of August 25th?"

"Yes, I did."

"What was the cause of death?"

"A subdural hematoma; in other words, bleeding in the brain. In his case, it was caused by a blow to the head over the eye."

"In your opinion, what caused the injuries?"

"I believe they were inflicted by a blunt instrument, like a rock or a club, but not something sharp. There was a lot of dirt in the wound."

"Thank you. Your witness, Counselor."

Mr. Price replied, "I have no questions, Your Honor."

Mutt wrote his notes while the next witness, Sam Turner, was sworn in and took the stand.

"Mr. Turner, please tell us about going to the Pratt house on the night of the attack."

"I heard Ruby—Mrs. Pratt—screaming for Coy Ratliff. It woke me up. I quick dressed, and made my way up to the house."

"Did you stop anywhere on your way to the Pratt house?"

"Yes, the Thompson house is on the way over there. I realized I didn't have a light, so I stopped and banged on their door to borrow a flashlight."

"The Thompson family was up?"

"Yes, they were up. They must have heard the screaming, too. Everybody did."

"And did you see Junior Edd Thompson?"

"Yes, he lent me the flashlight."

"You're sure you saw Junior Edd Thompson?"

"Well his mama and daddy was there, and his two brothers, and him. He's the one who gave me the flashlight."

"Thank you. Your witness."

Mr. Scott had now established that Junior was in the area and had been seen after the attack. Mr. Price had a little work to do.

"Mr. Turner, did you go to the Pratt house?"

"Yes."

"And how did Mrs. Pratt seem to you?"

"She was upset and talking a lot."

"What was she saying?"

"She was saying a man broke in the house through the kitchen window, and that he was a great, big fat Negro man."

"Thank you, Mr. Turner."

Judge Bobbitt looked at Mr. Scott. "Any further questions for Mr. Turner, Mr. Scott?" But Mr. Scott declined. Mutt was looking for clues in the jury's faces, but they kept their faces stony and expressionless.

Next up was Sheriff Munsey Hodges. Surely Mr. Scott could regain some ground with the Sheriff and with Mr. Allen, the SBI agent who would testify later.

"Sheriff Hodges, please tell the court about how Mrs. Pratt came to identify Junior Thompson as the attacker of her husband."

"On August 28, Agent Allen and I showed Mrs. Pratt a large book of mug shots. She identified Junior Thompson from those photos."

"Did she hesitate in deciding among the photos?"

"No sir."

"How else did she identify him?"

"We conducted a line-up of eight men at the Guilford County Jail. We did the line-up four different times, changing the clothing on some of the men each time. She identified Junior Thompson each time."

"Did she hesitate at all in her identification? Did she ever appear to be confused?"

"No sir."

"In your opinion, Sheriff, on the night of the murder, was there sufficient light for Mrs. Pratt to have seen her attacker clearly?"

"We conducted some tests in which we turned on the lights that she said were on when she entered the stairwell. We decided that it would have been possible to identify someone under those circumstances. We thought there was sufficient light."

"Mrs. Pratt has testified that she was sleeping upstairs when the noise of the intruder woke her up. Did you examine her room?"

"Yes I did."

"And did her bed look like it had been slept in?"

"Yes, it was wrinkled. It looked like it had been slept in."

"Did you interrogate Mrs. Pratt that night?"

"No. There were a large gang of men already out in the woods looking for the suspect. I decided I'd best get out there and do what I could to find the attacker. Unfortunately we didn't find him until later."

"Objection." Hamp Price stood up. "The witness is implying that the defendant was the attacker in the woods that night."

"Sustained. Jury will please ignore the witness's last comment. Please strike it from the record."

Mr. Scott continued. "After Mrs. Pratt identified Junior Edd Thompson as the attacker from the photographs, what did you do?"

"We put out a warrant for his arrest."

"How was he captured? Was he in his home?"

"No, he had run away. We had tips that he was in Virginia, and we used bloodhounds to track him. We were able to arrest him on September 3."

"Is running away something an innocent man would do?"

"Objection!"

Judge Bobbitt again decided with Mr. Price. "Sustained. Please rephrase the question, Mr. Scott."

"Was Junior Thompson wanted for any other crimes?"

"Objection. Other cases are not relevant to this one."

"Mr. Scott?" asked the judge.

"I'm establishing a pattern of disregard for the law, Your Honor."

"Overruled. Witness may answer."

"He had broken out of the Montgomery Correctional Center in Troy, in October, 1946."

"And for what crime was Mr. Thompson incarcerated?"

"Breaking and entering."

"When was that crime committed?"

"It happened on January 11, 1945."

"At what time of day?"

"Around midnight."

"Thank you, Sheriff Hodges. Your witness, Mr. Price." Mr. Scott had just let the jury know that Junior Thompson had been guilty of a late night burglary before.

Hampton Price approached the witness box. "Sheriff Hodges, when you arrived at the crime scene, was Mr. Pratt still there?"

"No, he had already been taken to the hospital."

"So you did not have the opportunity to examine the victim yourself, or speak to him, that night?"

"No sir."

"So you were not able to ask Mr. Pratt who the attacker was?"

"I saw Mr. Pratt at the hospital the next day. He was delirious. He couldn't say who attacked him."

"When you processed Junior Thompson after his arrest on September 3, what were the height and weight that you listed on the records?"

"Height was five feet, eleven inches. Weight was 145 pounds."

"Thank you, Sheriff."

Mutt scribbled frantically as the State called SBI Agent Robert Allen, who also testified that Mrs. Pratt had picked out Junior Thompson with no difficulty. The state then rested its case.

"Court in recess until 1:30." Mutt's stomach was rumbling. It had been a great morning. Mutt ambled outside, lit a cigarette, and thought about the events of the morning. Some other reporters tried to get his ear, but he moved away from them quickly, went to his car to eat his lunch, and start writing his article.

After lunch, the jury and most others returned to the courtroom looking satisfied from their meals, but not sleepy. All were anticipating what the defense arguments would be. Welcome to Act II.

The first witness for the defense was Edna Hoover, who had also lived on Price Road near the Pratt farm. Mr. Price had chosen a sympathetic person as his first witness, a chicken farmer who just so happened to be the victim's granddaughter.

"Mrs. Hoover, what is your relation to the victim, Mr. Pratt?"

"He was my grandfather."

"And how did you happen to go up to the Pratt house that night?"

"Coy Ratliff came for us, saying Mr. Pratt had been hurt real bad and needed our help. We weren't the first ones there, but we had a car and my husband went off for the ambulance."

"Did you hear Mrs. Pratt describe the attacker?"

"Yes. She said he was a great, big stocky Negro man."

"Did she mention Junior Thompson?"

"Someone, I don't know who, said maybe Junior Thompson had done it. We all knew he was around, home from prison. But she said, 'well, if that was Junior Thompson, he had grown considerably since she'd seen him last.'" Mutt saw the eyes of the jury members widen.

"Did you see the bed that Mrs. Pratt sleeps in?"

"Yes I did."

"Did it appear to have been slept in to you?"

"No it did not. The bed gave every indication of not having been slept in." Again, the jury's eyes widened and Mutt saw Mr. Scott's jaw tighten just a little. Mutt's mind started to race. If Ruby's bed hadn't been slept in, what was Mr. Price implying?

"Thank you, Mrs. Hoover. Your witness, Mr. Scott."

Mr. Scott had to keep Ruby's credibility in tact. "Mrs. Hoover, a lot of people were at the house that night. Did Mrs. Pratt ask that nothing be touched?"

"Yes, she did. She said, 'Y'all please don't touch anything until the police come.' She did say that, yes."

"Thank you, Ma'am."

Next up was Harold Hoover, Edna's husband. Hamp Price was going good, now. Mr. Price began, "Mr. Hoover, how did Mrs. Pratt seem to you when you arrived at the scene?"

"She was talking a lot about how the attacker got in the house, and that he was a big man. She said, 'he was as big as you, Mr. Hoover!' That's how I knowed he was a big man."

"And, if I may ask, what is your height and weight, Mr. Hoover?"

"Five-ten, and 248 pounds."

"Did you see Mr. Pratt before he was taken to the hospital?"

"Yes I did. He was lyin' on the floor when we got there, moanin' like."

"Did he tell you who attacked him?"

"No, but he called me by name, so I felt like he could have. But he just closed his eyes and shook his head; didn't say nothing else."

"Was he bleeding?"

"No, he wasn't bleeding. There was a lot of dried blood, on his face and clothes, and on the floor." Mutt sat forward and so did half the jury. The blood was dry? If the blood was dry, that meant he had been hit a lot earlier. Head injuries draw a lot of blood. It wouldn't have clotted up so fast.

"Mr. Hoover, you're testifying that Mr. Pratt was not bleeding when you arrived, but that he was covered with dried blood."

"Yes sir."

"In your opinion, was the light in the stairwell adequate for Mrs. Pratt to see the attacker?"

"No sir, it was just one light bulb, overhead. The attacker would have been kind of in a shadow to a person who was in that stairwell trying to see."

"Are you familiar with the dog that belongs to Mrs. Pratt?"

"Yes sir."

"Was the dog there?"

"No sir. That's a vicious little dog. Normally he barks like a son of a gun. But we didn't see nigh of him until late in the morning." This was incredible, Mutt thought. Junior's not on trial here, Ruby is.

"Thank you. Your witness, Counselor."

Mr. Scott looked purposeful as he rose. He was losing momentum quickly and he had to recover. "Mr. Hoover, you were among the first to arrive at the scene. What did Mrs. Pratt ask you to do?"

"She asked us to please get the officers and a doctor. I left in my car and rode over to the police station to get help. I knew he'd need an ambulance. Then I went round to notify some of the relatives, Mr. Pratt's children. I carried them to the hospital. Then I went back to Mr. Pratt's house."

"Thank you. No further questions."

The defense then called Coy Ratliff to the witness stand. "Mr. Ratliff, were you the first to arrive on the scene after Mrs. Pratt's cries for help?"

"Yes, I was."

"What did you see there?"

"Mr. Pratt was lyin' on the floor by his bed. His head had taken quite a blow, and he was moanin' in pain. There was blood all over the place."

"Was Mr. Pratt bleeding?"

"No, he had stopped bleeding. The blood was dry. It was all caked up on him."

"Did Mr. Pratt say anything to you?"

"No, he was injured and very confused. I'm sure he was in and out like. He had lost a lot of blood."

"Did Mrs. Pratt describe the attacker?"

"Yes, she said he was a great big, heavy-set Negro."

"Did you see her guard dog during the time you were there?"

"No, he wasn't nowhere to be seen."

"Did you attempt to see if you could identify an attacker under the lighting conditions that Mrs. Pratt described?"

"I did. I stood where she said she was on the stair and it was dark. I don't believe she could have seen the attacker. I couldn't tell my wife from my daughter when I tried it."

"Thank you, Mr. Ratliff. Your witness, Mr. Scott."

Mr. Scott approached Mr. Ratliff in the witness box and he was almost smiling. What was he planning? "Mr. Ratliff, when you were interviewed by Sheriff Hodges and Agent Allen about this crime, did you tell all that you knew?"

"No, I did not."

"And why was that?"

"I thought that the time to talk would be today, at the trial. I didn't want to tell nobody nothing until the jury could hear it for themselves."

"And did you suggest, Mr. Ratliff, that you should be put in a jail cell and that Mrs. Pratt should be put in an adjoining cell, and that officers could witness you questioning her?"

The image of such a scene caused a ripple of laughter in the court. Judge Bobbitt glared, reached for his gavel, but didn't use it. The spectators composed themselves quickly.

"Yes, I did. There were just things I wanted to ask her myself."

"Are you in law enforcement, sir?"

"No, I'm a farmer."

"Thank you, Mr. Ratliff."

"Redirect, Mr. Price?" asked the Judge.

Mutt could see that Hampton Price was not about to step into this pile. Too bad Mr. Ratliff hadn't said all he had known at the time. Mutt knew that Mr. Price would not risk asking him those things now. No lawyer asked a question if he didn't already know the answer to it, and this Ratliff fellow was a loose cannon at the moment.

"I have no more questions at this time, Your Honor."

"Very well. Court will adjourn until 9:30 tomorrow morning." The gavel dropped at 5:30 p.m., and Mutt rushed to get to his typewriter.

(2) They are parallel.

$$6 + 2 + 4z = 24$$
$$8 + 4z = 24$$
$$4z = 16$$
$$z = 4$$

Left: W. C. (Mutt) Burton from an undated newspaper clipping after he had received a press honor. The date is probably around 1958, 11 years after the murder trial.

Right: Mutt Burton in 1989. He died on December 2, 1995 at the age of 88. His column for the *Greensboro Daily News* had run for over 50 years. Photo courtesy of the *News and Record.*

$$3x + 2y + 4 = 15$$
$$3x + 6 = 15$$
$$3x = 9$$
$$x = 3$$

$$(3, 1, 4)$$

$$\dot{y} = 1 \qquad z = 4$$

$$2y + 4 = 6$$
$$2y = 2$$
$$y = 1$$

Chapter 14

The Trial, Day 2

Wednesday, November 5, 1947

"Your Honor, the defense moves for a nonsuit of both indictments, for first-degree murder and for first-degree burglary, and that all charges against this defendant be dropped."

"Motion denied. Let us hear testimony today, Mr. Price."

"Very well, Your Honor. The defense calls Mr. Coy Ratliff to the stand." Coy took the stand and nodded as he was reminded that he was still under oath from yesterday. Mutt saw that Hampton Price must have decided to save face after the humorous testimony from Mr. Ratliff yesterday. That testimony had made them both look foolish, and Mr. Price needed to recover.

"Mr. Ratliff, yesterday you testified that you did not tell the police officials all that you knew when they interviewed you about this crime. Is that correct?"

"Yes sir."

"You were the first to arrive on the crime scene. Tell us now, Mr. Ratliff. Did Mrs. Pratt describe the assailant to you?"

"Yes, she did. She said he was fat, heavy-set Negro."

"Is this something that you did not tell the officials at the time of your interview?"

"Yes."

"Thank you. That will be all." Mutt was impressed. This was the fourth witness who testified to Ruby's description of the attacker as a large man. Junior Thompson, sitting there in his oversized suit, was anything but. Mrs. Pratt was looking less and less believable.

"Care to cross-examine, Mr. Scott?" asked the judge.

"No, Your Honor."

"The defense calls Mr. Curtis Land." The large and lumbering Mr. Land was sworn in.

Hamp Price buttoned his coat over his large stomach as he approached Mr. Land. Really, thought Mutt, neither one of them had missed too many meals. "Mr. Land, please tell the court your occupation."

"I am deputy sheriff for Rockingham County."

"Were you, sir, the first law enforcement officer to arrive at the crime scene on August 25th?"

"Yes, sir, I was."

"What was Mr. Pratt's condition when you arrived?"

"He was on the floor, badly beaten, and he was bleeding from the head."

"Did Mr. Pratt say anything to you?"

"No. He appeared to be slipping in and out of consciousness."

"So he didn't identify his attacker to you?"

"No sir. He weren't in no condition to say anything sensible."

"Did you see Mrs. Pratt's bed in the upstairs room?"

"Yes."

"Did it appear to have been slept in to you?"

"Yes, it did." So far Deputy Land's testimony was matching the sheriff's. Mutt was waiting to hear why Mr. Price had called Mr. Land for the defense.

"Did Mrs. Pratt describe the assailant to you?" Ah, thought Mutt, here it comes.

"Yes, she did."

"Please tell the court what she said."

"She said he was as big as I was." Mutt could see some of the jurors shift their eyes from Curtis Land to Junior Thompson, making the comparison. Mr. Land had 100 pounds on Junior, easy.

"Would you tell us your weight, please, Mr. Land?"

"My weight is 235 pounds."

"Thank you, sir. That is all."

He'd done it again, thought Mutt. Ruby Pratt was either deeply mistaken or a liar. Either way, she did not appear to be a reliable witness.

Mr. Scott declined to cross-examine Mr. Land. Maybe he wanted this witness out of the witness box as soon as possible. The longer he sat there, the longer the jury had to look at his fat belly compared to Junior's skinny frame.

"The defense calls Mr. Jake Pratt." The victim's son, thought Mutt. This ought to be interesting.

"Mr. Pratt, will you please tell us your relationship to Mr. Tom Pratt."

"He was my father."

"Did you go to your father's house the night of the attack?"

"No. Harold Hoover came and told us of it. He carried me straight to the hospital."

"At what point after that did you speak to your father's wife?"

"During the day. She came to the hospital that morning where we all were."

"Did she describe the assailant to you?"

"Yes. She said he was a Negro; she said he was large, heavy-set, fat, stocky, and had long, slicked-back hair."

"She said all those things?"

"Yes, over the course of the day to whoever came by. She said it many a-time."

"Mr. Pratt, did you ever question whether Ruby Pratt had a good look at the assailant?"

"In the weeks after my father died, she moved out of the house. So we went over there, seven or eight different times, my brother and me, or my friends, to see what we could see in that light. We tried it at different times of the night."

"Could you identify someone under the lighting conditions she described?"

"No, I couldn't have. I think seein' anyone in that light was impossible."

"Thank you, Mr. Pratt. Your witness, Counselor."

Mr. Scott stood. Mutt guessed what his strategy would be. Mr. Price had been trying to make Ruby look guilty herself through her inconsistent descriptions, like maybe she wanted old Mr. Pratt dead to get his farm. Mr. Scott would have to show the jury that the Pratt children did not want to share their father's inheritance with her.

"Mr. Pratt, can you tell me please what your feelings were about your father's decision to marry Mrs. Ruby Pratt?"

"I didn't think it was a good idea."

"Why not?"

"I thought she was too young for him and wouldn't make him happy in the long run."

"What about your brothers and sisters? What were their feelings about it?"

"They didn't like it. None of us did."

"Did you try to prevent the marriage?"

"Yes, we tried to get him not to marry her."

"But you were not successful. Why not?"

"My papa always did what he had a mind to do. There was no talking him out of anything he set his mind to. We hoped he'd be happy."

"What was your relationship like with Mrs. Pratt after the marriage?"

"I'd say it was cordial. We had to accept what our father did, no matter what we thought."

"And since your father's death, did you try to have Mrs. Pratt removed as executrix of the estate?"

"Yes, because we learned that she was not legally married to our father. We didn't think she should be the executrix since she wasn't legally married to him. That didn't seem right to us."

"Thank you, Mr. Pratt."

Mr. Price approached the witness stand. "Mr. Pratt, to your knowledge, was anything taken or missing from your father's home after the night of the break-in?"

"No. I didn't find anything missing except a chop ax that he had on the back porch."

"Mr. Pratt, was your father in love with his wife?"

"He thought he was, in the beginnin'. It didn't last too long though."

Before Mr. Scott could object to this line of questions, Mr. Price ended it. "Thank you. That is all."

Mr. Price kept up the parade of witnesses—Stover Wynn, Smith Eggleston, Vera Ratliff—all of whom had heard Ruby describe the attacker as a "fat Negro." By Mutt's count, that was eight witnesses so far who had heard the "big, fat" description given by Ruby. Robert Barnes had particular credibility. Now a lumber dealer, he was the former Leaksville chief of police. He had also been the one to arrest Junior Thompson when he stole the guns from the midnight break-in in 1945. Yet, he, too, had heard Ruby describe the assailant as "heavy-set."

The testimony now turned in earnest on the lighting at the house. A Leaksville civil engineer, W. T. Combs, produced a scale drawing of the floor plan of the house. The drawing was meant to show that the light coming from upstairs would have been insufficient to identify another person. Garr Price and Tommie Patterson, who were neighbors and friends of Jake Pratt, also took the stand to testify to the lighting conditions. "You couldn't see a white man in that light, let alone a colored man," said Mr. Patterson. State Highway Patrolman Paul Smith testified that he thought it "might" be possible to see someone. (Then again, thought Mutt, it might not.) Would the jury believe that all these people had actually conducted these tests? Mr. Price had thought of that, too. Clay Jeffries, who was now living in the house, said he saw the tests take place by the various people but didn't take part in them and didn't know the results.

At 1:55, the defense rested its case. Mr. Scott re-called Ruby Pratt, Sheriff Hodges and Agent Allen to the witness stand to offer brief rebuttal testimony, but Mutt suspected that it was like spitting in the wind at that point. Mr. Price had done an incredible job of shaking the eyewitness testimony of Mrs. Pratt.

At 2:15 Hampton Price again addressed Judge Bobbitt. "Your Honor, the defense renews its motion for nonsuit of the indictments of first-degree burglary and first-degree murder, and asks that all charges against this defendant be dropped."

"In the matter of the first indictment for first-degree burglary, the motion is granted. In the matter of the second indictment, for first-degree murder, the motion is denied."

Mr. Scott protested, to no avail. "Nothing much was stolen, Mr. Scott," said the judge. "Let's focus on the crime we know occurred." And with that, part of Junior Thompson's future was decided in just fifteen minutes' time.

At 2:30 Mr. Price rose to begin his summation. Unconsciously smoothing his hair and clearing his throat, he began, "Ladies and gentlemen of the jury, I want to thank you for the careful way you have paid attention to the testimony in this case. My job is done for now, and now it is up to you. All of us in this courtroom, and in this community, want justice to be served. All of us would like to see the killer be punished. I have as much of an interest in that outcome as you do. You as the jury have been charged with determining the guilt of this man, Junior Thompson, based on the evidence that you have heard these last two days. What you must *not* do, ladies and gentlemen, is rush to judgment without considering the facts. What you must *not* do is punish the wrong person in your efforts to serve justice. What you *must* do is consider all the facts and all the testimony that has been presented here, without regard to your personal feelings about the case, to decide this man's fate.

"The case against Junior Thompson is based on the eyewitness testimony of just one person, the victim's wife, Mrs. Pratt. She was startled and frightened out of her sleep, entered a poorly lit stairwell to find a man attacking her husband. She thought she had a good look at the attacker before she turned her back on him to run back up a flight of steps. She later identified this attacker from photographs and a line-up, and never once wavered in her testimony that the attacker was any other than Junior Edd Thompson. There was a problem with this, ladies and gentlemen. She told many people on the night and day after the attack, people who testified before you, that the attacker was a 'large, heavy-set Negro with slicked-back hair.' As you can see sitting here before you, Junior Thompson does not fit that description.

"Now, I'm not saying that Mrs. Pratt was lying. She took an oath to tell the whole truth, and I believe that she did, to the best of her ability. But people make mistakes. In the dark of night, in an urgent and terrifying situation, she thought she knew what she saw. In the days that went by, her memory of the event seemed to change. And that is where we have a problem.

"Junior Thompson has been charged with first-degree murder, and to convict him you must believe that the evidence supports the verdict beyond a reasonable doubt. What is reasonable doubt? After careful consideration of the evidence, based on your common sense and reason, it is any questions that remain in your mind about the guilt of this defendant. To convict, the evidence must go *beyond* a reasonable doubt.

Do you not have reasonable doubt, ladies and gentlemen? Do you not question whether Mrs. Pratt could have been mistaken in her fright? If you question Mrs. Pratt's description of the attacker, compared to Junior Thompson who is sitting here, you must acquit. If you question whether it was possible to identify anyone in the light that was available in that stairwell, you must acquit. If you question whether Mrs. Pratt's memory played a trick on her, you must acquit. If you think it possible, based strictly on the evidence that you have heard in this trial, that someone else may have committed this crime, then you must acquit, and declare Junior Edd Thompson, 'not guilty.' Thank you."

Mutt had watched the faces of this jury during the Mr. Price's summation. Some heads were nodding slightly in agreement, the way worshippers might nod along with a preacher during his sermon. Mr. Price's delivery had been logical and spoken with conviction. As for Mr. Scott, he suffered a disadvantage because his summation wouldn't begin until tomorrow. On the one hand, he'd get the jury when they were fresh in the morning and paying attention carefully. On the other hand, these jury members would have a full night to consider the impact of Mr. Price's words. Mutt thought he knew how it would turn out.

As the jury filed out, the spectators gathered their coats, and Junior was recuffed for the walk back to the jail, Mutt gazed at Hampton Price in some awe. Mr. Price was a big man, to be sure, but to see him now, the senator was walking on air.

Chapter 15

The Trial, Day 3

Thursday, November 6, 1947

It felt like the afternoon of the last day of school. Everyone in the courtroom seemed edgy and distracted. Mutt, too. People seemed ready to call it a day before the day had even started. Mr. Scott had to do his summation, Judge Bobbitt had to instruct the jurors, and then the jury could deliberate. This trial had taken two days so far. Mutt wondered how long the jury would be out. He didn't mind waiting, though he hoped to make deadline with the verdict by tomorrow's paper. Waiting meant time to hang around and chat with his fellow reporters. Usually somebody had some good local stories, and with good stories came some good laughs, and it was all glue that kept him stuck in these small towns. Characters existed everywhere, but Mutt didn't think characters *like these* existed anywhere but here. If you weren't from here, you wouldn't understand it.

Here was one that got told: years ago, back in the 1930s, a trial had taken place right in this courtroom that involved a love triangle between Ida Lampkins, her husband, Dummy Martin (who was a deaf-mute, but that's not part of the story), and her boyfriend Danny Dean. One night Dummy Martin was shot and killed at Dean's upstairs apartment in Reidsville, and Danny Dean was put on trial for his murder. Just like in this trial, Danny Dean testified that a black man had entered his home, and had shot Dummy Martin who was standing at the base of the stairs. A Reidsville doctor testified that the angle of the bullet proved that the shot had been fired from the top of the stairs, not the bottom, as the bullet entered at the forehead and exited at the base of the skull.

Ida Lampkins, with her hard face and dyed blond hair, looked tough as nails and well capable of murder. Most people thought she deserved to go to jail based strictly on that mean face, but she was not the one accused of the crime. Her boyfriend Danny Dean was standing trial, and she testified in his defense. In the audience sat old Mr. Rakestraw, who attended the trial strictly for entertainment but who was almost totally deaf. Beside him sat Jim Lampkins, Ida's brother, afflicted with both a stutter and a lisp. As Ida was giving her testimony, Mr. Rakestraw announced to all within earshot, "She's a mean-looking woman." And Jim Lampkins, in an effort to defend her, said, "Thee my thith-ter." Mr. Rakestraw couldn't hear Jim, and again declared, "She's a mean-looking woman," to which the brother again replied, "Thee my thith-ter." Mr. Rakestraw continued to proclaim, "She's a mean-looking woman!" while the hapless brother was not heard. Finally someone reached around to Mr. Rakestraw, tugged his arm, and told him to pipe down, pointing out Jim Lampkins to him. Deaf old Mr. Rakestraw and J-J-Jim Lampkins were the butt of jokes for a long time after that. No harm was meant. People around here knew how to take a joke. Mutt had told many, and had been the subject of many, himself.

Mutt snapped out of his daydream as Mr. Scott rose to address the jury with his summation. Mr. Scott smiled at them, perhaps trying to compete with the friendliness that always exuded from Hampton Price. "Ladies and gentlemen of the jury, good morning. I want to thank you for your service to this court, to Rockingham County and the state of North Carolina. Without good citizens like you, we could not have a democracy.

"Ladies and gentlemen, Junior Edd Thompson stands before you accused of first-degree, premeditated murder. It is the state's view that Junior Thompson entered the home of his neighbor, Tom Pratt, with intent to steal from him. When Mr. Pratt woke up and tried to defend his home and property from an intruder, Junior Thompson clubbed him in the head. When Mrs. Pratt came down the steps, he fled, leaving his victim for dead. He then went home to hide, but realizing that he had been seen and would be caught, he ran away. That's all there is to it, ladies and gentlemen. No motive but robbery, no means but a rock, and no more heart than a monster."

Things had been going pretty well up to this point; the jury was paying attention. But right around here, Mr. Scott did an unfortunate thing. Not reading the jury and their impatience to leave, he launched into an hour and a half summation in which he seemed to retry the entire case, restating the testimony, offering rebuttals against the counter testimony, trying to point out holes in the defense arguments. Mutt thought it was like shadow boxing, punching the air with an opponent who's not there. Meanwhile, the jury's eyes were glazing over as they glanced at their watches. They were exhaling controlled sighs of boredom through their noses. They had heard all this already, and they may have resented being dragged through it all again. This wasn't a summation; it was the desperate struggle of a man who had lost his argument. Finally, Mr. Scott thanked the jury for their attention, and sat down. The jury members squirmed in their seats. You could almost hear them thinking, "Let's get going!"

Judge Bobbitt began at 11:30 to instruct the jury on points of law. Although Junior had been indicted for first-degree, premeditated murder, the jury could return with one of four verdicts: guilty of first-degree murder, guilty of second-degree murder, manslaughter, or not guilty. The judge was careful to define what each of those terms meant. First- and second-degree murder are basically the same thing. In both cases, the murderer has killed another person with "malice aforethought," meaning deliberately, intentionally, or recklessly killing another person. If a crime showed particular cruelty, premeditation, or if the murder occurs in connection with another crime such as robbery, the charge would be first-degree murder. First-degree murder carries a tougher sentence, and in this case, it could be the death penalty. Second-degree murder could be downgraded to manslaughter if it was thought that there were mitigating circumstances, such as provocation by the victim. That hardly seemed likely here, as old Mr. Pratt had been home minding his own business. And not guilty...well, Mutt was pretty sure the jurors knew what "not guilty" meant. It wasn't the same as innocent, but it meant that Junior would be cleared. Judge Bobbitt spent an hour and twenty minutes going over instructions with the jury. He was thorough and he was clear. The jury paid more attention to Judge Bobbitt, it seemed, out of respect, or awe, or even fear, of the judge. Nevertheless, that was a long hour and twenty. The jury and everyone else were getting tired. The court recessed for lunch at 12:50, and the jury began its deliberations at 1:30.

Mutt had expected to spend the afternoon with his press buddies, smoking cigarettes and drinking coffee from thermoses, so everyone was surprised when the announcement came that the jury had returned with its verdict in only one hour. The spectators, all white, had chattered excitedly while the jury deliberated, discussing the details of the case, deciding for themselves how they thought the verdict should go. They all hurried back into the courtroom, conversation and chatter having died away, replaced with an air of anticipation. These people couldn't wait to hear what was coming next.

"All rise." Judge Bobbitt re-entered the courtroom and took his seat at the bench. The jury came in looking eager, even a little nervous, as the foreman handed the slip of paper to the clerk, who handed it to the judge who read it silently. The judge nodded to the clerk, who then ordered, "The defendant will rise." Junior and Mr. Price stood together.

Judge Bobbitt asked, "Ladies and gentlemen of the jury, on the count of murder in the first degree, have you reached a verdict?"

"We have, Your Honor."

"What say you?"

"We, the jury, find the defendant, Junior Edd Thompson, not guilty."

"On the count of murder in the second degree, what say you?"

"Not guilty."

"On the count of manslaughter, what say you?"

"Not guilty."

The audience erupted into cheers and applause. Ralph Scott frowned, shook his head, and looked down at the table. Hampton Price beamed. Junior Thompson looked as if he had been struck by lightening, and let a smile come onto his face as the verdicts sunk in and he turned to offer his hand to his attorney. "Thank you, sir, thank you," was all Junior could muster. Ruby Pratt had left during deliberations, while Jake and Clyde Pratt smiled, nodded, and shook hands with one another. "We did it, Jake, we did it," Mutt heard Clyde Pratt say. "Yeah boy," said Jake, giving one firm nod of his head, "We sure did. Papa would be pleased." But Judge Bobbitt looked angry, banged his gavel, quickly stilling the audience's demonstration of approval. "This court is still in session! All quiet!" The audience, sufficiently rebuked, got quiet in a hurry.

Judge Bobbitt announced, "Junior Thompson is now remanded to Montgomery County to face charges on escape from prison and to complete his sentence associated with that escape. Bailiff, please escort Mr. Thompson to the custody of the Montgomery County deputies." Junior's smile dropped from his face. The happy spectators' jubilation was cut short, as if a shadow had passed over the room. They seemed to have forgotten about the escape charge. The momentary joy that had covered Junior's face was gone, too, and now the face hardened, the jaw tightening, his eyes going cold and looking straight ahead. The face seemed to say, "Some victory. What does anyone really care for me? I don't care none about you either." *Click! Click!* The bailiff snapped on the handcuffs, and Junior was a prisoner once more. If one moment in time can predict a person's entire future, Junior had just had his.

The Rockingham
County Courthouse
in Wentworth, N.C.,
as it appeared in
2005.

Chapter 16
Just Rewards
Friday, November 28, 1947

Ruby sat in her sister's parlor holding the unopened copy of the *Leaksville News*, which had just arrived. Everybody else was at work, and she'd be leaving to get to the mill in a little while. Ever since August, reading this newspaper had been a difficult and painful thing to do. Today, perhaps, would be different. It had been three weeks since the trial. Ruby had gone over it in her head a thousand times, but there was no way to undo what had been done. She had told her story as straight as she could, just as Mr. Scott had advised her to do. And look what happened! She'd been made to look like a complete liar about her description of Junior Thompson. She had been shocked at all the people who had testified against her, some people she thought had been her friends, like Coy. She thought friends stuck together. She'd think differently from now on.

Tom, who had once doted on her like a child, had turned into a spiteful old man, always calling her names and hollering just because she had wanted friends. Turns out those sons of his were no different. Cordial! Yes, it had been cordial, all right, as they had all made the unspoken agreement never to see one another. But they had been spiteful no matter what Jake Pratt said in the trial. Digging into her past, first of all, to make sure she couldn't get any of Tom's land. Who else had cooked for him, done his wash, swept his floor, slopped the hog, and listened, God Almighty, listened to him talk and talk and talk about the crops, his children, the neighbors, the war, for hour after lonely hour? Who had taken his wrath because he was old and she was young? They *had* gotten married, and to her mind that ought to count for something. It's true that her divorce wasn't final, but she hadn't known that. It wasn't her fault.

And to make matters worse, that horrible Mr. Price had dragged out her dirty laundry for everyone in the world to see! What did any of that have to do with Tom's murder? Why hadn't Mr. Scott objected? She'd been left to fend for herself up on that witness stand, feeling naked to the world. She had been on trial just as sure as Junior had. Her past was nobody's business, but you wouldn't know it here. Did everyone in this town have the right to pass judgment on her life? As much as she would never again utter the name of Hampton Price, she felt positively furious at Ralph Scott. Hampton Price had made her look like a Jezebel, and Ralph Scott had just sat there and let it happen, peering down his nose at her like she was beneath contempt. He had done nothing to come to her aid when that horrible man Price had come to ruin her reputation completely. Alone, alone, alone. Wasn't that the way it had always been for her? She felt herself go crimson again as she thought about it. She couldn't remember when she'd ever been so low.

And to top it all off, Jake and Clyde Pratt hiring that highfalutin lawyer for Junior Thompson! An escaped con! Couldn't they be satisfied with finding out that she and their father hadn't been legally married? That would have been enough for them to keep everything. They didn't have to humiliate her in public like that. No, they had to go and get the best lawyer in town just to completely sink her. They made their disapproval of her clear without ever saying a word, didn't they, standing by that nigger family over her, the person who had been their father's wife for five years. The town had gone crazy over that. Good Lord above! The talk! No matter what steps had been taken to get a better jury, she was sure everyone on the jury and everyone in town knew who had paid for Junior's lawyer. So here is what the jury thought: if Jake and Clyde Pratt, white men, the victim's sons, were paying for that colored boy's lawyer, he had to be innocent. That's all there was to it. She doubted if the jury even listened to anything else. She had heard that the courtroom cheered when the verdict came back. All those white folks happy to see that colored boy—that jailbird—get off! What was the world coming to? If she was grateful to herself for one thing she had done right, it was that she had not been there to witness that cheering. How much worse could it get?

It had been nearly impossible to go to work after that, or to show her face in town, but she had done it. She still had bills to pay and, well, if it was one thing that had always seen her through life, it was hard work. No one could fault her for laziness. Still, the newspaper accounts of the trial had embarrassed her. She had heard whispers when she walked by, seen the smirks when they addressed her, and felt the turned heads of people who seemed to know her even if she didn't know them. Thank goodness for her family. She had moved in with her sister as soon as she could manage it. She was happy to be shed of that whole farm and everything on it.

But today was a day to—well, if not to rejoice and be glad, maybe a day to hope for a fresh start. Today she held the rolled up copy of the *Leaksville News* in her hand and felt her heart thump. Part of her couldn't wait to see it; part of her feared to look at it. Several days ago a lady reporter, Beverly Robertson, had asked her to give an interview. Mrs. Robertson sometimes wrote articles for the Greensboro paper, even though she lived in town here. At first she said no, she couldn't possibly. Then it occurred to her that this would be her chance to stand up for herself a little bit, to regain a little respectability. This whole town, maybe this whole county, seemed to have arrived at the opinion that she was a gold-digger, a drinker, a liar, a cheat, an adulterer, a bigamist, and maybe even a murderer. Her humiliation could not have been worse. How was she to restore her reputation? How was she to convince people that she was all right? She decided to do it. If she could just tell her side of the story a little bit, maybe people would stop looking at her cross-eyed whenever she went to the store. Mrs. Robertson arranged to have a photographer come to her sister's house. Her picture in the paper! The photographer suggested putting Collie in the picture with her. That was a good idea! The trial testimony about her dog had been nonsense, how vicious Collie was and all that! The photo would show that Collie was just a little dog who wouldn't hurt a flea.

The lady reporter had been very kind to her and had taken the case seriously, asking many good questions. She felt she had made a good impression; in fact, she was sure of it. And sure enough, when the Greensboro paper had come out last week, it was a good start. The photograph looked nice–imagine her with her picture in the city newspaper!

She had clipped the article and could practically recite it, but she pulled it from the pocket of her sweater and re-read it again anyway. It started off this way: "Mrs. Ruby Pratt, 39-year old widow of Tom Pratt, 82, who was bludgeoned to death early on the morning of August 25, wants Governor Cherry to send help to continue the investigation into her husband's murder." Oh, that was good! And later it said a little more: "Mrs. Pratt, who was married to Mr. Pratt some five years ago–"(there was none of that stuff about them not really being married)–"said that she wanted the investigation reopened. She said she thought Sheriff M. S. Hodges and State Bureau of Investigation Agent Robert Allen had done an excellent job of investigation leading up to the arrest and trial of Thompson, but that the Governor should send help to continue the probe." And though Ruby hadn't actually spoken to the Governor herself, Mrs. Robertson had gotten a quote back from him, saying, "I agree that this crime should be solved and I will be glad to have the State Bureau of Investigation render such aid as may be possible in solving the case." How good to have all this in the newspaper! It proved that she was really interested in solving this, going all the way up to the Governor for help. And praising Munsey and Agent Allen proved how much she had cooperated with the investigation.

Munsey was quoted, too, saying, "We are continuing our investigation of this case and are probing all angles. We do not intend to stop until the murderer is caught and convicted." And then, bless him, Munsey had said– actually said to a reporter– "that the case was made doubly difficult to solve because of the number of rumors about the case as well as a lot of prejudice in the community." Well true enough! And was prejudice against the Negro race the problem? No! Everybody was on the side of the Negro this time. The prejudice and rumors had been against her, a divorcee, a woman who had tried too hard to make a free life for herself in this town of church-goers and do-gooders, who had all made up their minds about her. They had all pre-judged her–why, that's what prejudice meant, right? Now she realized that Munsey had seen that all along. She was grateful, grateful in her heart that someone, finally, had publicly defended her, even though he didn't mention her by name. Anyone with half a brain would know what he meant.

Mrs. Robertson was so easy to talk to that she just spoke right up. She added, "if another trial is held, the jury should be selected from outside of Rockingham from people who know nothing of the case and who have not known those involved." Could she have said it any plainer? She hoped the readers would take her message: a jury of strangers wouldn't decide the case before hearing the evidence. This trial was a joke. This trial was over before it began. Mr. Scott had presented no evidence except her testimony, and the jury hadn't been interested in hearing any, no-how. And she was able to say so, not in so many words of course, but say so, right there in black and white.

Ruby just loved how this Mrs. Robertson ended the article. "She feels that justice will rule in the end, and the murderer will receive his reward." That's right, that's just what she had said. We all face Judgment Day some day, and some day we all get what we deserve, good or bad. Ruby nodded to herself as she re-read that last sentence. But the self-righteousness she was feeling one minute was replaced by a shadow of doubt the next. Had Tom gotten what he deserved? Pangs of guilt flowed through her. Everyone makes mistakes, and she couldn't help it if her mistakes had had serious consequences. Things were in such a jumble; life was such a mess. Maybe God was punishing her now, with the way everyone in town seemed to have turned against her. Maybe she deserved it. Did she? Maybe she didn't. And anyway, God could sort it all out later. She couldn't think about it just now.

Fingering the article in one hand and gazing at the unopened *Leaksville News* next to her, she knew it was time to see what else had been written, this time in the hometown paper. The Greensboro article had been a lengthy article and a good one. A few people at work said they'd seen it and thought it was good. Well, it was a start anyway, wasn't it, to getting back to her old self? Maybe some people would start to see her side of things. For the first time in months she thought maybe she had reason to see a little sunshine. Not happiness, but something like it, maybe could come back into her life. She still hoped this article would put her in a better light. She looked back at the *Greensboro Daily News* article, said a silent 'thank you' to Mrs. Robertson in her mind, refolded it carefully, and put it back in her pocket.

She pulled the rubber band off the rolled up issue of the *Leaksville News*. Mrs. Robertson had told her that if there was space, the Leaksville paper might reprint it. Now everyone in Leaksville would see it, too. "Lookee here, Collie, we're going to see our picture in the newspaper again!" The dog looked up at her from the floor as she reached down to scratch his ears. She flattened the newspaper against her lap and began to look for the article. She was happy not to be on page one, at least; that was still more fame than she wanted. Turning to page two, it wasn't there, either, nor on page three. Didn't they print it? This wasn't a big newspaper, after all, rarely over 10 pages. And so she turned until she reached page eight, and there it was: in the two left columns, with a short article underneath. Her photo, large as life, right next to the weekly feature called Colored News. What...? Next to Colored News? She sat in disbelief for a moment; shook her head as if shaking it clean of cloudy thoughts, then she decided to read the article. It could still be good.

She quickly scanned the article. It began, "Mrs. Ruby Pratt, 39-year-old widow of Tom Pratt, 82, who was bludgeoned to death early on August 25, is shown above with her pet Collie, which is said to have been missing from the Pratt home at the time of the murder. The dog turned up soon after and had probably wandered off in the neighborhood." What? *Said* to have been missing? What were they suggesting? If this newspaper was trying to make a point about her dog, she wished they'd just come out and say it! Her indignation started to rise; she felt color starting to burn in her face. If the *Greensboro Daily News*, the biggest and best paper in this whole area, hadn't seen any reason to mention this fact, why was this little Dogpatch newspaper trying to make an issue of it? Her shoulders began to sag and her heart began to sink. But she read on.

"About two weeks ago a Superior court jury took only one hour to declare Junior Thompson, 17-year-old Negro escaped convict, not guilty of the slaying.

"Testimony at the trial was that Mrs. Pratt at first had described the slayer as a large man, weighing about 235 pounds. Later she identified Thompson as the assailant, picking his picture from several shown her, and reiterated her identification several times.

"Mrs. Pratt, who was married to Mr. Pratt some five years ago, said she wanted the investigation kept alive and that she hoped new evidence would be brought to light.

"Sheriff M. S. Hodges said this week the investigation is being pressed and that some new angles are being probed. The Sheriff added, 'We do not intend to stop until the murderer is caught and convicted.'

"Mrs. Pratt, who has moved from the Pratt home to live with relatives, feels that justice will rule in the end and the murderer will 'get his just reward.' She is a second shift worker for Fieldcrest here." And that was it. End of article.

It wasn't so much what they said, except about her dog, it was what they didn't say. Where was her request for Governor Cherry's help? They had left that out altogether! Why would they? And where was

Governor Cherry's quote offering assistance? Wasn't a quote from the governor good enough for their paper? Why had they left *out* her praise of the detective work? Where was Munsey's quote about the rumors and prejudice? Oh, they didn't want to be accused of that in this town! They also left out her statement about the jury selection coming from outside of Rockingham. They left out so much that she had said in the other article, so much she had wanted people to know. She felt she'd been silenced again, just like when any one of her past three husbands had told her to "shut up." Just like she were a child who had been told to be quiet and stop making a fuss. She reread the article and wondered if there was anything she could do about it. No, nothing. She couldn't call any more attention to herself now. That had been her one and only chance with the people of Leaksville.

And as she stared down at the page, her eyes kept drifting to the right: her picture right next to Colored News. She was numb for a minute as she took it in. Was that some kind of mistake, putting her in the back of the newspaper next to Colored News? Slowly, the reality sank in. It had been no mistake, no sir. She wasn't stupid. She knew it was a message to her, to everyone reading the newspaper, that she was second-class, that she was no better than the colored people. Tears of anger and humiliation welled in her eyes. They punish you in this town and you can't make it right. The tears spilled over her cheeks as she stood up, pacing and sobbing. The past five years of her life had been a nightmare. And since Tom's death, she had done everything she was asked to do and was supposed to do, only to see her life spin further and further beyond her control. Emotion she didn't even know she had filled her body; she felt like she was going to burst. She blurted out, "I hate this town! I hate this town!" She grabbed the newspaper from the sofa and tore it into bits, letting the scraps fall to the floor. Flecks of the paper clung to her sweater and shoes. She stood in the center of the parlor, amid the waste of the newspaper and the ruin that had been made of her life, and cried into her hands. She grieved for everything that had ever happened to her. She grieved for the loss of her school years, marrying too young to know better. She grieved for the wreck of the marriage with Charlie, years that should have been carefree and gay. She grieved for her mother. She grieved for the destruction of her plans for a secure life, and she even grieved for Tom, who had not been the answer she had been hoping for, but really shouldn't have died. Her life had changed forever. There was no going back. She didn't know how to go forward. She had no husband, no children, no home, no community, and not even her good name. How does a woman survive without those things? She wasn't even sure who she was anymore. She surely didn't know where to go from here.

Eventually the tears subsided. She sniffed, lifted her head, wiped the tears from her cheeks with the palms of each hand. She sat down, drew some deep breaths, and stared blankly at the wall for several minutes, then shifted her eyes to the shredded up newspaper on the floor. Well that was it, wasn't it? The sum of her life shredded on the floor. She felt shaky and empty. She tried to let peace enter her mind, but all she felt was blank. All her life she had been impulsive, had made crazy plans that had come to disaster. She knew she was going to have to begin again, and she'd have to be smarter this time, really smarter. She wanted the peace that she knew other people had, or contentment at least, but she hadn't the faintest clue how to get it. She knew what she didn't have, but what did she have? At first she couldn't think of anything. Well, she had her dog, good faithful little Collie, her true friend. And yes, she had her

194

$$\sqrt{2} = 1.414$$

$$\sqrt{3} = 1.7321$$

$$\sqrt[3]{2} = 1.26$$

$$\pi = 3.14159265358979...$$
$$\sqrt{\pi} = 1.77$$

family. She had her job. And she had her family name, Edwards. That was what she had.

She glanced at her watch. It was 2:15, time to leave for work. She needed to wash her face. Her mouth was dry; she wanted a drink of water. Not wanting to leave the indignity of her mess for her sister to find, she scooped up the newspaper scraps from the floor and threw them into the garbage bin. She flicked off the bits of newspaper that were still clinging to her sweater and shoes, straightened her shoulders and smoothed her dress. She walked out of the room, with Collie at her heels.

13

$$4^3 = 4 \cdot 4 \cdot 4 = 64 \qquad 4^3 = 64$$
$$4^4 = 256$$
$$4^5 = 1024$$
$$4^6 = 4096$$
$$6^{-4} = \frac{1}{6^4} = \frac{1}{1296}$$
$$6^{-1} = \frac{1}{6}$$
$$10^2 = 100$$
$$10^9 = 1,000,000,000$$
$$10^{-5} = 0.00001$$
$$e = 2.718281828459...$$
$$\sqrt{e} = 1.65$$

195

Ruby Pratt's photo in the *Leaksville News*. . .

...positioned next to the feature called "Colored News" in the last pages of the newspaper.

(12) $\sqrt{4x+21} - 6 = x$

$\sqrt{4x+21} = x+6$

$4x+21 = (x+6)(x+6)$

$4x+21 = x^2+6x+6x+36$

$4x+21 = x^2+12x+36$

$0 = x^2+8x+15$

$0 = (x+5)(x+3)$

Part 2

$x = -5 \quad x = -3$

Life After Murder

_____ *Verificare* (check)

$\sqrt{}$

$x = -5$ acceptable

$3 - 6 = -3$

$x = -3$ acceptable

⑩ $a^3 + b^3 = (a+b)(a^2 - ab + b^3)$

⑪ $\sqrt{3x+19} - \sqrt{5x-1} = 2$

$\sqrt{3x+19} = 2 + \sqrt{5x-1}$

$3x + 19 = (2+\sqrt{5x-1})(2+\sqrt{5x-1})$

$3x + 19 = 4 + 2\sqrt{5x-1} + 2\sqrt{5x-1} + 5x - 1$

$3x + 19 = 3 + 5x + 4\sqrt{5x-1}$

$-2x + 16 = 4\sqrt{5x-1}$

$-x + 8 = 2\sqrt{5x-1}$

$(-x+8)(-x+8) = (2\sqrt{5x-1})(2\sqrt{5x-1})$

$x^2 - 8x - 8x + 64$

$x^2 - 16x + 64 = 20x - 4$

$x^2 - 36x + 68 = 0$

$(x-34)(x-2) = 0$

$x = 34 \quad, \quad x = 2$

Chapter 17

Life Goes On

The weeks and years rolled by after the death of Tom Pratt, and a new normal without him became routine. Tom's six children all stayed in the Leaksville and Spray area. His grandchildren got married, had families of their own, worked at the mills, owned businesses, and a few went to college. Occasionally, they still wondered what happened on the night of August 25, 1947, but eventually the talk of it diminished, as there was nothing new to add.

Even though Sheriff Hodges had publicly stated that the investigation would continue, no further arrests were ever made for the murder of Tom Pratt. It seems as though the investigation was simply dropped.

Tom Pratt's farm was sold for $9,700 to Yancey Joyce, who owned land adjoining the farm when Tom died. Other income from the estate included rents, sale of hay and rye, tools, a hog and so on. Ruby received $25 for her share of the hog. No will was ever found; therefore, the property was divided equally among Tom's six children. After the burial and other expenses, each received $1,716.61.

Tom's oldest daughter Pearl was to married Dan Holland, who ran a dairy. Pearl Pratt Holland died in 1960. Pearl and Dan had two sons, Daniel B. (Deed) and W. H. (Peck), and a daughter Edna. Edna and her husband Harold Hoover, who were among the first to arrive on the scene of Tom Pratt's attack, continued to run a chicken farm. Edna and Harold had two children, Rebecca and Winfred (Wink.) Rebecca became a teacher. Wink, who had gone to his grandfather's house the night of the attack and waited with Ruby until help arrived, had a career in social work. He served on the Eden City school board for twelve years and the first Rockingham County combined school board for three years. He served two terms as the Commissioner on the Rockingham County Board of Commissioners from 1996 to 2004. In 2005 he received the first annual Duke Energy Citizenship & Service Award for outstanding service in the community.

Jake Pratt retired from Spray Cotton Mills in 1961 after more than forty years of service. He spent his entire career running slubbers, machines that draw loose assemblages of fibers into a single strand during the process of cotton yarn spinning. Jake and Josie Pratt, dedicated church workers, lived in Eden until their deaths in the 1970s.

When he was 21, Herbert Pratt, Jake and Josie's son, had gone with his dad and his Uncle Clyde to the meeting with Mr. Sharp, where he took notes and was briefly introduced to "Miss Susie." Herbert headed the Analytical and Applied Chemistry group at Fieldcrest Mills from 1946 to 1952. After that, he joined the DuPont Company in Wilmington, Delaware, and had a varied career in man-made textiles. In the 1970s, he became one of the earliest specialists in the forensic science of man-made fibers and helped solve a number of high profile murders in the United States and Canada, including the black child murders in Atlanta, the

Hillside strangler case in Los Angeles, and the Ted Bundy case in Florida. He retired from DuPont in 1985. Herbert's love of chemical history inspired him to gain National Historic Chemical Landmark status for the Willson Aluminum Company of Spray, North Carolina, where chemist Thomas L. Willson discovered an inexpensive method for making acetylene gas in 1892.

Clyde Pratt and his wife Fannie Sue had six children: Frances, Mildred, Milton, Ruth, Faye and Myra. Clyde was the long-time superintendent at the Leaksville Woolen Mill. He and Fannie Sue lived in Eden for the remainder of their lives. Clyde Pratt died in 1987.

Jim Pratt and his wife Evie Collins Pratt had nine children: Hovis, Elizabeth, Carroll, Hazel, Billy, Earline, Ralph and Joel. Jim Pratt, a long-distance truck driver, died in 1962.

Reid Pratt continued to work at the Fieldcrest sheeting mill in Draper until 1960, when he died of a heart attack while at work. He was 57. Reid's wife Custis remarried many years later, to become Custis Talbert. Now in her 90s, she still lives in Eden. Reid and Custis' daughter, Colleen Shropshire, also resides in Eden.

Betty Pratt married Martin Turner and they had one son, Ray. Martin Turner was owner of Turner Furniture Company in Leaksville, and was succeeded by his son Ray. Betty Turner died in 1998.

Munsey Hodges was sheriff of Rockingham County for five years, from 1946 to 1951. A fire at the Spray Courthouse and city jail occurred on March 17, 1950 in which six prisoners–five men and one woman–lost their lives. This tragedy ruined his career as sheriff. Munsey Hodges was personally sued for the wrongful deaths of these inmates, and was held personally liable for $25,000 to the victims' families, which he paid. He ran for re-election for sheriff and barely won, and a rematch was called. Munsey could not afford to re-run his campaign, and stepped aside. In 1951 he was appointed the acting postmaster of the Leaksville Post Office for one year, then the county tax appraiser until 1954.

While Munsey's career had had its ups and downs over the years, his younger brother Luther Hodges's career had been meteoric from his days at the Marshall Field textile mills in Leaksville, ending as vice president of the company in New York. Luther retired from Marshall Field in 1947 and spent one year as chief of the industry division of the Economic Cooperation Administration (the Marshall Plan) in West Germany. He returned to Leaksville and, at the urging of friends, ran for lieutenant governor. He took office in 1953. When Governor William Ulmstead died in office in 1954, Luther Hodges became Governor. He appointed Munsey to be district supervisor of prison camps with the North Carolina Prison Department. Munsey stayed in that position until ill health forced him to retire in July 1962. Meanwhile, Luther Hodges served as governor until 1960, during which time he founded Research Triangle Park, now one of the largest research complexes in the world. Later, Hodges served as secretary of commerce in the cabinets of presidents Kennedy and Johnson. Luther Hodges died in 1974.

Bobby Vernon, a successor to Munsey in the Sheriff's department, declared that Munsey Hodges was the one of the nicest and most trustworthy people you could ever want to meet. "If he said it was snowing, you needn't go to the window and look." Munsey took the success of his famous younger brother in stride. "Munsey," he was once asked, "did you hear the governor's speech last night?" "Nah," he deadpanned. "I didn't have to hear it. I wrote it." Munsey Hodges died in August, 1962, at the age of 68. His wife Zell, six sons, and two daughters survived him.

Susie Sharp worked with her father James Merritt Sharp from 1929 to 1949 and was introduced to Jake, Clyde, and Herbert Pratt in the 1947 meeting with her father. She was the first, and for many years, the only female lawyer in Rockingham County, beginning a lifetime of breaking barriers for women. She never married. In 1929, a good fifteen years before women were allowed on juries, Susie Sharp was the judge in the courtroom, very often the only woman there. In her first trial at the Rockingham County Courthouse, she faced none other than district attorney and legendary eccentric Alan Denney Ivie Jr. (who coincidentally had sold his father's farm on Price Road to Tom Pratt.) Mr. Ivie began his summation to the jury with the following remark: "Gentlemen of the jury, the presence of sweet womanhood in this courtroom today rarefies the atmosphere." She reportedly remained amused by that comment for the rest of her life.

In 1949, Susie Sharp was appointed the first female superior court justice in the state of North Carolina. In 1962, she became the first female associate justice of any state supreme court in the nation. In 1974, she was appointed chief justice of the North Carolina Supreme Court, also a "female first" in the nation. Among her many honors and accolades, *Time* magazine put her on its cover on January 6, 1976, as one of twelve "women of the year" for 1975.

Susie Sharp said in a 1979 interview, "I broke the ice. I hope I made it a little easier for women who want to be lawyers and judges. But no one else can have the fun, the pleasure and the shock of being first." Her father and law partner, James Merritt Sharp, died on August 2, 1952. Susie Sharp died on March 1, 1996, at the age of 88.

Ralph James Scott, the Rockingham County solicitor, failed to get a conviction for Junior Thompson, but that hardly slowed him down. He was re-elected solicitor again in 1950 and 1954. He resigned this position in 1956 when he was elected to the United States Congress, to represent the fifth congressional district. He served from 1957 to 1967, declining to run for a sixth term. A staunch fiscal conservative, he felt ineffective in the face of "overwhelming liberal forces" in control of the House. "Any gimlet-eyed nitwit that we meet on the street today knows that he can't live beyond his means; no less so can the federal government if it is to retain the confidence of the American people and the respect and confidence of the world at large." In 1980 he donated fifty acres of land to Stokes County in Danbury, North Carolina, to build a new courthouse and county building. He died in 1983.

Robert A. Allen was born in 1913 and was 34 years old when he helped track down Junior Thompson in the Virginia woods in 1947. A native of Reidsville, he served as the Reidsville chief of police and as an agent for the North Carolina State Bureau of Investigation from 1946 to 1951. He died in 1969 at age 56.

J. Hampton (Hamp) Price was born November 20, 1899, and grew up in Stoneville, North Carolina. Perhaps like many college students today, he spent too much time socializing and not enough time studying. After one year at Guilford College in Greensboro, North Carolina, he transferred to Washington and Lee University, where his first-term grades were abysmal. He made a C and an E in commerce I and II, a D in politics, and Fs in English and hygiene. However, he did win an oratorical medal, which perhaps foretold his career in law and politics. He earned his LLM (Master of Laws) in 1924.

Price was a member of the state Democratic Executive Committee and a delegate to the national convention in Philadelphia in

1948. He served six terms in the North Carolina senate and was elected president pro tem, the state's third highest office, of the 1943 Senate.

Price and his wife Sallie Hester (Lane) Price never had any children. However, Price's law partner in Leaksville, Floyd Osborne, and his wife Elizabeth (Fulcher) Osborne, named two of their own children "J. Hampton Price" and "Sallie." Hamp Price died in 1972.

William Clarence Burton, the reporter at the trial, made his byline W. C. Burton, though everyone knew him as Mutt. He started his career in 1936 with the *Greensboro Daily News* (now called *The News and Record*) and, except for the three years he spent in the army, stayed there until retirement, writing his last column a few months before his death at age 88 in 1995. Journalism and theatre appeared to be equally important to him, and he enjoyed a distinguished career in both. He was inducted into the North Carolina Hall of Fame in Journalism in 1994 and received an honorary doctorate of fine arts from the University of North Carolina at Greensboro (UNCG) in 1981. He published *Christmas in my Bones* in 1991 at the age of 83. The North Carolina Theatre Conference awarded him a distinguished career award for a lifetime of service to theatre. In this account of Tom Pratt's murder, when Mutt says that the theatre taught him "to see as well as to look, to taste and to swallow," the words are Mutt's. According to an editorial that ran after his death, he had made that comment in a lecture, saying, "The theatre teaches us to really observe and get pleasure from the simple everyday things. It teaches us to see as well as to look, and taste and swallow. We really don't take time to look at one another. We take too much or granted. We don't really see things." In his 60-year acting career, he appeared throughout the southeast, at venues including the UNCG theatre, and Western Carolina's Parkway and Flat Rock playhouses. In 1979 he appeared in the movie *Being There*, which starred with Shirley MacLaine and Peter Sellers. His daughter Martha Jane Wilkinson described him as "the quintessential southern gentleman—a bon vivant who never met a stranger."

William Haywood Bobbitt was elected resident judge of the fourteenth judicial district of North Carolina (Charlotte), a position he held until 1954. It was in this capacity that he served as the judge in Junior Thompson's murder trial. He was appointed associate justice of the North Carolina Supreme Court in 1954. He preceded his dear friend Susie Sharp as chief justice, serving from 1969 to 1974, and recommended her for the post when he retired. Bobbitt and Sharp had a close, lifelong friendship. According to A. C. Snow, another friend, "For over 25 years, this friendship sustained the two of them through good times, difficult times, and tragic times. Throughout them all, they were there to share each other's sparkling wit, their keen interest in all things legal and governmental, and to comfort, support, and buoy each other in times of crisis." Even after the death of his wife Sarah in 1965, Bobbitt and Sharp never married. William Bobbitt died on September 27, 1992, at the age of 91.

In 1728, a Virginia aristocrat named William Byrd was sent to survey the region of the Dan River Valley in order to settle boundary disputes between the colonies of Virginian and North Carolina. Byrd was awed by the natural beauty and bounty of the area that later became the cities of Leaksville, Spray, and Draper. He wrote, "This is a land rich even unto the fabled lands about Babylon. The air is wholesome, and the soil equal in fertility to any in the world." In 1733 he received a land grant of 20,000 acres. Saying it was the most beautiful area he'd ever seen, he described it as the "Wonderful Land of Eden." In 1707, after the Revolutionary War, John Leak was authorized by the state to lay off a town on a tract of his land on the north side of the Dan River, which he named Leaksville. In 1967, the towns of Leaksville, Spray, and Draper merged to form a new incorporated city. They called their new city "Eden."

$$-x + 5y + z = -18$$
$$4x - 5y + 3z = 34$$
$$x + 5y - z = -10$$

$$-x + 5y + z = -18$$
$$4x - 5y + 3z = 34$$
$$\overline{3x \qquad + 4z = 16}$$

$$5x + 2z = 22$$

$$3x + 4z = 16$$
$$5x + 2z = 22$$
$$3x + 4z = 16$$
$$-10x - 4z = -44$$
$$\overline{-7x = 28}$$
$$x = 4$$

$$(4, -3, 1)$$

$$12 + 4z = 16$$
$$4z = 4$$
$$z = 1$$

$$-4 + 5y + 1 = -18$$

Chapter 18

Edward Thompson, Outlaw

1968

$$5y - 3 = -18$$
$$5y = -15$$
$$y = -3$$

By 1968, 17-year old Junior Edd Thompson had become 37-year old Edward Thompson. What passed after the Tom Pratt murder trial were two decades of increasingly reckless and violent behavior.

Although acquitted in the Tom Pratt case, Junior Thompson returned to the state prison farm in 1947 to finish serving his 1945 sentence for burglary, with two years added for his escape. But instead of using the "get out of jail free card" handed to him by Hampton Price and the Pratt family to start a fresh life, he managed to escape from jail again. He broke into a Reidsville school and was found by Reidsville police hiding out there, eating in the cafeteria. While Rockingham County authorities and the State Bureau of Investigation were looking all over Rockingham County for him, the Reidsville police didn't recognize who they had. Sheriff Axsom happened to go to Reidsville to confer with their police, and who should he find sitting in the city jail but Edward Thompson. The Reidsville police said no photo of him had been circulated. Thompson was tried on the charges in Reidsville, then sent back to state prison.

He didn't stay there long. On October 30, 1950, he drew two concurrent ten- to fifteen-year sentences for breaking, entering, larceny and receiving. He appeared again in Rockingham Superior Court on February 18, 1956, on three charges of breaking and entering. He drew three concurrent sentences of nine to eighteen years, but again, did not serve the full sentence. On September 16, 1960, he came before Wake County Superior Court and received eighteen months for felonious assault. Surviving records do not indicate when he was released from his sentence on that charge.

On October 17, 1966, he received a two-year sentence in Hendersonville Mayor's Court for assaulting a female. For at least the third time in his life, he escaped.

On January 9, 1967, Buncombe County Superior Court handed him to a two-year sentence for larceny under $200. He must have escaped again, because on March 31, 1967 he drew a three-month sentence on an escape charge in the same court. He was sent to a state prison camp at Hendersonville and was released on May 7, 1968.

Two days later, on May 9, 1968, he kidnapped Dr. William Alexander, a Hendersonville, North Carolina physician, and his wife, stealing Dr. Alexander's car. After forcing them to drive him around for several hours, he released them, but not before forcing Dr. Alexander to inject himself with morphine, probably to subdue him. The couple was otherwise unharmed. A Hendersonville police officer, Millard Reed, was shot at when he and another police officer entered a house in which they believed Thompson to be hiding. Thompson escaped by firing a wild shot from a revolver and exiting through a window.

On June 16th in the town of Green River, North Carolina, he kidnapped Michael Beddingfield, 20, and a 17-year old girl whose name was not released, and raped the girl. Thompson forced Beddingfield to drive, but Beddingfield intentionally crashed his own car near a Morganton, North Carolina, rest stop where several truck drivers were parked. Thompson escaped on foot.

One week later, on June 23rd, Thompson kidnapped 22-year-old Robert Lewis and a 14-year old girl. He raped the girl twice, robbed Lewis at gunpoint, stole their car and kidnapped them, with the girl in the car and Lewis bound and locked in the trunk. They were later released and the car was abandoned in Yadkin County, North Carolina. A pick-up truck was then stolen in the same area.

Frustrated law enforcement officials were desperate to catch Thompson. Henderson County Sheriff James Kilpatrick made an unusual request of the court, which was granted. On June 25, 1968, Buncombe County Superior Court Judge W. K. McClean had Edward Thompson declared an "outlaw." This seldom-used nineteenth-century statute made it legally allowable for any citizen to shoot and kill Thompson with impunity if he did not surrender to citizen's arrest. As such, every person in the state had just become a deputy. Anyone with a gun would be allowed, without penalty, to shoot and kill Edward Thompson. In 1968, North Carolina was one of the few states in the country that still had such a statute on the books.

Up until this point federal agents were not involved. On July 2, 1968, a federal warrant was issued against Edward Thompson charging unlawful flight to avoid prosecution. This charge allowed the FBI to become officially involved in his pursuit. The FBI was probably alarmed by the legal and law enforcement precedent that might be set if a citizen were allowed to kill Edward Thompson.

If Thompson was aware of his new legal status, it didn't slow him down. On Monday, July 15, he entered the home of Hester Freeman, 50, of Roanoke, Virginia, and held her, her daughter Hester, 17, and her niece, Matilda Love, 13, at gunpoint. About that same time a young friend, Joanne Ellen Davis, also 13, came to visit. Thompson forced her to get her father, J. Howard Davis, 49, to come inside from his parked car. He held all of them hostage.

He then forced Davis to drive everyone to an abandoned cinderblock house, where he separated the girls from the adults. He shot the adults in the head, killing them instantly. When the girls asked about the shots, he told them he was taking some "target practice." The girls didn't know the adults had been murdered.

The stolen pick-up truck was found on Wednesday, July 16 in Roanoke, Virginia, near the bodies of Hester S. Freeman and J. Howard Davis.

When Davis didn't return home from dropping off his daughter at the Freeman residence, his wife went looking for him. She found the Freeman house empty, with lunch on the table and a pot of coffee boiling on the stove. Davis's 1968 green Dodge was gone. Davis's brother, too, had gone looking for him. He told the *Greensboro Daily News*, "The coffee pot was still on, the bread was out, the tomatoes were out, the butter was out and it didn't look good to me." He added that there were no signs of violence but that the back door had been left open.

Hundreds of police officers searched the Roanoke area as well as Rockingham County, again using bloodhounds and setting up roadblocks, but to no avail. Rockingham County Sheriff Carl Axsom, who had been part of the posse that had arrested Junior Thompson in the Tom Pratt case, said Thompson "knows all there is to know about this area. When I was deputy sheriff in 1948[*] we ran him through the woods with bloodhounds. He was a hard one to catch."

Thompson first raped the oldest girl, Hester, near the scene of the Freeman and Davis murders, though none of the girls knew of these homicides. He then bound all three girls, covered their mouths with tape, and put them in the trunk of the Dodge. He drove them seventy miles, to North Carolina, stuffed in a trunk on a ninety-one degree day. According to newspaper accounts, he drove them to "an abandoned clay-and-timber tobacco barn near the end of a dirt road outside Eden." He raped one of the 13-year old girls there.

He next took the girls to a nearby country store, where he bought milk, cakes, and candy for his supper, and then returned the girls to the abandoned barn, where he declared he would shoot them all. He had with him two rifles and a .32-caliber automatic pistol. But he changed his mind, telling them they were more useful as hostages. They spent the night in the car. The girls had not eaten or slept in two days.

The next morning, he raped the 13-year old girl again. After buying some gasoline, he drove, with the three terrified girls in the back seat, to his family home on Price Road, now owned by his younger brother Pete, 33. Neither Pete nor Weldon had seen "Junior" since 1955, thirteen years before. Pete said, "He came in, shook my hand, asked how I was doing, asked if any police was looking for him. I said every police in the country is looking for him and he said he had to go." Thompson left and Pete called the police immediately.

---

[*] Sheriff Axsom misspoke. It was 1947.

Thompson then headed to Black Bottom (a neighborhood in Eden) in search of Weldon. Weldon's wife Lennis saw him first but did not recognize him. Seeing the three white girls in the back seat, she said she "thought it was somebody that had a boy chauffeuring for 'em." But when he removed his sunglasses, she knew who it was and called to Weldon. Weldon greeted him and said, "Why don't you go and give up?" Thompson replied sarcastically, "Huh, will I?" Lennis Thompson had meanwhile whispered the numbers of the license plate to her granddaughter who scratched them into the dirt. As Thompson drove off, Lennis called the police.

All morning and afternoon police swarmed the area in search of Thompson and the kidnapped girls. Thompson was spotted at various times but escaped by driving across a field or by making violent U-turns in the road. Sometime that afternoon, he raped the other 13-year old girl.

Bernard Young, a retired Rockingham County law enforcement officer, spotted Thompson on Route 220 South, heading from Eden to Greensboro, and called the Greensboro police. Mr. Young was quite certain that it was Thompson because he, too, had been involved in the search for Junior Thompson in 1947, when he worked for the sheriff's department. Raymond Yokley, an employee of the State Highway Commission, also spotted the car as it came speeding south down Route 220. He trailed the car until it entered the city limits, then called the police.

The Greensboro police quickly stopped all northbound traffic and set up a roadblock on the southbound side, ordering a dump truck to block the path of the road. Drawing their pistols, Officers R. V. Tadlock and W. N. Smithey quickly pulled Thompson from the car by his arm with a pistol to his head, removing a .32-caliber pistol from Thompson's holster. Officers S. I. Rhodes and W. E. McNair emptied two shotguns found on the floor of the car. They were able to capture Thompson peacefully and rescue the terrified girls. One newspaper account said that Thompson appeared to be confused.

Thompson allegedly said to the police, "If I had gotten to my gun, things wouldn't have happened the way they did." Sheriff Axsom confirmed it. "If he has a gun and you don't have one, he's mean, but if you have one and he doesn't he's just like a kitten." Indeed, when finally cornered with no way out, Thompson surrendered as quietly as he had in 1947 when he was hiding in the Virginia cornfield, wanted for the murder of Tom Pratt.

Police this time took no chances that Thompson would be able to escape again. While in the Guilford County jail, two officers stayed in the cell with him throughout the night and he was not allowed visitors, though it is unlikely that anyone came to see him. The elevator leading to the jail was not allowed to stop on any floor other than the first, where the sheriff's department was situated. No trusty–trusted inmates given special privileges–was to open the glass door unless a uniformed deputy stood outside and gave permission. When Thompson left Guilford County to be transferred to the Buncombe County jail in Asheville, he rode in a police car with a partitioned rear seat, handcuffed to an officer.

Federal, North Carolina, and Virginia law enforcement officials haggled over where Edward Thompson would first face charges. He was charged with two counts of murder and three counts of kidnapping in Virginia, and a combined fifteen charges of kidnapping, rape, and robbery in North Carolina. It was decided that Hendersonville, North Carolina, would try him first on the charges of rape and kidnapping. Virginia authorities as well as other jurisdictions in North Carolina hoped to try him also, but in fact they never did.

The news of Thompson's arrest made the front page of *The Washington Post* on July 18, 1968. The fact that he had been declared an outlaw by the State of North Carolina was seen by many as reckless and dangerous in and of itself. All it would have taken for a tragedy to occur would be a case of mistaken identity. A broader issue was that a suspect, no matter how heinous the crime, should have the opportunity to stand trial, as guaranteed by the Constitution. On Thursday, July 18, the *Greensboro Daily News* ran a lead editorial decrying the century-old statute, stating, "that statute in effect legalized vigilante justice. It permits, under law, the execution of a suspect without a trial. ... If anything, the apprehension of Edward Thompson proved how utterly unnecessary this statue is. ... The police did their job well, and in so doing they demonstrated that the job should be left to them."

Prior to the Edward Thompson case, the statute—North Carolina Statutes Section 15-48, originally enacted in 1866—had not been invoked since 1960. It was declared unconstitutional by a federal district court in 1976 and repealed in 1997.

On July 22, Thompson was taken to Dorothea Dix (mental) Hospital in Raleigh, North Carolina, for mental tests and observation, and was kept under maximum security. He was deemed fit to stand trail.

At 3 p.m. on September 24, 1946, while Junior Thompson was serving time in a state prison camp for burglary, Monroe M. Redden was meeting with President Harry S Truman at the White House as part of a meeting with Democratic congressional and senatorial candidates. Monroe Redden won that election, serving as a United States representative of North Carolina's twelfth district from 1947 to 1953.

After that he resumed his law practice in his native Hendersonville. On July 18, 1968, Superior Court Judge Harry Martin appointed the 66-year old Mr. Redden to serve as Edward Thompson's court-appointed attorney. So, for at least the second time in his life, Edward Thompson was defended by a well-known politician. But this time the evidence was overwhelming. Thompson was convicted on October 18, 1968.

Thompson entered Central Prison in Raleigh having received a combination of consecutive and concurrent sentences for his crimes. His incarceration summary showed sentences for robbery (ten years, sentence began October 18, 1968), kidnapping (life sentence began on May 15, 1975), kidnapping and rape (concurrent life sentences were to begin on October 7, 2003), larceny and receiving (ten-year sentence was to begin October 14, 2005), kidnapping (life sentence was to begin on November 9, 2033), and kidnapping (sentence was to begin July 31, 2074). Given that he would have been 143 years old in the year 2074, these dates were meant to guarantee that he never would be released from prison. And this time, he wasn't. He spent the rest of his life, twenty-one more years, behind bars. He died of AIDS on July 18, 1989, at the age of 58. His remains were cremated.

Thompson's two mug shots appeared in 1947 and in 1968 in the *Leaksville News*.

Thompson Is Captured by Greensboro Police

Thompson's capture on Route 220 South outside of Greensboro on July 16, 1968. News of the arrest of the outlaw made page 1 of *The Washington Post*.

Photo courtesy of the *News and Record*

Chapter 19
Ruby Edwards

Ruby Pratt moved out of the home she had shared with Tom shortly after the murder and went to live with relatives. As she had done after her separation from Charlie Corum, she resumed the use of her maiden name, Edwards. As she hadn't legally been married to Tom Pratt, it was the right thing to do. Another motive, undoubtedly, was to dissociate herself from the Pratt family, the trial, and the reputation she had earned. Ruby Edwards had to reinvent herself one more time.

In 1956, she joined the Floyd Missionary Baptist Church and became an active member. She attended church every Sunday, sharing a pew with her two sisters, Lillie and Lucille. She liked to cook and sew, and she made many close friends within the congregation. When Lucille became sick, Ruby cared for her until Lucille's death in 1988. Ruby never remarried, never had children and she never left Eden. She continued to work for Fieldcrest until her retirement.

When Edward Thompson's crime spree made the papers in 1968, it recalled the 1947 murder of Tom Pratt. Although newspapers re-told that story, including "Mrs. Pratt's" testimony, she was not identified as the current Ruby Edwards. It is unlikely that reporters knew who she was. If anyone asked her to be interviewed for the articles, she must have declined. However, she undoubtedly felt some vindication that the man she once accused of murder was, in fact, proven capable of it. Unless, of course, she secretly knew that Edward Thompson had not murdered Tom Pratt.

Ruby Edwards had finally become someone that a small town could accept. She obeyed the social norms that church members were expected to follow. She had law-abiding friends, took care of her family, worked hard and was a good neighbor. Perhaps she underwent a full religious conversion, considering her fifty years of church attendance and the peaceful life she led with her sisters. Her former pastor said, "What I saw of her indicated that she was a very fine woman. She was faithful in attendance to the church and quiet in her demeanor. There was no harm in her."

One thing seems certain: few if any of her friends later in life knew that she had ever been Ruby Meeks, Ruby Corum, or Ruby Pratt. Few if any knew she had been married to a man who had been murdered. Those who discovered the truth undoubtedly were disinclined to believe it. One of Ruby's acquaintances, in fact, later lived in what had been Tom and Ruby Pratt's house, but in the years of their knowing one another, Ruby never told the woman that she had lived in that house for five years. One can only surmise that embarrassment or shame kept her from revealing her past. How would she explain to people why she had married a 77-year old man, forty-five years her senior? How would she explain why she had not inherited the farm? How would she describe the trial, and why the jury rejected her testimony? Better to leave it alone and hope that no one remembered. New friends would know nothing of it.

Christian friends would accept her and love her even if they knew her past, and, as churchgoers, gossip was frowned upon. Whether due to a sincere Christian faith, a desire to be accepted, or sheer terror of being found out, Ruby finally found a way to make her life work. The final reinvention of herself took hold and lasted for the rest of her life. Person after person said that she was a good, sweet and kind lady.

Every person in the world has a life story that is as unique as a fingerprint. Our culture, our experiences, our relationships and our choices create these stories. We carry them in our hearts, and good or bad, they make us who we are. Each new day adds to the story. What survives over time? What do we bring with us as we age? What myths and habits do we hang on to? What memories cling to us? What do we rub out and hope to forget? Ruby's life had been turbulent during the twenty years between her teens and mid-thirties. After that, her new identity was one that no one could question or scorn. Did any part of the young, reckless Ruby survive throughout her life? Did a small part of her miss the days of parties and the attention from male friends? Did she ever look back fondly on that life? One friend said Ruby liked to wear too much make-up and cologne. Was this small clue a subtle act of defiance to convention? Was it a tribute to her former self? Was she still hoping for male attention? Did her heart really change, or did she just act better?

Ruby Edwards died on March 27, 2001, at the age of 91, and is buried behind the church that she attended weekly for fifty years. Having found little happiness in her marriages, she seemed to have found some measure of peace by conforming to the conventions of the good people of Rockingham County, North Carolina. She appears to have lost the checkered reputation that had dogged her for so long, building a new level of respect from people who met her later. It seems that Ruby Edwards lived simply but lived well, and she lived long enough to outlast the notoriety of Ruby Pratt and the murder on Price Road.

Ruby Florence Edwards, in a photo for her church annual. A former pastor said, "She's a good Christian lady– there's no harm in her."

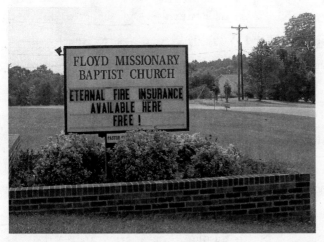

Ruby Edwards became a lifelong, faithful member of the Floyd Missionary Baptist Church.

Chapter 20

Who Killed Tom Pratt?

The North Carolina State Bureau of Investigation possesses a file, housed, no doubt, in some rarely used storage room, that contains notes and possibly physical evidence concerning the Tom Pratt murder case. According to an SBI attorney, private citizens are not allowed to see such files. Technically, the case remains open.

What could be of interest in the file that isn't already known? According to newspaper accounts about the capture of Junior Thompson on September 3, 1947, a blood-stained khaki coat and a blue sweater matching the description of Junior's clothing were found at the home in Virginia in which he was hiding out. Those accounts said that the coat and sweater gave bloodhounds the scent to track Junior. One assumes the SBI conducted blood-type matches between the blood on the coat, Junior and Tom Pratt. A positive blood-type match between Tom Pratt and Junior's coat would support the possibility that Junior killed Tom, but hardly prove it: millions of people share the same blood type. The blood could have come from any one of a number of people. If Junior and Tom shared the same blood type, it would have been impossible to know, by 1947 technology, whose blood it was. But DNA testing available today is specific to the individual and almost certainly would prove Junior's guilt if Tom's DNA were on Junior's coat.

According to an SBI attorney, even if there is a blood-stained coat in an evidence box, the blood would have deteriorated beyond testing usefulness by this time. Still, this is a testable assumption. What's in it for the SBI and State to conduct these tests? Isn't it always desirable to close a case? Is it not good public relations to always serve justice? Why not test the coat? There is a simple and practical answer. Everyone associated with this crime has died. There is nobody to bring to justice. While satisfying curiosity may be a compelling reason for historians, it tends not to be for bureaucrats.

The coat and sweater were not part of the state's evidence at the trial. Why not? Perhaps the clothing belonged to someone else. Perhaps the blood on the coat was an animal's, or Junior's alone. Perhaps the sheriff's department failed to collect blood samples from Tom Pratt, either at the scene or in the hospital. Perhaps the tests failed to support the premise that Junior was guilty. Perhaps the clothing was lost. Newspaper accounts said that the home of James Penn had been searched while he was not at home. Did the officers have the proper search warrants? If not, Hampton Price may have had the evidence suppressed for the trial. At any rate, any compelling evidence about the clothing would have been presented at the trial–the bloody coat itself could have been shown as evidence–yet there was no mention of it at all. If the clothing was used to track Junior with the dogs, it probably did exist, but perhaps the blood on it was just rumor.

Oddities and Questions

Custis Pratt had stayed awake on the hot night of August 24, 1947, because she couldn't sleep. Well after midnight, now August 25th, she saw a car come slowly up her road, then turn around and come back by. In hindsight, she felt certain that someone was checking to see if Reid's car were there. Was it the sheriff, who knew about the contentious relationship between Reid and his father, checking to see if Reid was home with an alibi? Was it someone else, hoping to blame the murder on him? Was it a coincidence? She never learned who it was. Custis always felt, however, that if Reid had not been home that night, he would have been accused of murdering his father.

Sheriff Hodges suggested to reporters that Tom knew his attacker, but there was no way to know if that could have been true. If Ruby is to be believed, Tom turned on the light when he heard an intruder. How would anyone know if he recognized the killer? If so, he died without naming him (or her). Harold Hoover said Mr. Pratt was aware enough to call him by name, so why didn't he name his attacker? Was he too confused? Was he ashamed to say? If it was a stranger, couldn't he have offered any description? And why did Hodges suggest that Tom knew who it was?

What happened to the ax that was kept on the back porch? It was never found, even with twenty men combing the woods around the house.

Coy Ratliff was the first to arrive at the scene of the crime, responding to Ruby's cries for help. He admitted he did not tell all he knew to the investigators, thinking that the time to tell his story would be on the witness stand. Ralph Scott, the solicitor, managed to make him appear quite foolish, and Hampton Price was able to recover just a little when he elicited more testimony from Ratliff that Ruby said the attacker was a large man. But what else did Coy Ratliff know that he never got a chance to say? Why did Coy want so badly to question Ruby himself?

Tom's granddaughter Hazel said that her Aunt Betty, Tom's youngest daughter, said she thought she knew who the killer was, but Betty wouldn't say it. Hazel regretted that Betty died without ever learning her theory. Why wouldn't Betty tell? Betty was a good Baptist. She would not gossip and she would not "tell tales" without any proof. Her theory of the murder died with her.

The Case Against Junior Thompson

If Junior was the guilty party, the likeliest motive was burglary. Junior's prior crime (in 1945) of a midnight breaking-and-entering (to steal guns and ammunition) proved that he was capable of it. If he was the culprit, he probably did not expect to encounter Tom Pratt face to face. When he did, he slugged him hard, with a club or a rock. However, he stole nothing. Having been seen by Ruby, he fled quickly. He went home to plan his next move, or to gather some things for his escape, when Sam Turner, a neighbor who wanted to help in the manhunt, unexpectedly showed up to borrow a flashlight. After that, he ran.

Does knowing what became of Junior in later years add to an aura of guilt? In hindsight, does he now appear to be the guilty party? He never held any regard for the law and became increasingly violent. Robbery, kidnapping, rape, and murder were his legacy. Why should anyone today think that he was innocent of murder in 1947? For one thing, nothing was stolen. Two, he knew the Pratt family (though admittedly, given his later history, that might not have mattered.) Three, it would seem to stretch plausibility that he would return home after an attack like that, especially after having been seen. Fourth, and most important, Ruby's physical description of the attacker differed significantly from Junior's appearance.

Another motive for Junior might have been revenge. On September 5, 1947, the *Greensboro Daily News* printed one line in an article that said, "[Tom] Pratt had testified against the Negro at a burglary trial shortly before the alleged murder," but this statement was not followed up with any details of the prior crime or trial. The statement makes no sense. Junior was a prison escapee. If he had been on trial at any time during the 10 months between breaking out of prison and this murder, he would have been kept in jail, not free to roam around and commit more crimes. There was no burglary trial "shortly before the alleged murder."

The rumor changed a little but was basically repeated on July 24, 1968, when *The Eden News* interviewed Sheriff Carl Axsom, who had participated in the bloodhound search of Junior in 1947 and was part of the manhunt in 1968. The article stated, "at the time of his arrest on suspicion of murder, Thompson was an escapee from prison on charges of breaking and entering, where the testimony of Tom Pratt, the murdered man, had helped send him. Thompson was said to have been quoted as saying 'he would get even with the old man.' " It's odd that these statements turn up in 1968 but not in 1947. If they were true, a clear motive could be established linking Junior to the attack on Tom Pratt. Court records of the 1945 burglary listed the witnesses as L. E. Davis, whose home was burglarized, police officer S. L. "Pug" Carter, and police officer Robert Barnes, but not Tom Pratt. No evidence could be found that Tom Pratt ever testified in any trial against Junior Thompson. The Pratt grandchildren could not remember their grandfather ever being involved in such a trial. There are two big reasons not to believe this rumor. One, this information would have been used in the trial to establish motive. Two, if Tom Pratt had testified against Junior, Jake Pratt would have known about it, and Jake and Clyde never would have paid for Junior's attorney.

One has to conclude that Tom Pratt never testified against Junior, and that Junior's vow of revenge never happened. Where did Sheriff Axsom get this information? If Junior said it, who heard him? Did the sheriff's department deliberately start this rumor to implicate Junior? How else might this rumor have started?

Just as time seemed to gel rumors into "fact" by 1968 regarding Junior's vow of revenge, at that same time a Mary Cox Cassell was quoted in *The Eden News* as saying, "I was on the jury that tried him [Thompson] for the murder of old Tom Pratt nearly twenty years ago. Pratt, who was in his 80s, was killed by a blow on the head with an ax. He was known to carry a lot of money." In 1947, the female jurors were listed as Mrs. A. R. Williams, Mrs. W. L. Patterson, and Mrs. Marion Caudle (alternate). Apparently, the women jurors were listed under their husbands' names, and women's names often change over time. Still, who is Mary Cox Cassell? Second, the jury heard testimony that he was killed with a blunt object, not an ax. If Mary Cox Cassell sat on the jury, she would have known that. Third, Tom Pratt would not have been known to carry a lot of money. Frequently in debt, he always lived meagerly, trying to stretch his money. Fourth, he was attacked in his home at night, not out on the street. But newspaper stories carry enormous weight. Once words are in print, they are deemed to be true. Given his violent crimes in 1968, the tide of opinion seemed to turn against Junior.

The Case Against Ruby Pratt (or someone she knew)

If Ruby had been inclined to murder, inheriting Tom's land would have been a good motive. Was she really capable of premeditated murder? Another theory is that the murder was not premeditated, but was the result of a spontaneous quarrel between Tom and one of her male friends who had come to the house. What is the evidence that Ruby either premeditated murder or helped to cover one up?

First of all, she married him, a man forty-five years her senior. Because they fought all the time and she maintained her distance from his family, it did not seem to anyone (but Tom) that she loved him. Why did she marry him? For security? For money? To escape some other situation? But she did. And when five years passed and he was still healthy, and she was so miserable, perhaps she looked to speed things along.

Ruby was never accused of murder. But questions asked at the trial pointed a finger away from Junior's direction and onto Ruby. Some testified that Tom Pratt's blood was dried around his face when help arrived; others said he was still bleeding. Head injuries typically bleed profusely. If the blood was dried, then the assumption was that Ruby had waited to call for help. Why? Was she simply trying to assist him herself and couldn't manage it? Was she waiting for the killer to get away? Or was Tom, in fact, still bleeding?

Some testified that her bed had been slept in; others said it had not. If her bed had not been slept in, why not? What had she been doing? The implication is that she was assisting the killer. But maybe the bed had been slept in, as she said.

Wink Hoover, who was 15 when he waited with Ruby on the night of the attack, found two things odd that night. One, she kept offering to show him the overturned butter churn outside the house where the intruder climbed in. Wink himself was afraid that night, and even holding a shotgun, was not about to go outside. It was strange to him that she wanted to go out and show him the churn. Wasn't she afraid? Or had the butter churn been a ruse? Second, the broken oven door was held closed with a stick that was propped against the opposite wall of the narrow kitchen. Thinking about it later, Wink wondered how a large man would climb in the window without knocking over the stick. Was the intruder going to stop and replace it? Or had it never been moved?

Ruby's dog was missing on the night of the attack. Was the dog confined somewhere so that the killer could do his work without arousing the neighbors? Or did the dog simply have the run of the property and happen not to be in the area when the attacker came?

Tom Pratt's father had had a will, and Tom Pratt's children had assumed that their father did, too. Wills were not always filed with the court in those days, but still could have been considered valid. Was there a will? If so, what happened to it?

Ruby's statements about the attacker were inconsistent. On the night of the attack and the next day, she described a "large, heavy-set Negro with slicked-back, wavy hair." Within a few days she identified the short-haired, small-statured, 145-pound Junior Thompson as the attacker. Despite the obvious discrepancy, Ruby stuck to her accusation of Junior Thompson. Using a Negro scapegoat to cover up a white person's crime was hardly unusual. Perhaps her description had been completely fabricated, but when she learned that Junior Thompson had fled the area, or that he had escaped from jail, she accused Junior instead. Or maybe she simply was a poor eyewitness, terrified in a poorly-lit stairwell, at seeing someone attack her husband. Did she see a person whose show of brute force made him appear to be twice his size? Once she was on the witness stand, did Ruby's poor reputation cast a longer shadow over her credibility?

232

Rumors about Ruby

It's been told in the Thompson family that Ruby's bloody dress was found in the well. It's a great example of a rumor starting with a kernel of truth. The well was indeed searched, at the request of Jake Pratt, to look for the missing chop ax. Nothing was found–not an ax, not a bloody dress.

Some said that Ruby had been taken to Raleigh for a lie detector test that she failed. Lie detector tests had been in use since 1917, but have not been considered sufficiently reliable for the results to be admissible in court. But the bigger question is, if she were not on trial, why would she have taken a lie detector test?

Ruby was reputed to have attended and thrown many parties with people of questionable character. Presumably there's truth in that; Tom frequently stormed to his daughter's to complain about such behavior. The parties reputedly were pretty wild, with plenty of alcohol. Many said Ruby had a boyfriend, and over and over again people named Sheriff Munsey Hodges. Many people did not think Sheriff Hodges was aggressive enough in pursuing the case. Perhaps people speculated that he was helping her cover a crime because they were romantically linked. Is this how these rumors started? No one knew any of this for sure, as no one had any direct eyewitness contact of these events. Other people have said that they would be very surprised to learn that Munsey had acted in an improper fashion. Whether these particular stories were true or not, Ruby's unconventional behavior made her the topic of talk which would dampen her credibility when she most needed to appear trustworthy–on the witness stand.

A curious entry showed up in Herbert Pratt's notes from the meeting he attended with his father Jake, Uncle Clyde, and attorney Jim

Sharp. The note said, "'Evidently somebody has talked too much; we found a rock in the cook stove, but didn't want it told just yet.' quote Beverly Robertson, quote Bob Allen.' " Beverly Robertson was the reporter who wrote the final article about Ruby in which she appeared in the photo with her dog. Apparently Robertson was following the case more closely than anyone realized. From what Herbert Pratt remembers of the meeting with Sharp, Jim Sharp said that according to Robertson, who heard it from Agent Allen, the SBI found a rock in Ruby's stove—an unusual place for a rock—which presumably could have been the murder weapon. Did Robertson, a reporter, hear this from someone, ask Allen about it, and he confirmed it? Did she then confide it to Mr. Sharp? Was she looking for a second confirmation? Mr. Sharp certainly had no vested interest in this criminal matter. He was hired to look into the marriages and did so. He was highly respected and professional; he would not have divulged information he did not think to be true. Would Agent Allen plant a rumor with a reporter? To what end? No one else was ever brought up on charges.

Fifty-five years after the death of Tom Pratt, one of his grandsons said, "I used to see Ruby up at the Texaco station, and she never could look me in the eye. That li'l ol' colored boy no more'n killed Old Pa than I did." Was Ruby's shame an admission of murder or its cover-up? Did she lie to protect someone? Or was her shame in manipulating an old man for the independence she thought he could give her, being a poor wife, and making him miserable in the process? If she were guilty of murder or accessory after the fact, would she have asked the governor to keep the investigation open? Could she really have been that brazen? Did she ever tell anyone a different story of what happened that night? If so, no one ever came forward.

And then there's this:

A person who wished to remain anonymous told one reliable source for this book, "I know who did it. He's dead and his children are dead, but his grandchildren are alive and would be hurt by the knowledge." That rules out Junior Edd Thompson, who did not have children. Would that person please come forward to solve the case in respect of Tom Pratt?

Tom Pratt lived a long life, had many years with his beloved Nettie, and raised seven children. He experienced joy and hardship, tragedy and grief, yet always looked for ways to make his life better. His impulsive optimism took over his sense when, at age 77, he fell in love with the most unlikely woman. His final years brought him bitterness, not comfort, but he did not leave. Then one hot, summer night, without warning, he finally faced the one obstacle he could not overcome: a person who would callously take his life, with no more regard for him than for a worm on tobacco. Who did this to him and why? Someone was telling the truth; someone was lying. From the moment it occurred, the truth crumbled into fiction; the fictions became fact, and the questions remain unanswered. There seems to be no one left who can say, and likely, no one ever will.

Tom and Nettie's final resting place, at the El Bethel Presbyterian Church cemetery, in Eden, North Carolina.

Chapter Notes

The following notes expand on the information in the story. Whereas the story contains fictional elements in dialogue, these notes are factual and help shed light on the people and events around the story.

Notes on Chapter 1: Junior Thompson

Edd and Reeves Thompson (Junior's parents) and their family lived on Price Road about three miles outside of Leaksville, North Carolina, in an area known as El Bethel named for the local El Bethel Presbyterian Church. Edd Thompson Sr. worked at the Fieldcrest Textile Finishing Mill in the sheet finishing division. He was in charge of large equipment and machines that mixed starch in 300- to 500-gallon tanks to be pumped into machines for application to the fabric. Edd Thompson would have had to read the formulas for mixing the starch and other ingredients and follow the various "recipes" that would be required for different fabrics. It was a difficult and respected job due to the amount of materials involved. Edd and Reeves had three sons, Weldon, and Junior Edd and "Big" Pete. Edd and Junior looked alike: tall, wiry, dark-skinned and not weighing more than 150 pounds. Reeves and the other two boys looked alike: heavy and light-skinned. According to people who remembered them, there was no way you could mistake Junior for his brothers.

The Thompson property was in front of the Pratt family farm on Price Road. Tom and Nettie Pratt lived about 300 yards back from the road, slightly northwest of the Thompson property. Sometime after Nettie died in 1936, Tom built a smaller house on his property "down in the cow pasture" that was directly north of the Thompson property about 250 yards away. Tom rented the original house to Coy and Vera Ratliff, tenant farmers.

Edd Thompson Sr. worked occasionally as a farm hand for Tom Pratt. Tom Pratt's grandchildren, cousins Hazel Estes and Wink Hoover, remember playing with Junior as they spent time at the house, picking apples in "Old Pa's" orchard or visiting on Sundays. There was no animosity across racial lines, and in fact, cooperation and perhaps friendship existed between the families. According to Carl Thompson, whose father was a distant cousin to Edd Thompson, "the people who lived on Price Road were both black and white. They were a close people."

The events and conversations at the Thompson house on the night of the attack are speculative, but Sam Turner did testify to seeing Junior there when he stopped to borrow a flashlight on his way to the Pratt home.

Although Edd Thompson Sr. had a good job, his son Junior had been incarcerated in 1945 for a burglary charge in the Montgomery Correctional Center in Troy, NC, at about the age of 14. About two years into his term, in October, 1946, Junior escaped from a prison road gang. Apparently he just came home, and if the authorities really looked for him, they didn't look there. He would have been about 16 at the time of his escape. He was apparently home for about ten months when the Tom Pratt murder occurred, on August 25, 1947. It's not known what he told his parents about his being home.

Junior was captured by the posse on September 3, 1947. The authorities suspected that Junior was hiding at the home of James Penn, a friend who lived about a half mile from Route 220 in Ridgeway, Virginia. Police officers searched the Penn home while no one was there. According to newspaper accounts, they found a bloodstained khaki coat and a blue sweater on a corner of the front porch. While two officers remained at the Penn home, the other four officers split up following two trails, as bloodhounds followed the scent. Junior was trailed into the Virginia woods. When found, the "hungry and bedraggled fugitive" (as described by the *Greensboro Daily News*) offered no resistance to arrest. Agent Robert A. Allen of the North Carolina State Bureau of Investigation fired one shot into the air to communicate to the others that Junior had been captured. On questioning, Junior denied any connection with the Pratt murder but admitted that he had been near the home on the night of the murder and had heard Ruby scream.

SBI Agent Robert Allen and Henry County, Virginia, Deputy Sheriff Obie Wells made the arrest. The Rockingham County officers in the posse were Chief Deputy B. J. Carter, Carl Axsom, Marshall Clark, A. J. Talbot and Charles C. Case. (Years later, Carl Axsom became sheriff, and this would not be his last encounter with Junior Thompson.) Junior was taken to Martinsville, Virginia, waived extradition and was jailed in North Carolina to await grand jury action.

Notes on Chapter 2: Tom Pratt

Tom Pratt's date and place of birth were March 29, 1866, in Henry County, Virginia.

Tom Pratt's parents were William Frederick (Fred) Pratt (1832-1897) and Lucy Elizabeth (Bettie) Martin Pratt (1846-1935). Their eleven children were: William Thomas Pratt (Tom) (1866-1947), Sarah Frances (Fannie) (1868-1951), Nancy Kinnie (1870-1941), Samuel Andrew (Sam) (1873-1957), John Richard (1875-1955), Maggie (1877-1961), M. Frederick (Fred) (1878-1954), Robert James (Jim) (1880-1956), Charles Fields (Charlie) (1881-1961), Harvey Judson (1883-1954), and Annie Dell (1886-1959). They lived on land currently marked as Rockingham County Road 1562, no longer owned by the Pratt family. However, a small Pratt family cemetery is there, where Tom's parents, some other relatives, and his daughter Alma are buried.

John Motley Morehead (1796-1866) was governor of North Carolina from 1841 to 1845. His son, J. Turner Morehead, established the cotton and woolen mills that became the central industry of Leaksville, Spray and Draper for most of the twentieth century, and so he was indeed the richest man in Rockingham County. He became overextended, however, in the early 1900s and had to declare bankruptcy.

In "The History of the Willson Aluminum Company, Spray, North Carolina," Herbert T. Pratt wrote:

To cover his debts, Morehead apparently borrowed from banks as well as the community. The will of William Frederick Pratt (1832-1897), a well-off farmer and great-grandfather of the author of this article, contains the following provision: "The note of Major Morehead, who I think is an honest man, and will pay the note in full, this note when collected I wish to be divided equally between my wife and children. . ." (Rockingham County, N.C., Wills, Book F, p. 73, January 21, 1897.) The amount of the note was not given, but family tradition has it that it was never paid.

Tom's mother Bettie had been well educated, but his father, despite his success in business, had not learned to read or write until late in life. Although Tom made his living through carpentry and farming, he liked to stay informed of world events. At one time he subscribed to both the *Atlanta Journal Constitution* and the *Kansas City Star.*

Laura Nettie Morgan was born to James Morgan (1818-1894) and Sallie Hyler Norton Morgan (1827-1900). Their children were William T. (b. 1846), Eliza C. (b. 1849), Mintora T. (1853 -1901), Mary L. (b. 1854), James R. (b. 1856), Robert R. (1858-1893), Charles Anthony (1861-1907), Roxey A. (b. 1863), Laura Nettie (1866-1936), and Sarah E. (b. 1889).

James Morgan, Nettie's father, owned a grist and flourmill on Buffalo Island Creek above the present NC 770 bridge. He was also licensed by the federal government to distill whiskey, paying a tax on what he sold. A seal on the bung of the whiskey barrel proved that the tax had been paid. But Mr. Morgan had whiskey barrels with bungs on both ends. One end had the seal; the other end didn't. When the tax revenuers came around, he made sure they saw the end with the seal. The federal agents apparently never detected his trick.

Tom and Nettie's children were: Pearl Pratt Holland (1887-1960) married to Dan Holland; W. Alma Pratt, (1891-1908); Thomas Boaz Pratt (Jake) (1896-1973) married to Josie Smith Pratt (1898-1975); Clyde Milton Pratt (1898-1987) married to Fannie Sue Cox Pratt; James R. Pratt (1901-1962) married to Evie Collins Pratt (1902-1974); Robert Reid Pratt (1903-

1960) married to Custis Talbert Pratt (now Clifton) (1915 - ____); Betty Hyler Pratt Turner (1907-1998) married to Martin Turner.

Nearly everyone in the county had a nickname. Nicknames often followed a person's profession or physical appearance, and weren't always kind. Two photographers in town were Picture Price and Photo Adams. Boss Rakestraw was a mill overseer. Crip Purdy was a restaurant owner who had a deformed leg, and Tan Martin was a red-headed store owner. More can be found at www.leaksville.com. Tom's children's nicknames were Peedly (Pearl), Jake (Tom Boaz), Toug (Clyde), Duck (Jim), Reidy (Reid), and Monk (Betty.)

For all the hard times and apparent differences in their personalities, Tom and Nettie had a good marriage. Their granddaughter Hazel Estes said, "They were just a loving couple."

Leaksville was a town of many contrasts. One of them was that despite of the nicknames, there was also a certain formality to how people addressed one another. Even relatives often referred to each other by their surnames. Josie Pratt called her father-in-law "Mr. Pratt" as a sign of respect. Harold Hoover called Tom "Mr. Pratt." Even though Tom was his wife's grandfather, he would have never addressed him as "Old Pa" the way the other grandchildren lovingly did. Herbert Pratt remembers his first job promotion at Fieldcrest Mills. Women he'd known all his life, who were friends with his mother, now addressed him as "Mr. Pratt," even though he was half their age. His education and position at the mill earned him that new level of respect. Munsey Hodges and his two brothers were another good example. Munsey, as sheriff, was referred to as "Sheriff Hodges." His younger brother Luther, who held a highly respected position at Fieldcrest Mills, was called "Mr. Hodges," and later, of course, "Governor Hodges." Pity their older brother Dave who ran a highly successful Shell gasoline station. He was known simply as "Old Man Dave Hodge"–"Hodge" without the "s" at the end. On the social ladder, he wasn't anybody.

Tom had worked for D. E. Moore Company, a carpentry and millwork firm. Among Tom's papers when he died were the many mortgage notes for loans, including the loan for $15.40. And he did indeed own a Ford touring car that he never learned to drive.

Tom built his first house on the land he had inherited from his father, where he lived with Nettie and their young family. They sold it in 1910 so that they could move to town. He bought the property at 109 Johnson Street in Leaksville and built the house there, which is still standing. In 1930, they sold the house at 109 Johnson and moved to the farm on Price Road, where they lived the remainder of their lives.

The deed to the property said, "Beginning at an iron stump, a corner of Polk Thompson, with J. A. Pratt and running thence with the line of J. A. Pratt and T. R. Pratt, N. 85 degrees W. 1304 feet to an iron at the root of a fallen white oak..." The adjoining property of J. A. Pratt and T. R. Pratt belonged to some distant cousins of Tom's, but they didn't live there. Polk Thompson was Edd Thompson's father and Junior Thompson's grandfather, but he was not living there at the time of these events.

The "company store" was the Spray Mercantile Company, which was housed in a large building in the midst of the mills. Built around 1900, it is sometimes known as the "the country's first mall." On a basement level was B. H. Edwards Meat Market. On the first floor of the three-storied building one would find the Rufus Ray dry goods store, a grocery store, a furniture store, a drug store, the post office, and the medical offices of Dr. John B. Ray and his nephew Dr. Philip Ray. On the second floor was the sheriff's office and police station, Spray Recorder's Court, the medical offices of Dr. A. F. Tuttle, and several law offices. Men would often go to the recorder's court for entertainment, but if they were lucky, they might get chosen for jury duty and be paid twenty-five cents. The court was presided over by Judge Henry P. Lane. The roller rink was on the third floor, above the courtroom. The roller rink was open to any white person, but provided entertainment for many mill employees, a number of whom were often teenagers.

It's not known whether Reid Pratt repaid his parents for the $1000 they paid to his daughter's mother. Receipts totaling $1000, written to the clerk of the court, were found among Tom Pratt's papers.

Dump Ivie's given name was Allan Denny Ivie Sr. (1873-1927). Why he was called "Dump" is not known. He was well-known in the county because he had been a prominent attorney, justice of the peace, and a two-term state senator. The son, Allan Denny Ivie Jr. (1907–1987) became a district attorney for the area that included Rockingham County and had a reputation for being rather eccentric. He was a tall, slightly overweight man with thick, long gray hair who wore seersucker suits with bat-wing collars all year round, long after the styles had changed. The "paper trail" of the land deal between Allan Ivie and Tom Pratt was found in Tom Pratt's papers.

Tom and Nettie purchased eighty-six acres from Allan D. Ivie Jr. on June 2, 1930, and immediately sold four parcels of it, probably to raise some cash. The house itself was built in 1813, according to a date stone set in the chimney. They sold fifteen acres to Harold Hoover, two acres to "Patterson" (first name unknown), one acre to Fletcher Pratt (nephew to Tom), and four acres to "Edwards" (first name unknown), possibly one of Ruby's brothers. Since this sale occurred many years before Tom and

Ruby began "courting," it is not known whether Tom knew Ruby at this time. Ruby would have been 19 years old and still legally married to Carl Meeks. After all the sales, Tom and Nettie were left owning sixty-four acres of land.

Herbert Pratt remembered the work that went into preparing the property to make a working farm. He was also my source for describing how tobacco was raised before the days of modern machinery and "factory" farming.

A cord of wood measured four feet high by four feet wide by eight feet long.

The amount of tobacco that one farmer was allowed to grow was restricted after Franklin Roosevelt became president in 1932, as a way to keep competition and prices up. Bills of sale from Tom Pratt's papers to the tobacco warehouses show varying amounts of tobacco produced. In 1945, Tom sold 688 pounds of differing quality for between thirty-five cents and forty-seven cents per pound, totaling $319.54 for his crop. Two years later, the year he died in 1947, he sold 304 pounds for only $55.04. The price per pound was only between eleven cents and twenty-nine cents, probably due to broken leaves, which could be used for snuff but not cigarettes.

A later owner of the property cut down the apple orchard to grow tobacco, but a few apples trees still stand.

Jake and Reid were on "short time" at the mill during some of the 1930s, when the mills had to cut everyone's hours back or go out of business. They used the extra tune time to help their father on the farm.

Nothing more is remembered of "Aunt Caroline" than what is written here, including her last name. Herbert Pratt remembers her "strange" (i.e., Chicago) accent, and that at times he could not understand her. Clyde Pratt did take her to church with his family.

Custis Clifton told me the story of how she met Reid, and that Old Mammie clearly was playing matchmaker.

Notes on Chapter 3: Tom and Ruby

No one really knows how Tom and Ruby came to be a couple. Ruby's family lived not far from Tom's farm. Tom could have easily known her from the sale of his garden vegetables or from seeing her on his walks. But how he approached her, or she him, so that it would come to pass that they would marry, is unknown. The scenes in which Tom bought the ring and proposed to Ruby are also pure fiction, though obviously they had to have discussed it in order to do it. What is not fiction was that Tom was smitten with her. His grandchildren and some great-grandchildren remember that he was head over heels.

Tom's actual age at the time of obtaining the marriage license in Wentworth was 77, although the license said 78. The information was written in script, not typed. Did Tom forget how old he was in all his excitement?

There were separate marriage registers by race ("white" and "colored"). On June 12, 1967, the Supreme Court unanimously ruled that states could not bar interracial marriages. The North Carolina General Assembly did not officially repeal the ban until 1977.

Ruby listed her marital status as "divorced" on both marriage licenses, so Tom had to have known she had been previously married at least once. Whether he knew about both ex-husbands is unknown.

Cultural and social mores were extremely strong and largely defined by religion. Protestant church teachings dictated the value systems of most people, including those who were not church-goers. These were fervent, unwavering beliefs in (a) the resurrected, living Jesus; (b) the teachings of the Bible; (c) a personal relationship with Jesus through prayer; (d) actions a person must take to "be saved" (that is, go to Heaven); (e) what constitutes sin; and (f) that Heaven and Hell were real places, not allegorical symbols. These beliefs created powerful standards of acceptable and unacceptable behavior. People who deviated from these standards would pay a social price. For example, in the mill, people were addressed by their titles and surnames–Mr. Jones, Mrs. Brown. But if woman had an illegitimate baby, the other workers might address her using "Miss" plus her first name, for example, "Miss Clara." It was a subtle insult, but its message would not be lost.

The book *Eden, Past and Present, 1880–1980*, by James E. Gardner, provides excellent descriptions of the mountain people who moved to town to work in the mills, and the mores they brought with them. According to Gardner, in the late nineteenth and early twentieth centuries, "a strong puritanical view apparently was held in regard to such activities as dancing, using tobacco, card playing, divorce, keeping stores open on Sundays, drinking, gambling, and swearing and cursing. By mid-century, some shift was evident in what was regarded as sinful conduct. Dancing, the use of tobacco, card playing (as distinct from gambling), divorce, and keeping stores open on Sunday came to be viewed more tolerantly. However, drinking, gambling, and swearing and cursing were still virtually universally condemned" (page 162). With regard to tobacco use, Herbert Pratt disagrees with Gardner. He recollects that most men smoked or chewed tobacco, even the church elders. Frivolous young women smoked, but not older married women. Then there was "Granny" Owens, who lived across the road from Harold and Edna Hoover, who smoked a corncob pipe.

Oddly enough, though drunkenness was considered sinful, making whiskey was not (nor was "taking a dram," as long as it did not lead to drunkenness). This attitude reflected the highly independent ways of the mountain people, who viewed moonshining as their right, and felt that the law was infringing upon that right.

Another term that was commonly understood was the phrase "good people." Everyone knew that "good people" were those who did "anything they could to help in sickness and other troubles," and were honest, reliable and hardworking. "Bad people" were those who drank to excess, gambled, and failed to support their families. Anything, in fact, that interfered with wage-earning work or "took away from the family" was considered morally offensive (Gardner, page 165). A person who ran out on his family was considered the lowest of the low.

According to the 2000 census, Rockingham County had a population of approximately 92,000 people covering 572 square miles. The Eden telephone directory in 2003 covered the towns of Danbury, Eden, Madison, Mayodan, Reidsville, Ruffin, Sandy Ridge and Stoneville. In it, the Protestant church listings include Apostolic, Assemblies of God, Baptist, Independent Baptist, Southern Baptist, Church of the Brethren, Christian, Church of Christ, Church of God, Church of God in Christ, Community, Episcopal, Evangelical, Friends, Holiness, independent, interdenominational, Methodist, Moravian, nondenominational, Pentecostal Holiness, Presbyterian, United Methodist and Wesleyan—totaling 128 entries. There was one Catholic Church, one Church of Jesus Christ of the Latter Day Saints, and no temples, synagogues or mosques.

It would be safe to say that Protestant belief systems continue to dominate the region.

Notes on Chapter 4: Ruby

"Everybody" in Leaksville had a Karastan rug, which was similar in style to a Persian carpet. "Everybody" had one because they were manufactured there, and Karastan is one of the few mill companies left in Eden to this day.

Herbert Pratt never understood why his grandfather built the house so that the narrow stairs came down into the tiny alcove-sized bedroom instead of turning to end up in the living room. Maybe Tom didn't plan to use the upstairs except for storage. The lights operated on pull-chains, not wall switches. His bedroom light was centrally located on the ceiling and was connected by a string from the pull-chain to the end of his bed so that he could turn it on and off from bed.

Jim Sharp obtained Ruby's work record through 1947 when he investigated her marriages. A person close to Ruby told me she had been a bobbin winder, which was also written in Herbert Pratt's notes about her occupational record. I have also heard that she was a burler in the rug mill. Of course it's possible that she had several jobs over her long career.

According to Herbert Pratt, mill workers would literally run to their cars at the end of the shift, but often came in early for the luxury of using the toilets. They had outhouses at home. Houses started to be updated at the end of World War II.

Much has been written about life in mill towns in the South. In Leaksville, Spray and Draper, there was generally a sense of loyalty to the mills. Marshall Field, later called Fieldcrest, operated six textile mills for yarn, gingham, sheets, cotton and woolen blankets, and hosiery. The

Spray Cotton Mill, the Leaksville Cotton and Woolen Mill, and the Morehead Cotton Mill also drew people in from neighboring counties because of work opportunities that didn't exist elsewhere. The mills provided living wages, housing at lower rents, education for the children, recreational facilities, and health care for employees. A $7,500 grant from the Marshall Field Company, along with loans from Spray Cotton Mills, the Carolina Cotton and Woolen Mill, and other sources, allowed the opening of Leaksville Hospital in 1924, which also had a nursing school. During the Depression, the mills shortened their hours rather than lay people off. Even though their paternalistic approach to workers became controversial over time, the economic opportunities provided by the mills allowed many people to enjoy a much better life for themselves and their children.

Fieldcrest Mills worked closely with town leaders and civic organizations such as the Lions Club to sponsor activities that promoted civic pride. The pageant that was scheduled to take place in the fall of 1947 was one example. It included a play about town history with a cast of about 150 drawn from the towns and was held in the ballpark.

Mr. Tolbert was Ruby's foreman at Fieldcrest and served as a character witness for the prosecution at the trial.

Herbert Pratt described the process of cone winding to me. The number of cones one winder could produce on a shift would vary depending on the diameter of the yarn and the number of winding positions on the equipment, typically about forty, and the frequency of yarn breakage.

The "dope wagon" was what we would call a "coffee wagon" today. It sold Coca-Colas and sandwiches. The caffeine and sugar in Coke helped keep the employees alert. The machines never stopped running

250

and employees were paid by what they produced, so employees didn't stop to eat. They just ate "on the run."

Ruby had a reputation for socializing. One person told me, "She was notorious for going around with different men." Another one said, "She had a boyfriend who drove her everywhere–to the trial and everywhere." Regardless of the specifics, her socializing became the basis of many fights with Tom. He'd calm down at Pearl's house and then go home again.

I don't know the date of Ruby's mother's death (Lillie Edwards), but her youngest sister Lucille was born in 1930 (1930-1988). Ruby listed her mother as "deceased" on the marriage license in 1943. I have speculated about the nature of the relationship between Ruby and her father, Ruffin Edwards.

Ruby married Carl Meeks (who filed for divorce but didn't complete it) on April 8, 1926 when she was 16. She married Charlie Corum on November 4, 1933, when she was 23.

The circumstances of Ruby's first marriages are not known; the section describing why she married those men is pure speculation. I don't know how she met them, why she married them or why the marriages ended. I don't know whether Mr. Corum worked at the mill. There was one clue to the marriages in Mutt Burton's newspaper article about Ruby's trial testimony. It said, "She appeared confused about whether her second husband had obtained an annulment of their marriage after finding out about the first husband but declared she believed herself to be legally free at the time of her marriage to Pratt." The phrase "after finding out about the first husband" indicates to me that she had kept her first marriage a secret from her second husband, and that Price questioned her about the circumstances of her divorces.

I also don't know why Ruby would have married a man forty-five years her senior when she married Tom Pratt, but one suspects that after two failed marriages, she may have become fairly cynical about the nature of "true love." It was not uncommon for older men to marry younger women, even up to twenty years' younger, as the men established their farms or businesses, then married young women. However, even by standards of the day, forty-five years had to have been a stretch.

The first marriage license for Tom and Ruby was returned unused to the Rockingham County Courthouse, but no one knows why. Were they just too busy to get around to getting married within the sixty-day time frame? Or did one of them send it back after an argument? Either way, they didn't marry until December 13, 1943.

No one in the Pratt family knew the circumstances of Tom's and Ruby's wedding. Many people assumed the worst of her, that she somehow tricked him into thinking they were legally married by forging some papers and "fixing up a little ceremony somewhere." I doubt that Tom would have been that naïve, though he did seem blinded by love. On a hunch, my father suggested we take a ride to the courthouse in Henry County, Virginia, as Martinsville was known for "quicky marriages" in those days. Based on the previous license that was returned in August, 1943, we started looking through the marriage registers beginning that same month. We quickly came across the entry that ended part of the mystery that had hung on for over fifty years. Tom and Ruby had, in fact, gotten married on Monday, December 13, 1943. The look of shock on my father's face was priceless.

The person who married Tom and Ruby was listed as J. P. McCabe in the Henry County, Virginia, marriage register. It can be assumed that it is the same Dr. McCabe who was pastor of the First

Baptist Church in Martinsville, Virginia in the 1940s. They may have married in a church, but it is just as likely that Dr. McCabe performed weddings at the courthouse on his days off for a little extra money. That he was listed repeatedly in the register would suggest that this was so.

On both marriage registers (the one from Rockingham County, North Carolina, and the one from Henry County, Virginia,) Ruby listed her last name as "Edwards" and her marital status as "divorced." Apparently she resumed using her maiden name after each divorce. Tom would have known that she was married before, at least once.

Leaksville radio station WLOE first aired on 1490 AM on December 20, 1946 and has been in continuous broadcast since that time. The call letters stood for the "Wonderful Land of Eden," prescient to the change of the town name in 1967. In 1990 WLOE merged with WMYN of Mayodan (call letters which stood for, "We Make Your Name.") The current format is information, talk, and Christian broadcast.

Notes on Chapter 5: The Attack

This chapter is deliberately ambiguous. What really happened in the few minutes before this chapter begins? I wish we knew. Much of the information in this chapter comes from newspaper accounts and from interviews with the few people who remember it.

When Ruby tried to get help for Tom, it's thought that she ran up the lane yelling, or screamed, to summon Coy Ratliff, the tenant farmer who lived on the Pratt property about 150 yards away. While telephone lines were rapidly being installed in the towns, they were still rare out in the rural areas where Tom and Ruby lived. One of Governor Greg Cherry's campaign platforms in 1945 was the expansion of telephone and electrical services. *The Leaksville News* printed the cartoon shown below on

October 30, 1947 (used with permission). It summed up the new arrival of telephones to the country town:

THE LEAKSVILLE NEWS, LEAKSVILLE, N. C.

"I CAN HARDLY WAIT."

J. Holt

Notes on Chapter 6: Death of Old Pa

Information for this chapter came from interviews with the Pratt family, from newspaper articles and from reviewing Tom Pratt's death certificate.

Custis's account of how her father was shot and killed at a church picnic up in the mountains was both fascinating and tragic. The Presbyterian church to which they belonged believed in predestination, meaning that if it was your time to die, you would die. If it were not your time to die, you would live. Men shot at each other recklessly– almost as a game, believing fully that their lives were in the Lord's hands regardless of their own behavior. Custis was the oldest child, about four years of age, when the four faithful (and drunk) men were shot and killed that day. For an interesting account of people who lived in Buffalo Mountain, Virginia, just over the North Carolina state line, in the early years of the twentieth century, see Richard C. David's book called *The Man Who Moved A Mountain* (Philadelphia, Fortress Press, 1970).

By today's standards, Tom Pratt was at the house for a considerable amount of time, badly injured, before help was to arrive. But even if help had arrived sooner, he probably would not have survived. Large masses of blood were collecting around his brain, and there was no neurosurgery in those days, at least not at the Leaksville Hospital, that could have saved him. Wink Hoover and Colleen Shropshire have said that Old Pa was semiconscious when they saw him, though they couldn't get him to say much. It is consistent with a subdural hematoma that this was possible, since the internal blood loss that would eventually lead to coma and death could have been occurring slowly.

Tom Pratt died at 6:30 p.m. on August 25, 1947, less than twenty-four hours after the attack. The death certificate lists the cause of death as "fracture of skull, intracranial injury, subdural hemotona [sic]."

There are several inaccuracies on the death certificate, making one wonder whether the paperwork was put aside to be filled out on another day. The mistakes are as follows:

• The length of the hospital stay says "48 hours." This is incorrect, since he was brought in around 1:30 a.m. on August 25 and died about 6 p.m. that same day.

• The name of the attending physician, R. P. Harris was typed, not signed, although "signature" is designated for both the physician and the informant.

• A section of the certificate is designated to be filled out if death was due to external causes, including accident, suicide, or homicide, along with the means of injury. This section was left blank.

• Tom Pratt's name was listed as Tom W. Pratt, but his true name was William Thomas Pratt.

• Ruby's listed age, 35, was incorrect. She was 36.

• The "informant" was listed as Tom W. Pratt, Jr. (also typed, not signed). However, Jake Pratt's real name was Thomas B. Pratt.

• Most important, the date of death was listed as August 26. The correct date, August 25, was verified by funeral home records of when they received the body. This was critical because death occurred within twenty-four hours of the assault. This fact makes the criminal charge murder.

The many mistakes on the death certificate stand in stark contrast to today's standards, in which precise laws and regulations must be strictly followed. The handling of the crime scene is another example where the investigative techniques appeared to have been so casual that any physical evidence that was obtained likely would have been rendered useless.

Notes on Chapter 7: Munsey Hodges

Source material for the chapter included a newspaper article delineating the content of Sheriff Hodges's report to the county commissioners, and Munsey Hodges's obituary. I'm speculating that this unsolved murder would have stolen the thunder of his first-year success at the commissioner's meeting, as people's attention and questions would have been drawn to the murder. It is true that the commissioners as well as other unnamed persons offered rewards for the capture of the murderer.

The newspaper article describing Hodges's report to the commissioners listed his accomplishments as described in the text. "Execution notices" refers to the process of collecting a payment that has been ruled upon by judge in a lawsuit.

The Leaksville mayor was John Smith, who served from 1947 to 1955, and again from 1963 to 1967, when Leaksville, Spray and Draper merged. Many years later, Mayor Smith's daughter Irma married Sheriff Hodges's son Troy.

Bootleggers would move the moonshine across state lines to avoid arrest. If the North Carolina sheriff were coming, they'd put the whiskey in their truck and move it into Virginia. The North Carolina sheriff would have no jurisdiction in Virginia. Of course, if the Virginia sheriff were coming, they'd move it back again to North Carolina. According to Herbert Pratt, one enterprising man, Ernest Mabes, actually built a store that straddled the Virginia and North Carolina state lines. He could move his whiskey stock (moonshine) across state lines without ever having to leave his store.

Deputy Curtis Land was an informal standard of measurement around Leaksville. It was a common expression that any particular person might be "not as big as Curtis Land, as big as Curtis Land, or bigger than Curtis Land." Everyone knew who he was and how big he was, too.

Notes on Chapter 8: Munsey and Ruby

This chapter is speculative regarding Munsey's interview of Ruby, though certainly he would have interviewed her, probably repeatedly. Did he suggest to her that Junior was a likely suspect? Did she hear somewhere else that Junior was a prison escapee, and did that gave her the idea? Did she think it over and decide that it had been Junior, not a large man, after all? None of this is known. We do know that she never wavered from her accusation of Junior once she named him; yet Junior did not match her description of the attacker at all.

What does seem clear is that Munsey appeared to focus all his attention on capturing Junior Thompson despite of Ruby's description of the attacker as a large man. Whether Munsey interrogated other "large men" is not known. Other than Ruby's eyewitness identification of Junior, no other physical evidence was presented against Junior, making Solicitor Ralph Scott's case a difficult one.

Enough people suggested a romantic liaison between Munsey and Ruby that I hint of it in the story. However, of the few people who still remember the events of 1947, no one could give me any direct information about it. It all was hearsay. Rather than treat this rumor as fact (though it would have made for a juicier story), I have been intentionally ambiguous about it. These were, after all, real people, to whom we should give the benefit of the doubt.

Notes on Chapter 9: The Line-up

Junior was held in the jail at the Guilford County Courthouse in Greensboro, about thirty miles south of Leaksville. This may have been for his own protection, or it may have been due to a lack of confidence that the local jail could secure him.

According to newspaper accounts, the line-up did include eight men who exchanged some items of clothing between identifications. Ruby was asked to identify the attacker four times. The investigators apparently took extra steps to ensure that the defense could not punch a hole in the identification process.

Notes on Chapter 10: Jake and Clyde

This conversation between the brothers, or something like it, had to have taken place in order for events to unfold as they did, but exactly what was said is my speculation.

Herbert Pratt remembers that his parents Jake and Josie had a large photograph of his grandmother Nettie hanging in their bedroom. At the end of a visit, Tom would say "I want to go see Nettie before I go," and he would stand for a few minutes looking at it.

If Ruby had been legally married to Tom and there was no will, she would have received a "child's part" of the inheritance. In other words, according to the laws of the day, a second wife would share equally in the inheritance with the children from the former marriage.

"Well-Digger Jones" was a real person who searched the well on Sheriff Hodges's orders and at Jake Pratt's request. He was aptly nicknamed for his profession. It is not known what his real name was.

One rumor that was floated at that time was that Ruby's brother Marion had inquired about Tom Pratt's bank account the day after the attack. I have no idea if this is true, but it was said at the time. And even if it were true, the reason could have been innocent enough: Ruby may have had to pay a hospital bill or thought she had to pay for a funeral (the payment came out of the estate.)

The state of North Carolina has employed four methods of execution. It used hanging until electrocution was invented in the early part of the twentieth century. Electrocution, which was considered a more humane method than hanging, was used until 1935. It used lethal gas from 1935 until 1972, when the Supreme Court abolished the death penalty. In 1976, this ruling was overturned and the death penalty was reinstated as a states' issue. North Carolina continued to use lethal gas from 1976 until 1983, when it switched to lethal injection.

Jake and Clyde's decision to pay for Junior's defense, given that they were living in rural North Carolina in 1947, was momentous. Racial divide was gripping the country, not just the South. The issue loomed in the background of all events, from political (the denial of voting rights; segregation), to economic (denial of job opportunities to blacks), to social (how people addressed one another). For example, the *Greensboro Daily News* ran a photo of 20-year old Iris Alexander with the caption, "Dated Negro." A Wisconsin college student, she had been evicted by her landlords for dating a "Negro" student. In fact, anti-miscegenation laws that made interracial marriage illegal were on the books until 1967, when the Supreme Court overturned them. North Carolina was one of fifteen states that still had such laws on the books at that time. Most people just accepted it as "the way it was." In the Leaksville area, race relations were without heat—the Depression had served as a great equalizer, in that nearly everyone was poor. There was little or no Ku Klux Klan activity until some years later, when the civil rights movement gathered steam. However, lynchings were not unheard of, and if any black man had been found in the woods behind Tom Pratt's house on the night of the attack, vigilante "justice" likely would have prevailed. Just think of the headline that ran in the *Madison (N.C.) Messenger* after Junior's acquittal: "Negro is Acquitted of Murdering White Man." How often was the testimony of a white witness, no matter how flimsy, challenged when it came to a black defendant?

On the other hand, Jake and Clyde had grown up living and working side-by-side with black men and boys on the farms, and they were friends. Jake and Clyde's willingness to defend a black person against murder did not happen because they were what we today call "liberals." These were men who followed a conservative moral code on all the matters of the day. They were patriotic, politically conservative, and firm believers in the Protestant work ethic. They went to church, Bible classes and prayer meetings, and did not drink, swear, play cards or tell "dirty jokes." As such, their decision to defend Junior came from their religious convictions, which taught them to "do unto others as they would have others do unto them" and from a profound sense of fairness and justice they believed should prevail regardless of race. However, the same moral code that led them to support Junior Thompson would have also led them to suspect Ruby of wrongdoing. They had definite ideas of what was proper behavior for women and men. Her behavior was outside those bounds. While she was definitely inconsistent in her description of the attacker, one also has to assume that some prejudice against her came into play in their decision. Apparently, most of the community agreed with them.

The Tri-City Directory for Leaksville, Spray and Draper was a precursor to a telephone directory. It listed the names, addresses, and occupations of every adult in the three cities. Consistent with the South's obsession with race, listings for black citizens had a © after their names, for "colored."

Justice Sharp told the story of the elderly black man coming to visit her "just to see what a woman lawyer looked like" when she was appointed superior court judge. The story was printed in the newspaper in 1949.

It always has been part of the folklore of this story that Jake and Clyde Pratt paid the attorney fees for Junior Thompson. This is what Herbert Pratt had always thought. However, in going through Jake Pratt's papers, he said he could find no financial receipt for or record of it. Jake Pratt never had a checking account and paid cash for everything. It is possible that Hampton Price did the work *pro bono*. It is also possible that the Pratts gave Edd Thompson Sr., the funds to cover the cost. It would have made sense to stay one step removed from that attorney-client relationship, and perhaps to allow Mr. Thompson to "save face" in accepting charity. (Mr. Thompson could then pay Mr. Price himself.) There is one other reason to think that the Pratt brothers did pay for the attorney. One day I said to Carl Thompson, Junior's distant cousin, "Carl, I've always heard that my grandfather paid for the attorney, but I really have no proof of it." Carl said, "Well, they did!" "How do you know?" I asked. "Because my family always said they did!" That's proof enough for me.

Notes on Chapter 11: A Few Answers

The date of the chapter is approximate. The visit to Jim Sharp occurred sometime that fall. There is a date of December 2, 1947 on Herbert Pratt's notes, and he remembers the car ride there (in his Uncle Clyde's car) to have been quite cold. However, Jake Pratt testified in the trial that they tried to have Ruby removed as executrix, which suggests that they had already spoken to an attorney about it. Perhaps there was more than one meeting.

Notes on Chapter 12: Jury Selection

Source material for this chapter, and the following ones on the trial, came from indictments, criminal dockets and court records related to jury selection–including the Order for Special Venire–and jury pool list. The jury pool list featured the name of each potential juror, the town of residence, and for some people, an abbreviation "(Col.)" after the name. I was stumped as to what "Col." could mean. Once again I was confronted with the issue of race: "Col." meant "colored." It is another stark reminder that Jake and Clyde Pratt took an extraordinary step when they crossed the color line to pay for Junior's defense attorney.

The Order for Special Venire expanded the jury pool to 75 names. Each name is listed with the hometown. Three of the names have a note next to them that say, "Dr. Ct" or "Doctor certificate." Presumably, these people brought in a doctor's note to be excused. It so happens that all three of them were women.

Names as listed: 1. N. L. Case, Madison; 2. John M. Jones, Reidsville; 3. Joe Ben Hodges, Reidsville; 4. W. R. Barnes, Reidsville; 5. A. R. Gunn, Wentworth; 6. Joe F. Baugn, Mayo; 7. Marion Caudle, Mrs., Mayo; 8. Mrs. H. W. Stanfield, Williamsburg *(Dr. Ct.)*; 9. Mrs. G. H. Miller, Reidsville; 10. C. L. Combs, Draper; 11. Ben Aiken, Col., Leaksville; 12. Marvin McMichael, Draper; 13. E. H. Jones, Reidsville R-5; 14. Robert Dalton, Col., Mayo; 15. Orien Knight, Madison; 16. J. F. Burgess, Draper; 17. Mrs. Hunter Carter, Simpsonville; 18. E. P. Rothrock, Leaksville; 19. Bennie Williams, Williamsburg; 20. Mrs. E. V. Stephenson, Madison; 21. Mrs. Senola Neal, Col., Reidsville; 22. Joseph Brown, Draper; 23. Monroe Pinnix, Col., Williamsburg; 24. Mrs. P. G. Beville, Simponsville; 25. T. J. Fargis, Reidsville; 26. W. J. Crowder,

Ruffin; 27. Monroe Alley, Mayo; 28. H. J. Frye, Mayo; 29 H. F. Hankins, Mayo; 30. Hugh T. Lea, Leaksville; 31. J. W. Childrey, Reidsville, R-2; 32. Harry Hylton, Ruffin; 33. John W. Gwynn, Reidsville; 34. F. R. Price, Mayo; 35. John Allen McDonald, Mayo; 36. Harry Knight, Mayo; 37. R. E. Snead, Mayo; 38. Walter Stone, Reidsville, R-3; 39. J. A. Moore, Williamsburg; 40. Clyde Comer, Mayo; 41. Aubrey Leake, Mayo; 42. A. Herman Simpson, Reidsville R-2; 43. G. A. Dillon, Madison; 44. Dillard Peay, Reidsville; 45. J. F. DeLancey, Reidsville; 46. J. Henry Roberts, Mayo; 47. Mrs. Fleeta Scales, Col., Reidsville; 48. Dan G. Taylor, Leaksville, *Excused by Judge*; 49. M. B. Newman, Draper; 50. J. W. Barber, Draper; 51. Roy Flynn, Madison; 52. Mrs. B. B. Gentry, Simpsonville, *Dr. Ct.*; 53. J. D. Pyrtle, Leaksville; 54. G. A. Barham, Reidsville; 55. Mrs. O. A. Rothrock, Reidsville; 56. Mrs. John D. Crowder, Wentworth, *Deceased*; 57. D. W. Shelton, Spray; 58. Mrs. R. W. Crutchfield, Reidsville, *Dr. Certificate attached*; 59. Mr. G. Lee Somers, Reidsville; 60. Rodney West, Reidsville; 61. B. E. Ivie, Leaksville; 62. D. Y. Adams, Wentworth; 63. Mrs. Jessie Tuttle, Madison; 64. Jonothan Baynes, Wentworth; 65. Clyde Zimmerman, Williamsburg; 66. D. G. Huggins, Leaksville; 67. Mrs. Sam L. Eisenberg, Leaksville; 68. Mrs. James Edd Carter, Wentworth; 69. J. H. Leasure, Col., Leaksville R-1; 70. M. D. Rakes, Leaksville; 71. Mrs. W. L. Patterson, Williamsburg; 72. Mrs. Julia Mullins, Col., Reidsville; 73. Russell Draper, Wentworth; 74. Walter Gillespie, Reidsville; 75. Geo. A. Whitten, Leaksville.

Incredibly, the actual trial transcripts were purposely and completely destroyed, as was the practice in those days when a person accused of a crime was acquitted. W. C. ("Mutt") Burton's newspaper accounts are the only record I have of what actually occurred in that courtroom, and I am grateful for his detailed descriptions. Without it, I'd hardly have a story to write.

Apparently it was not an uncommon practice for young children to serve the state by choosing juries. The Order for Special Venire for the state of North Carolina against Junior Edd Thompson states "...that 75 scrolls be drawn from Jury Box No. 1 by a child under ten years of age and the names so drawn shall constitute the special venire and the Clerk of this Court shall insert the names appearing on the scrolls so drawn..." On October 29, 1947, Douglas Taylor, five years old, who had been approved by the court, did indeed select the jury for this trial in the presence of Junior Thompson and his attorney. He was paid one dollar by the county commissioners of Rockingham County for his services. Douglas Taylor's father, Captain Taylor, was warden for the State Prison near Wentworth.

A posse of both Rockingham County deputies and Henry County, Virginia deputies were on the trail of Junior Thompson during the week but unable to track his exact whereabouts without bloodhounds. Sheriff Hodges attempted on three occasions to borrow bloodhounds from Orange and Randolph counties, but each time was told the dogs were not available. When he made it publicly known that failure to get the dogs was impeding progress, Captain J. M. Barnes, supervisor of prison camps for the Fifth District, sent them immediately, along with a keeper trained to help animals track their quarry. The dogs were kept at State Prison Camp 509 near Wentworth.

Jury selection only took a few hours, which was very fast by today's standards for a murder trial. I have speculated about the questions the attorneys asked while screening potential jurors. I think it is possible that women were questioned about whether they felt they were able to listen to grisly details of a murder.

The jury was sequestered at the Belvedere Hotel in Reidsville. The trial took place in Wentworth, and the jury undoubtedly was transported there by bus or in deputy police cars.

I don't know if Judge Bobbitt's instructions to the jury included a reference to the women who had been empanelled, but he did offer a quote to a newspaper that it was, to his knowledge, the first capital case in North Carolina with women on the jury. He must have thought it notable.

Notes on Chapter 13: The Trial, Day 1

The description of how Junior Thompson was dressed for the trial is true. The suit was similar in style to Hampton Price's, and hung on Junior just a little bit big.

Ruby and Dr. Harris had testified twice already. The first time was at a preliminary hearing against Thompson on September 19 in the Recorder's Court in Spray on charges of first-degree burglary and murder. Judge Herman Peters presided over this hearing in an overflowing courtroom. Probable cause was found against Junior Thompson, and the case was bound over to superior court at Wentworth for the grand jury. The grand jury met in Rockingham County Superior Court in Wentworth on October 27, 1947. R. A. Clark was the foreman, with Judge William Bobbitt presiding.

The Rockingham County Courthouse in Wentworth was built in 1907 after the previous courthouse burned down. The wings were added in 1938. The jail, directly across the street from the courthouse, was built in 1910 and was used as a jail until the 1970s (it is now used for storage.)

Funds for a new courthouse to be built a few miles from the present one were approved in the fall of 2006.

Newspaper accounts of the murder trial list Ruby's age as 39, as does the interview with her after the trial. Tom Pratt's death certificate lists her as spouse, with her age as 35. The Social Security Death Index lists her birth year as 1909, while her grave marker lists her birth year as 1911. Assuming that her grave marker is correct and that she was born on February 11, 1911, she would have been 36 years old when Tom Pratt was murdered. The newspaper accounts said that Tom was 82, but he was 81.

Notes on Chapter 14: The Trial, Day 2

The testimony as described in the three trial chapters was taken from W. C. ("Mutt") Burton's columns in the *Greensboro Daily News*. Except for a few incidences, I don't know exactly what was said, but all the names and the substance of the testimony is factual. Nothing has been inserted. Coy Ratliff did indeed testify that he had asked the police officers to lock him in one jail cell and Ruby in an adjoining cell so that he could question her himself.

I have speculated as to what Mr. Price and Mr. Scott said in their summations. We do know, however, that Mr. Scott's summation lasted ninety minutes, and we can guess that it irked the jury.

Notes on Chapter 15: Trial, Day 3

The story about Mr. Rakestraw is true, but it wasn't Mutt Burton's story. Mr. Rakestraw, Ida Lampkins, Dummy Martin, Danny Dean and Jim Lampkins were real people. Herbert Pratt attended the trial when he was about 12 years old with his dad Jake, and witnessed the exchange. It was Jake Pratt who tugged on Mr. Rakestraw's sleeve and got him to understand who the stuttering man was, and to be quiet.

Solicitor Ralph Scott failed to get a conviction. What evidence had he really presented? All he had was Ruby's testimony. Was the word of a white woman against a black man so sacrosanct in those days that he thought nothing more would be required? Was Mr. Scott overconfident, or was he unable to present any further evidence, such as Thompson's clothes found at his hideout? The verdict pleased people in the courtroom and the community, either because they agreed with the Pratt brothers that Junior had to be innocent, or as a way to punish Ruby for what was considered to be immoral behavior. However, most people also felt that Ralph Scott had not been very aggressive in prosecuting this case.

Hamp Price, the defense attorney, ruined Ruby's credibility with the jury by not only attacking her eyewitness description, but by questioning her reputation through his line of questions. Junior Thompson never took the stand in his own defense, a wise move by Price. The immature and unsophisticated Thompson may have become easily rattled on the witness stand and made to appear guilty, whether he was or not. The jury took only one hour to reach its verdict.

Mutt Burton reported the audience's reaction to the verdict this way: "After lunch recess, the jury took the case at 1:30 p.m. When, an hour later, the jury returned the verdict of not guilty there was a brief ovation from the main floor of the courtroom filled with white citizens. The demonstration of approval was stilled by a sharp rap from Judge Bobbitt's gavel." Thank you, Mr. Burton, for that vivid description.

The Leaksville News was founded in 1924 by J. S. Robertson. In 1943, Robertson named his son, Richard Robertson, editor-in-chief. Beverly W. Robertson, Richard's wife, sometimes wrote freelance newspaper articles that appeared in the local daily newspapers such as the *Greensboro Daily News* or the *Winston-Salem Sentinel.* At some point in the late 1940s or early 1950s, in between having children and doing freelance writing for the local dailies, Mrs. Robertson became the managing editor of *The Leaksville News*. Mrs. Robertson says that although her job mostly involved typing, she did a little bit of everything–except clean the bathroom. *The Leaksville News* changed its name to *The Eden News* in 1967 and remained a weekly paper until 1972, when it became semi-weekly. It became a daily paper in 1980. Mr. and Mrs. Robertson are retired and have homes in Eden and Virginia.

Greensboro, North Carolina's major daily newspapers were the *Greensboro Daily News* (founded in 1909) and the *Greensboro Record* (founded as *The Daily Record* in 1890). The two merged in March 1982 to be called the *Greensboro News and Record*. In 1992 the name changed to the *News and Record.*

The Leaksville News did not try to compete with the big city dailies. Its readership wanted local stories about local people and events–who had a birthday bash; where a revival meeting was to be held; news of the mills, schools, churches, clubs, boards; police activities; obituaries. A wonderful example of local news comes from the following article, reprinted here, first printed on October 23, 1947:

*****

Season's First Coon is Taken After Battle

The first coon of the season was treed and killed early Saturday morning on the Walter Bratcher farm on Troublesome Creek. He was a fine, big 12-pound coon and he put up a furious fight before the dogs finally conquered him.

The hunting party from Leaksville was composed of Bull Russian, Sam Reynolds, Sandy Frazier, and Bud Shelton, with five dogs, including Old Drum, battle-scarred veteran of many a clash with denizens of he woods and swamps. Mr. Bratcher joining the party and brought his young dog which, after it was all over, he said he had gained much good experience.

It was 3 a.m. before the dogs scented their game and treed him. The coon was high up a huge oak tree about the size of one of those big trees in the yard of Burton Grove School. It was a perfectly sound tree, valuable for lumber. Mr. Bratcher, the owner, did not hesitate. 'Cut her down,' he called, 'get your axes.'

They chopped and chopped and chopped. It took three hours before the big tree gave up the ghost. When it thundered to the ground Mr. Coon was with it, securely ensconced in a recess of the upper limbs. The dogs pounced, but they backed up quickly. In the hollow limb the coon was protected, all but his face. He bit every dog that came within range. One of the dogs was covered with blood. Finally Old Drum, who with a pal named King had led the fight, dived in and pulled the coon out.

And they said it wasn't a good night for hunting, either.

*****

One has to admire that the article contained not only the names of the hunters, but also the names of their dogs.

This chapter about Ruby was based on two newspaper articles that ran in the *Greensboro Daily News* (approximate date November 16, 1947) and *The Leaksville News* (November 27, 1947.) Beverly W. Robertson wrote the article that appeared in the *Greensboro Daily News* as a freelance reporter. It was then excerpted for the Leaksville paper. By reading the two articles side-by-side, it is obvious that *The Leaksville News* article is simply a summary of the *Greensboro Daily News* article. Interestingly, Robertson's name was dropped from the byline when it was printed in the Leaksville paper. A copy editor may have edited the article for space; still, it is interesting to see what was added and what was left out. Besides adding the information about her missing dog, the Leaksville paper also added information about Ruby being a second shift worker for Fieldcrest Mills. People today might imagine that the job information was an insult ("just a factory worker.") In fact, the residents of Leaksville were grateful to Fieldcrest for their jobs and proud of their association with the company, whom they felt treated them well. So this particular quote, beyond simply stating the facts, implies to me a certain mark of respect for Ruby's employment.

The Bill Hawkins Studio was a photography studio that existed for a short time in Leaksville. *The Leaksville News* didn't have its own photographer, so if a photo was needed, local studios were contracted to provide it.

The various terms used to refer to race were changing. *The Leaksville News*, a small weekly newspaper, referred to black citizens as "colored people." During that same period, the more cosmopolitan *Greensboro Daily News* used the term "Negroes." The term "black" did not come into usage until the 1960s.

Proving that segregation was everywhere, including the newspaper, "The Colored News" feature was apparently a new one in 1947. In the September 11, 1947 edition of *The Leaksville News*, the following notice was placed:

*****

Correspondent Wanted to Write Colored News. Wanted–correspondent to write and bring in news about activities of colored people. The pay is small but here is an opportunity to see what you write in print. It is not necessary but preferable, that you have a telephone. Any colored person interested may contact The News office at its location.

*****

Today, we would view the "Colored News" feature as racist and such a job notice would be illegal. However, by the standards of the day, a feature called "Colored News" may have been seen as progressive. After all, without it, there might have been no news of the black community in the paper at all. By late September 1947, one Maxine Allen was writing these articles.

Why had Ruby agreed to be interviewed for the article featuring her? What were her reactions to seeing her words in print? My chapter gives those speculations, but it is pure fiction. Perhaps she was perfectly happy with both the *Greensboro Daily News* story and the truncated version in *The Leaksville News*. I don't know, but I strongly suspect, that *The Leaksville News'* decision to run her article in the back of the paper next to "Colored News" was indeed a mild rebuke. I believe that Ruby suffered deep humiliation with the very public revelation of her past marriages, and the fact that the jury came back so quickly with a "not guilty" verdict, clearly not believing her sworn testimony. Questions floated then, as now, about whether she was directly or indirectly involved in the murder. I do think she was trying to promote the opinion that she was a "good person." I think that the second, edited version of the article did not let her make that case as effectively as the Greensboro article. I think she would have been disappointed, at least, in the Leaksville version. I think it possible that she found it very upsetting for the reasons described in the chapter.

Notes on Chapter 17: Life Goes On

After his death, Tom's children sold his farm to Yancey Joyce who owned adjoining property. Yancey was owner, with his brother Frank, of the Floyd Hill Furniture Company on The Boulevard in Leaksville.

Notes on Chapter 18: Edward Thompson, Outlaw

According to Carl Thompson, Edward Thompson's distant cousin, many in the black community were both afraid of Thompson and somewhat enthralled to have seen him. Many claimed to have seen him "around" whether they had or not, wanting bragging rights.

One person who did not want to see him was Carl Thompson's brother, another Edward Thompson. (Carl and Edward's father was also named Edward.) This cousin Edward had just returned from serving in Vietnam, and was quite alarmed to hear about Junior's outlaw status. Having the same name, being from the same county, and being roughly the same age as the outlaw, he had every reason to believe he could have been shot by just about anyone. He went to the police to identify himself, but he didn't rest easy until his cousin Junior was behind bars.

Carl Axsom, the Rockingham County sheriff, came under some fire in the press when he was accused of missing an opportunity to capture Edward Thompson. One article appeared on Sunday, July 20, 1968 in the *Winston-Salem Sentinel*. The article suggests that Edwards was in the Eden area before going to Virginia to murder Freeman and Davis and to kidnap the girls on July 16th. If Axsom had caught Edwards, the article suggested, those crimes would not have occurred.

According to the article, a witness named Dusty Hamlin, who lived alone in the Price Road neighborhood, claimed to have gone to bed early on Sunday evening, July 14. He awoke around 10 p.m. to the sound of snores. "I switched on the light and there was this outlaw fellow in the bed beside me. It was him, all right. I've known him for years—ever since he was a boy. He woke up, too, when I turned on the light. I asked him, 'Where's your gun?' 'I hid my gun outside,' he told me."

Hamlin said he sneaked out of the house when Thompson fell asleep again. He ran down the road and encountered the local grocery store owner, Bobby Robertson, and his wife, in their car. They brought him back to his neighborhood and let him off, then went to report the sighting to the police. "We told Deputy John Gallimore and the one-armed jailer [George Weatherford], who were on duty at the time, that Thompson was asleep in Dusty's house. Then we came back on home and went to bed." Gallimore did investigate the outside of the house, saw that it was dark and quiet with no signs of a disturbance, and did not enter.

The Eden police maintained that Thompson was in the Roanoke, Virginia area at that time, and that these reports were false. Sheriff Axsom explained, "We have received all kinds of reports. We had one call that he was down in the woods off Price Road with a woman who was screaming her head off. We went down there and found a donkey braying. He was

274

also supposed to have been out back of somebody's house, but it turned out to be a dog in a trash can." Other callers reported that Thompson had been seen on the roof of Morehead Memorial Hospital, in an old barn on Price Road and in a home in the Blue Creek section of Eden. As for Dusty Hamlin who claimed Thompson was in the bed with him, Sheriff Axsom had this to say, "He was drunk at the time. He was drunk the next morning. He was drunk that night, and he is drunk now. Practically everyone on Price Road knows Dusty tells all sorts of tales when he is drunk."

Monroe M. Redden Sr. (1901 - 1987) graduated from Wake Forest College law school in 1923. He practiced law in his hometown of Hendersonville, North Carolina, and became active in the Democratic Party there. Working his way up through party committees, he was elected to Congress from the Twelfth District and served from 1947 to 1953. He then returned to Hendersonville, resumed his law practice, and was the president of the Southern Heritage Life Insurance Company from 1956 to 1959, and chairman of the board of directors of Home Bank and Trust Company.

Judge Harry C. Martin (born in 1920) appointed Monroe Redden to be Edward Thompson's defense attorney in 1968. At that time, Martin was resident superior court judge for Buncombe County, having been appointed by Governor Dan K. Moore in 1967. In 1982, he was appointed associate justice of the North Carolina Supreme Court by Gov. James B. Hunt, Jr. This was the second judge in Edward Thompson's life as a criminal defendant who went on to sit on the North Carolina Supreme Court.

Prison records for North Carolina inmates are available on the internet. Death certificates are available through the Bureau of Vital Statistics for a small fee.

Edward Thompson's birth date is recorded in prison records as June 18, 1931. Listings of Thompson's age are not consistent throughout court documentation or newspaper accounts. The earliest court record that could be found, dated January 11, 1945, stated his age to be 15. However, in January 1945 Junior would have been only 13. Therefore it is possible that his first jail time was served starting at age 13. Tom Pratt's murder occurred in August 1947, when Thompson would have been 16. Newspapers all stated his age as 17.

He had one disciplinary infraction on his prison record, on March 14, 1988, for weapon possession.

According to his death certificate, Edward Thompson died of pneumonia and CMV (cytomegalovirus) secondary to an AIDS infection. Substance abuse might partially explain his increasingly violent behavior. The incidence of AIDS nationwide in prisons is higher than in the general population because of the large number of people who have risk factors for HIV. Of course, it is not known how he contracted the virus while incarcerated, but he may have shared a contaminated syringe while abusing drugs. According to a 1997 Emory University document, the number of prison deaths from AIDS was 325 in 1985 and 4,588 in 1994. Thompson died on July 18, 1989.

Notes on Chapter 19: Ruby Edwards

Source material for this chapter came from people who knew her later in life. I have not revealed their names in order to protect their privacy.

Bibliography

"A Dozen Who Made a Difference," *Time*, January 6, 1976.

"Attorney Is Selected for Outlaw's Defense," *The Greensboro Record*, July 19, 1968.

Baldwin's Tri-Cities Directory for Leaksville, Spray and Draper, 1949.

Bledsoe, Jerry. *Bitter Blood.* New York: Onyx, 1989.

"Bloodhounds Join Search for Killer," *The Reidsville Review*, September 3, 1947.

"Bloodhounds Track Down Negro Wanted for Brutal Slaying of Thomas Pratt," *The Leaksville News*, September 11, 1947.

"Bobbin Winder, Machine (tex. prod., nec; textile)," *Dictionary of Occupational Titles*. Code: 681.685-104,

<www.occupationalinfo.org/68/681585014.html>.

"Bobbitt, William Haywood." Manuscripts Department Library of the University of North Carolina at Chapel Hill, Southern Historical Collection, #4637, William Haywood Bobbitt Papers Inventory, <www.lib.unc.edu/mss/inv/b/Bobbitt,William–Haywood>.

Burton, W. C. "Bloodhounds Join Hunt for Rockingham Escapee," *Greensboro Daily News*, September 3, 1947.

Burton, W. C. *Christmas in my Bones.* Asheboro, North Carolina: Down Home Press, 1991.

Burton, W. C. "Court Nonsuits Charge of Burglary and Denies Same Motion in Murder Court in Wentworth," *Greensboro Daily News*, November 6, 1947.

Burton, W. C. "Mrs. Pratt Points to Junior Thompson as One Who Left Murdered Man's Room," *Greensboro Daily News*, November 5, 1947.

Burton, W. C. "S. B. I. Called In on Pratt Murder Case by Rockingham County Sheriff," *Greensboro Daily News*, August 27, 1947.

Burton, W. C. "Thompson Seized in Virginia as Bloodhounds Trail Negro," *Greensboro Daily News*, September 4, 1947.

Burton, W. C. "Young Leaksville Negro Innocent; Mixed Jury Returns Quick Verdict," *Greensboro Daily News*, November 7, 1947.

"Burton, W. C. 'Mutt,' "North Carolina Journalism Hall of Fame," <www.jomc.unc.edu/specialprograms/famejournalism.html>.

Cheney, Jr., John. L. North Carolina Government 1585-1979. A Narrative and Statistical History. North Carolina Department of the Secretary of State, 1981.

"Complete Text of Sentinel's Controversial News Story," *The Eden News*, July 24, 1968.

"Correspondent Wanted to Write Colored News," *The Leaksville News*, September 11, 1947.

Covington, Jr., Howard E. and Ellis, Marion A., eds. *The North Carolina Century, Tar Heels Who Made a Difference, 1900-2000*. Charlotte, NC: Levine Museum of the New South, 2002.

"Dated Negro," *Greensboro Daily News*, November 2, 1947.

"Defense Opens Case at Thompson Murder Trial in Wentworth," *The Reidsville Review*, November 5, 1947.

"Eden Fugitive Wanted in Rape, Kidnapping Case," *The Eden News*, June 26, 1968.

"Eden is Combed for Outlaw," *The Greensboro Record*, July 16, 1968.

"Ex-Sheriff Dies at 68; Rites Set," *Greensboro Daily News*, August 8, 1962.

"Five Men, Woman Suffocate in Jail at Spray," *The Advisor*, December, 1958.

"Four Daily News Writers Receive Press Honors," no reference, clipping from vertical file on W. C. Burton at the Reidsville Pubic Library, probable date 1958.

"FBI Joins Search for Man Charged with Kidnap, Rape," *Greensboro Daily News*, July 3, 1968.

"Fieldcrest Communities Plan Pageant," *Greensboro Daily News*, Tuesday, Sept. 2, 1947.

"Former Rockingham County Sheriff Succumbs Monday," *The Leaksville News*, August 9, 1962.

Freeman, Franklin. Presentation Address of the Late Chief Justice Susie Sharp's Portrait, June 11, 1996. <www.aoc.state.nc.us/www/copyright/sc/portrait/sharp1.html>.

Gardner, James E. *Eden: Past and Present 1880-1980*. Friends of the Eden (North Carolina) Public Library, 1983.

"Grand Jury to Get Pratt Murder Case," *The Leaksville News*, October 2, 1947.

"Grand Jury Rules No One to Blame in Accidental Death of Six at Spray Jail," *The Leaksville News*, March 23, 1950.

Griffin, Jeri; Scott, Zelma; Carter, Bob; Seybert, Rich; and Osborne, Peggy. *Postcards from Rockingham County North Carolina*. Wentworth, N.C.: Rockingham County Historical Society, no publication date noted.

"Held in Murder," *Greensboro Daily News*, September 6, 1947.

Henry County (Virginia) Marriage Register, December 13, 1943.

"Hodges, Luther Hartwell," *The Columbia Encyclopedia Sixth Edition*, 2000.

"Hodges, Luther Hartwell,"

<www.itpi.dpi.state.nc.us/governors/hodges.html>.

Hoyle, Bernadette W. "North Carolina's First Woman Judge to Add Luster to Bench," *Greensboro Daily News,* June 26, 1949.

Index to the Dictionary of North Carolina Biography, Created by the Staff of the Olivia Raney Library.

<www.web.co.wake.nc.us/library/locations>.

"Injury Fatal to Tom Pratt," *Greensboro Daily News*, August 26, 1947.

"Intensive Investigation Made to Locate Assailant of 81-Year Old Tom Pratt," *The Leaksville News*, August 28, 1947.

Irons, Ken. "Luck, Precision Factors," *The Greensboro Record*, July 19, 1968.

Irons, Ken. "Tight Security Surrounds Outlaw," *The Greensboro Record*, July 17, 1968.

Jay, Peter A. "Trail of Abductions, Murders, Rape Lead to Capture of Outlaw," *The Washington Post*, July 17, 1968.

"Junior Edd Thompson Murder Case Goes to Superior Court Jury," *The Reidsville Review*, November 6, 1947.

"Junior Edd Thompson Murder Trial Begins in Superior Court," *The Reidsville Review*, November 4, 1947.

"Jr. Thompson 'Not Guilty' in Pratt Case," *The Leaksville News*, November 12, 1947.

"Justices Upset All Bans on Interracial Marriage; 9 – 0 Decision Rules," *The New York Times*, June 13, 1967.

Kaiser, Robert G. "Police Retrace Outlaw's 28-Hour Trail of Terror," *The Washington Post*, July 18, 1968.

"Mattresses in Spray Jail Being Made Fire Resistant; Safety Measures Adopted," *The Leaksville News*, March 30, 1950.

"Morehead, John Motley,"

<www.itpi.dpi.state.nc.us/governors/morehead.html>.

"Munsey S. Hodges Elected Rockingham County Sheriff by 1,984 Vote Majority," *The Leaksville News*, November 7, 1946.

"Negro Escapee Captured After Intensified Search," *The Reidsville Review*, September 4, 1947.

"Negro is Acquitted of Murdering White Man," *The Madison Messenger*, November 13, 1947.

News Summary: "Former Justice Dies," The Insider, North Carolina State Government News Service, Monday, March 4, 1996, Vol. 4, No. 44. <www.ncinsider.com/insider/1996/march/insd0304.html>.

"No Developments in the Murder Case," *The Reidsville Review*, September 2, 1947.

North Carolina Biographical Clippings I. The University of North Carolina at Chapel Hill Libraries. <www.lib.unc.edu/ncc/ref/b75/b75I.html>.

"North Carolina Civil Rights Time Line," Tar Heel Junior Historian 44 (Fall, 2004), copyright North Carolina Museum of History, Division of State History Museums, Office of Archives and History, North Carolina Department of Cultural Resources. <www.king-raleigh.org/history/NCcivilrightstimeline.htm>.

Obituary of J. Hampton Price, *The Eden News*, January 5, 1972.

Obituary of Ruby Florence Edwards, *The Eden News*, March 28, 2001.

Obituary of W. C. Burton, *The Reidsville Review*, December 3, 1995.

Obituary of W. C. Burton, *The Greensboro News and Record*, December 2, 1995.

"Outlaw's Car Found in Yadkin County," *The Eden News*, July 10, 1968.

"Outlaw's Hearing Planned," *The Greensboro Record*, July 18, 1968.

Paul, C. A. "Without a Gun, 'Like a Kitten;' He's Been in Trouble Most of His Life," *Greensboro Daily News*, July 18, 1968.

Pocahontas Bassett Baptist Church, Church History. <www.kimbanct.com/~csdeans/pocahontaschurch.htm>.

Pollack, Kent. "Police Snare Outlaw, Rescue 3 Teen Girls," *Greensboro Daily News*, July 17, 1968.

Pollack, Kent. "Thompson is Moved to Buncombe Jail," *Greensboro Daily News*, July 18, 1968.

Pratt, Herbert T. "The William Frederick Pratt Family Cemetery." *Rockingham County Historical Society, Inc. Newsletter*, Series III, no. 74, September 30, 1994, pp. 14-16.

Pratt, Herbert T. "The History of the Willson Aluminum Company, Spray, North Carolina 1891-1986." *The Journal of Rockingham County History and Genealogy*, Vol. XVII, No. 1, June, 1992, pp. 1 -26.

"Pratt Killer Identified as Negro Escapee," *The Reidsville Review*, August 29, 1947.

"Price, J. Hampton," *The Alumni Directory and Service Record of Washington and Lee University*, 1926.

"Profile of Judge Herman Peters," *The Leaksville News*, August 19, 1954.

"Progress Made by Sheriff's Department in Past Seven Months is Shown in Report," *The Leaksville News*, August 28 1947.

Ramsland, Katherine, "The Polygraph." <www.crimelibrary.com>.

Rasmussen, Wayne D., ed. *Agriculture in the United States, A Documentary History, vol. 1*. New York: Random House, 1975.

"Recent Spray Jail Tragedy Should Not Be Used As An Election Campaign Issue," *The Leaksville News*, March 30, 1950.

Robertson, Beverly W. "Widow of Murdered Man Asks State Aid in Hunt for Slayer," *Greensboro Daily News*, no date; clipping from Josie E. Pratt papers.

Rockingham County Bicentennial Commission, *Historical Sketches and Photographs*, Eden, North Carolina: Style-Kraft Printing, 1985.

Rockingham County (North Carolina) Marriage Register, 1921-1945. Book 10, page 1327.

Rodenbough, Charles Dyson, ed. "William Sterling Ivie Family," article 556, page 319, *The Heritage of Rockingham County North Carolina*, The Rockingham County Historical Society, 1983.

"S.B.I. to Investigate Pratt Murder Case," *The Reidsville Review*, August 27, 1947.

Schlosser, Jim. "Ex-Lawman Claims Tip," *The Greensboro Record*, July 18, 1968.

Schlosser, Jim. "Outlaw Jailed Often," *The Greensboro Record*, July 17, 1968.

"Scott, Ralph James," Biographical Dictionary of the United States Congress, 1774-Present.
<www.bioguide.congres.gov/scripts/guidedisplay.pl?index=5000184>.

"Scott, Ralph James," *Stokes County (North Carolina) Natives*, biography #859.

"Search Continues for Murderer of Tom Pratt; Bloodhounds Sent Here," *The Leaksville News*, September 4, 1947.

"Search for Fugitive Continues; FBI Join in Wide-Scale Manhunt," *The Eden News*, July 3, 1968.

"Season's First Coon is Taken After Battle," *The Leaksville News*, October 23, 1947.

Seitz, Katrina Nannette. *The Transition of Methods of Execution in North Carolina: A Descriptive Social History of Two Time Periods, 1935 & 1983.* (Ph.D. diss., Virginia Polytechnic Institute and State University, 2001).

"State Senator J. Hampton Price, Prominent Lawyer and Citizen," (photograph) *The Leaksville News,* February, 1944.

Stewart, Alva W. "A New Togetherness," excerpted on <www.leaksville.com>.

Stone, Amy. "An Epidemic Ignored," Public Health, Spring 1997. <www.whsc.emory.edu/_pubs/ph/phspr97/epi.html.>

Sullivan, Nick, "Axsom Denies Men Muffed Chance to Nab Eden Fugitive," *The Eden News,* July 24, 1968.

"The First Woman to Serve," *The Leaksville News,* September 18, 1947.

"The Henry County Caller," Henry County Baptist Association, April 2003, Vol. 4, Issue 1. <www.churchfirst.net/hcba/newsletter/may03.pdf>.

"The 'Outlaw' Apprehended," *Greensboro Daily News,* July 18, 1968.

"Thompson Now in Raleigh Hospital for Mental Tests," *The Eden News,* July 24, 1968.

"Thompson Will Have Hearing Here Friday," *The Leaksville News,* September 18, 1947.

Trantham, Doug. "Eden Fugitive Apprehended," *The Eden News,* July 17, 1968.

Trantham, Doug. "Flight to Avoid Justice is Story of Outlaw's Life," *The Eden News,* July 24, 1968.

"Two Women on Jury for Trial of First Degree Murder Case," No reference, clipping from Custis Clifton personal papers. Approximate date November 5, 1947.

"Va. Urges Fast Trial of Outlaw," *The Washington Post,* July 20, 1968.

"W. C. 'Mutt' Burton, columnist and colleague," *Greensboro News and Record*, December 2, 1995.

"Widow Identifies Pratt Murderer from Photograph," *Greensboro Daily News*, August 29, 1947.

"Widow Identifies Thompson in Line-up at Guilford Jail," *Greensboro Daily News*, September 5, 1947.

"Widow of Murdered Man and Her Pet Collie," *The Leaksville News*, November 27, 1947.

<www.bioguide.congress.gov/scripts/biodisplay.pl?index=R000104>.

<www.leaksville.com>.

<www.nccourts.org/Courts/Appellate/Supreme/Portrait/Portrait.asp?Name=Martin>.

<www.politicalgraveyard.com>.

<www.rockinghamcountyhistory.com>.

<http://www.trumanlibrary.org/calendar/main.php?currYear=1946&currMonth=9&currDay=24>

<www.vitalrecords.dhhs.state.nc.us/vr/holdings>

WLOE home page, <www.wloewmyn.com>.

⑧

$$_{50}C_3 =$$

$$\frac{50!}{47!\ 3!}$$

$$= \frac{50 \cdot 49 \cdot \overset{8}{\cancel{48}}}{\cancel{3} \cdot \cancel{2} \cdot 1} = 19{,}600$$

⑨ Factor

$$x^3 - 8$$

$$(x-2)(x^2 + 2x + 4)$$

About the Author

Alison Pratt, Ph.D.

Alison Pratt is a native of New Castle, Delaware who grew up going to her grandparents' home in Leaksville, later called Eden, during summer vacations of her childhood in the 1960s. The moss around the base of the gigantic willow oak was thick and cool on bare feet, the rope swing was dangerous and exhilarating, and the lawn chairs were always ready for visitors. The garden yielded bright, red tomatoes and sweet, juicy cantaloupes. Granddaddy's Chevrolet Impala never had a speck of dirt. The wooden shed was a place of mystery. Though not used, the rusted water pump in the back yard could still bring forth water. The velvet couch in the parlor was scratchy, but no one sat in there anyway. The black and white television set could barely get any stations. African violets and spider plants filled the sunny kitchen breakfast nook. Grandmama's biscuits and jams were homemade. Her snow-white hair was worn in a bun and she always wore dresses. Granddaddy's pocketknives were as sharp as razors and his gold tooth shone when he laughed. The front porch swing was a good place to read. The little fan whirred on the linoleum floor; and the back screen door opened and closed with a particular squeak of the spring. Alison remembers all this and more.

Dr. Pratt is psychologist in private practice in Long Island, New York. She is married to Steve Hetzel and has a stepson, Sean, and a son, Reid.

(6)

$$15x + 5(3{,}500 - x) = 27{,}500$$

$$15x + 17500 - 5x = 27{,}500$$

$$17{,}500$$

$$10x = 10{,}000$$

$$x = 1{,}000$$

There were 2,500 energetic and exuberant ~~child~~ minors at the park that day.

①

200 feet

X

50 feet

$$c^2 = a^2 + b^2$$

$$200^2 = 50^2 + x^2$$

$$3\cancel{44},000 = 2500 + x^2$$

$$- 2500$$

$$\overline{37,500} = x^2$$

$$x = \sqrt{37,500}$$

$$x = \underline{193.65} \text{ feet}$$

④

34

30 yards

100 yards

104 yards

104
34
———
4 16
3 120
———
3536 yards

3536
3000
———
536 yards

⑤

quarters $= 5x$

dimes $= x$

nickels $= x + 3$

pennies $= 9x - 2$

Quarters dimes nickels pennies
$$125x + 10x + 5x + 15 + 9x - 2 = 1503$$

$$149x + 13 = 1503$$
$$-13$$
$$149x = 1490$$

$$x = 10$$

50 quarters

10 dimes

13 nickels

88 cents

②

$4x - 3$ $3x - 2$ miles

x

$4x - 3 + 3x - 2 + x = 11$

$$8x - 5 = 11$$
$$8x = 16$$
$$x = 2$$

5 miles   4 miles

2 miles

③

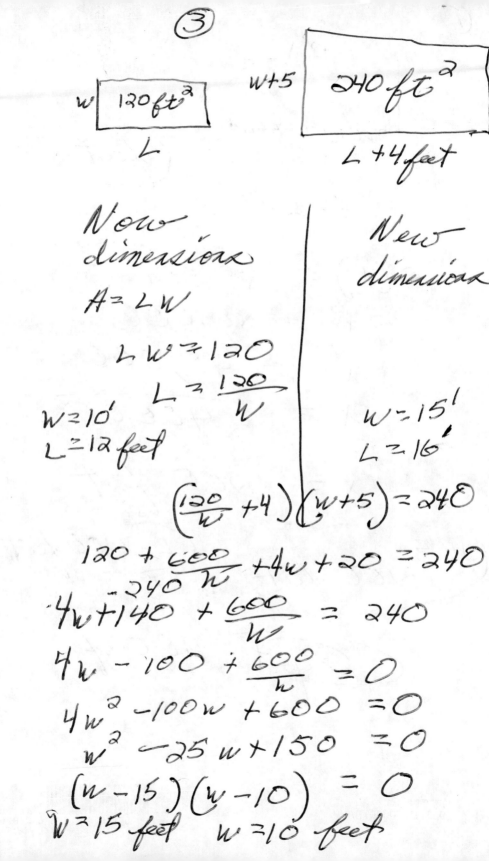

w | 120 ft² | $w+5$ | 240 ft² |

L | $L+4$ feet

Now dimensions

$A = LW$

$LW = 120$

$L = \dfrac{120}{W}$

$W = 10'$
$L = 12$ feet

New dimensions

$W = 15'$
$L = 16'$

$$\left(\dfrac{120}{W} + 4\right)(W+5) = 240$$

$$120 + \dfrac{600}{W} + 4W + 20 = 240$$

$$4W + 140 + \dfrac{600}{W} = 240$$

$$4W - 100 + \dfrac{600}{W} = 0$$

$$4W^2 - 100W + 600 = 0$$

$$W^2 - 25W + 150 = 0$$

$$(W - 15)(W - 10) = 0$$

$W = 15$ feet $W = 10$ feet

①

2x

X [   ] X

~~river~~
river

(feet)

$$A = LW$$

$$2x(x) = 80,000$$
$$2x^2 = 80,000$$
$$x^2 = 40,000$$
$$x = \sqrt{40,000}$$

$$x = 200 \text{ feet}$$

(W = 200 feet)   (L = 400 feet)

(800 feet)   '400 fe